Falling

LOVE'S OWN TIMELINE
BOOK ONE

STEPHANIE PHILOMENA

Cover Designer: Sam Palencia, Ink and Laurel

Editor: Sam Stringert, @samspeededits

Stephanie Philomena did not use AI to imagine or write the story of
Falling, nor will she use AI for future writing projects.

For my best friend, Helen.
Thank you for the chicken impersonations and gorilla races at work, the spontaneous meals together, your daily phone calls to check I haven't imploded from self-publishing, and your unconditional love.

&

For those who take the brave path in love...

&

For my niece, who is far too young to read this book.
Plum is the essence of you.

Triggers & Glimmers

'Glimmers and triggers are opposites in that
glimmers spark positive feelings
while triggers spark negative ones.'

Trigger Warnings

Death of brother by rock climbing accident,
off page, six years prior.
Death of parents by drunk driver,
off page, nearly twenty years prior.
Parent abandonment mentioned.

Glimmers

Warm, cozy autumn vibes.
Loving, supportive relationships.
Low-stress conflict.
Halloween – this is more for me!
Preparation for and celebrating
Friendsgiving/Thanksgiving.

CHAPTER 1
Rhys

"You getting me home... I know I embarrass you when I repetitively compliment your resourcefulness, but this is pure witchcraft," I speak quietly into my cell phone as to not be that person you hear shouting their conversation like they are the only person on Earth.

My assistant knows I have a high level of respect for her vast skillset, but getting me out of Texas and around the storms ripping through the Bible Belt today is truly miraculous. Some would look at Sophie's age, her disability, and underestimate her talents and intelligence, but those people are worthless to me. I have fired employees, walked away from business deals, for their utter foolishness.

"I appreciate the sentiment, but you can give it a rest."

I may not be able see Sophie, but I still sense her eye roll.

"I never want you to think I'm taking you for granted or for someone to steal you from me." I know she can hear my smirk through her phone.

"Impossible. You pay me too much to leave you. Besides,

after all these years together, your compliments have become white noise to me."

"Ouch."

"You'll live. Have you boarded?"

"I'm walking the jet bridge now. Thanks for getting me an aisle seat."

"I know you need the leg room. Sorry first-class wasn't available, but this flight shouldn't be full."

The line of passengers is shuffling along, slowly, yet moving enough to know it's not a full flight. There are only a few people behind me, so the middle seat could be vacant.

"Chicago to Buffalo is a short flight. Doesn't matter."

"Then my job is done."

I'm greeted with a smile by a couple female flight attendants eyeing me up and down. Flight attendants will size up a passenger to determine if they will be helpful in an emergency, but this is a completely different sizing up. I know that look. You don't have to be conceited to know that look, just receive it thousands of times in your life.

"You know, there's only an hour left in the workday. Why don't you go home?"

"Packing up now!"

As I wait for a few people ahead of me to get settled in their seats, I can hear desk drawers opening and closing through the phone.

"Have a great weekend, Sophie. You definitely earned it."

I'm moving again and my seat is easy to spot seven rows back on the left. *Yes!* The middle seat is empty. I see only a glossy, dark brown head of hair at the window seat.

"I'd tell you to have a great weekend too, but I know you're just going to get work done from this trip."

"Got to go, Soph."

Not a lie, but I hang up before I get the work-life balance lecture.

Again.

Some variation of this lecture started around year five of Sophie's employment, when we started getting really comfortable with each other. Approximately fifty-two Fridays per year for the past five years, maybe six now. That's a lot of lectures. I understand where her heart is. Sophie's an eldest sibling too. And a parent. I may not have kids of my own, but I know about parenting and caring about the life choices of the people you love.

I drop my leather messenger bag into my seat before sliding my black carry-on into the overhead bin, pull out my laptop and slip it into the front seat pocket. As I pick up my bag and take my seat, I glance at my row companion, because she has the most beautiful long hair I've ever seen. Shiny, deep, dark chocolate waves all the way down her back.

After shoving my bag under the seat in front of me and buckling my seatbelt, I allow myself another glimpse. All I see is hair because the woman's head is bent over a hardcover book, her hair curtaining her face. She is dressed casually in all black with hot pink sneakers. The only other standout is her long fingernails painted black with something orange on them. Pumpkins? No. Jack-o'-lanterns. That's right. Halloween is next week.

If she's noticed I'm here, she hasn't let on.

I wonder what she's reading.

The sound of the cabin door closing snaps me out of a curiosity I have never had for a fellow passenger. And I fly often. Not as frequently as I used to when I was based out of Manhattan the two years after college, eighteen years ago. My first business was soaring high then, but I was working sixteen-hour days to create something lucrative. Sophie would have keeled over if she knew me back then.

I switch my phone to airplane mode and slip it into my inside jacket pocket just as the plane begins backing up. Maybe I'm more tired than I thought, because I have no control over my eyeballs tracking the woman's movements. As she turns to look out the window, her book closes enough for me to read *The Gods of* in silver foil script against the black dust jacket that looks like the stars of a galaxy, but I can't see the rest of the cover.

The cabin lights are off. It's a cloudy day and the sun is already making its descent. With my seatmate's overhead reading light on, I can see a bit of her reflection in the window. Her eyes. Large. Doe-like. Looking right at me.

Damn! Caught!

I pretend to look out the window too, but I know she knows I was looking at her. All I can do is face forward, lean my head back, and close my eyes as I feel the plane taxi the runway, then the force of takeoff. I don't open my eyes again until the flight attendant announces we can use the in-flight Wi-Fi, but I did sense my row companion shift in her seat. She probably resumed her reading.

I retrieve my laptop from the front pocket and set it up on the tray table, ready to get back to work, but my eyes catch something new in the peripheral. I take a full-on glance and notice four things before returning my eyes to the laptop screen.

The full title of her book.

She swept her hair over her shoulder.

I can see her stunning profile.

And she has the cutest smirk on her lips.

Shit! Did she see me look?

I am facing my laptop, hands hovering over the keyboard, but my now-obsessed eyeballs are straining far right.

I think that twitchy smirk on rosy lips is a reaction to whatever she's reading.

After I log onto the Wi-Fi, I search *The Gods of What We Take for Granted.*

Pretty high rating. Romantic fantasy genre. First book of a series. Published this year. Sounds like an interesting story.

Huh.

Story contains explicit sex.

Huh.

Extremely explicit sex.

"Are you usually this interested in what strangers read?"

Well, fuck.

I should be embarrassed, but I'm too busy tasting the sound of that voice. It's the perfect sweet and salty snack. A voice made to equally soothe and to speak filthy things.

Double fuck.

When I turn to face that voice, she's still reading, but her smirk has upturned closer to a real smile. And now that I'm really looking at her, she's seriously beautiful to my wandering eyes, and probably to a whole lot of people.

My own smile is making an appearance. "Only when the stranger is..." *Don't say attractive!* "...so engrossed as you are."

The blonde flight attendant halts at our row to offer beverages and snacks, but we both decline and she moves on to the row behind us.

I turn to look at my seatmate who is now looking at me.

Seriously fucking beautiful.

I can't even begin to describe the color of her eyes. Maybe redwood, no, that's too light. I guess reddish brown, if I had to put a name to the color. I don't know. But her eyes are clear, and expressive in a, *I know she's laughing at me even though she's not,* way.

"It's a really good book."

That voice! "By your expression, I'm sure it is."

She tilts her head slightly. "Do you like fantasy novels?"

"I can't say I have ever read one."

"Do you read for pleasure?"

"When I have the time." *That's a lie!* I couldn't tell you when the last time I read a book for fun.

She takes a pointed look at my laptop screen. "By your research there, is this a book you might be interested in?"

"I'm not completely sure."

I think she glances at her current page number before flipping back a few pages, then hands the open book to me.

"Interested in a few sample pages?"

Normally I would decline the offer and get work done, but there is something about this woman's offer. I need to know what is holding her interest.

As I reach for the book, my eyes dip down to what looks like mischief on her lips before she turns her face to look out the window. When I contemplate her reflection, she's not looking back at me, but if I had to guess her expression... teasing?

After reaching up to turn on my overhead light and closing my laptop, I skim down the first page of the chapter. Someone named Tru and another character named Analise. Just before midnight. Thunder and lightning. The smell of petrichor.

Wait!

There is no way this woman, a stranger, someone who is seated two feet away and will be in said seat for the next hour, would give me a sex scene to read.

I turn the page as casually as I can.

Tru and Analise are actually getting it on.

Now, I am hyperaware of every move I make. I will not give the instigator seated to my right the satisfaction of seeing me squirm. Instead, I read how Tru goes down on Analise. In explicit detail. I hate to admit it, but Tru has serious skills.

I can't help wonder if the temptress still gazing out the window, pretending to ignore me, likes to be eaten out this way.

Analise comes hard. Tru's dick is harder.

Fuck! This is hot.

Okay. I can play this game too. First, I have to stop reading or I'll be in the same condition as Tru and I cannot allow that to happen. Not one throb behind the zipper. But I can pretend to read.

My eyes slowly scan the words without registering them, but my lizard brain manages to land on random words like 'nip' and 'breast' and 'thrust' and 'moan.' I still understand exactly what Tru and Analise are up to, but my reaction is restrained.

Lucky for me, it only takes another minute before the devil woman finally turns to face me, leaning in to check what page I've just turned to.

"Hey! You're reading farther than where I left off."

I hold up a finger for her to wait as my eyes slowly meander down the page to the end, then onto the next. Out of my peripheral, I can see the woman's knee start to bounce and I'm trying really hard not to laugh.

When I feel holes burning into my skull from her glare, I snap the book shut and hand it back to its owner. "That's quite a story you're reading."

She places the book on her lap, not an ounce of embarrassment in her amused expression. "It is. Everything this author writes is...interesting."

"Is she your favorite writer?"

"I don't really have any favorites. I'm more of a mood girl."

"Is that just in the books you read?"

"In many things."

My eyes narrow. No favorites? She's got to be kidding. "No favorite color? Food? Vacation spot?"

She shrugs in reply, expression unchanged, giving me nothing. Yet her body has shifted in her seat, angled to face me as much as her fastened seatbelt will allow. I rarely engage in conversation with a stranger during travel, but I'm intrigued and, yes, part of the reason is she's fascinating to look at. All bravado and beauty.

I angle my body to comfortably face her. What I don't do is allow my gaze to dip below her chin. I won't be *that* guy.

"So, you don't like anything more than another thing in the same category?"

The smile she tosses me is just as open as her posture, brightening those mesmerizing eyes, illuminating flecks of gold I didn't see before. Instantly addicting. There's less than an hour remaining of this flight and I'm wondering how many times I can coax that smile out of her.

"There are exceptions, but my mood rules many of my choices, especially in books." Her voice is all sparkly with humor.

I nod and offer a smile of my own, but I'm positive mine isn't going to electrify a major city at night the way hers could. "You make your choices based on what you like in the moment."

Her eyes are so expressive. I see recognition spark. "You understand."

"Let's see if I do. Instead of asking what your favorite food is, I could ask what mood you're in for dinner or what you're craving right now."

"Steak tacos."

Zero hesitation. I like that. Is it wrong for me to get sexy vibes knowing she's a carnivore who likes messy foods?

"If you could pick a place to vacation today, where would it be?"

"Orlando or Anaheim. Preferably Anaheim."

I must have the most confused expression on my face because hers turns extra amused with mock irritation. "It's Halloweentime at Disneyland!"

I shake my head in disbelief. "I did not see that one coming."

She giggles and I feel it zing through my chest.

"Why would you prefer Anaheim?"

"I'm Southern California born and bred, so Disneyland will always be near and dear to my heart."

"Is that where you're traveling from?"

"Disneyland?"

I give her an exaggerated frown that she actually took the easy joke and I get rewarded with another giggle. It is akin to winning at a custom slot machine, put in wit and out pours pure gold.

"I live in Los Angeles."

Damn. She might as well live in Singapore. Even though I don't have time for any type of thing, I feel the sting of disappointment.

"What brings you to Buffalo?"

"A couple reasons. I have family in Buffalo. I try to spend as many Halloweens with my niece I can since her parents are Halloween-clueless."

I take a pointed look at the fingernails resting on the armrest. "I kind of figured you for a Halloween fan."

"And you're not?"

"I consider myself on the fence."

She is faux aghast. "You and I could never be friends."

"That's harsh." I am faux offended.

"If you're that desperate for friends, I could teach you the charms of Halloween."

"I might be open to that."

"Might? Then you're not desperate enough."

I wonder if she's dressing up for Halloween. This nanosecond of a thought leads to a series of images flashing through my mind of scantily clad costume options.

I am a fucking pig. I subtly shake my head to empty these absurd thoughts. When I come back to focus, her eyes have narrowed as if she's searching through my mind, wondering where I went. She really doesn't want to know. Yet, after reading that chapter –

No way! Not going there!

"You stated you have a couple reasons for this trip. What's the second?"

She doesn't answer right away, still assessing me, then her voice morphs into a more serious tone. "Business. My sister," she pauses a beat before continuing, "in-law owns a wellness center and we have been wanting to work together for a while. I'll lead some meditation classes at her studio while I'm in town. It's something Alex has been wanting to test with her clients."

The sister-in-law hesitation isn't lost on me. Is it a new marriage? Wait. Is she married? I didn't see a ring.

"So, you teach meditation in LA?"

"Yes. It's one tool I offer. I'm a wellness coach."

I have never heard of a wellness coach before nor do I know how to inquire about it without receiving a sales pitch. She's studying me, spying my confusion or determining her angle.

She continues, "Have you ever tried meditation?"

"No."

Yes, I heard the slight edge to my no, but she's still smiling. Not the full wattage smile from moments ago, but she remains relaxed. A practiced smile.

"It's a good tool to have in your personal wellness kit. It's not just to alleviate stress."

"Oh, I've heard of the benefits of meditation from my sister."

"Smart sister."

Carys would instantly love this woman.

"She is smart. And she has suggested meditation to me over the years, but I haven't gotten around to it." I wish I didn't say that. I can only imagine the convincing argument that's coming next. Not the direction I wanted our conversation to steer toward.

"Well, then, sounds like you have the information you need."

Not the reply I was expecting at all. Maybe she isn't great at selling herself, because I definitely opened a window of opportunity for her even with my unfriendly 'no.'

"Since you live in Los Angeles, I assume it's your business home base as well." I guess I can't believe she's not taking the bait. Perhaps she's baiting me. If so, she's damn good.

"Pretty much. But I fly all over the US and have done work in Costa Rica and Portugal as well. Private and corporate." She eyes my obvious business attire. "Do you travel for business a lot?"

She's not interested in the hard sell. Nor the soft sell. "I used to, but not so much anymore."

"I've cut back on my work travel, too. Don't get me wrong. I love what I do, but I'm more selective on which jobs I take."

"Work-life balance. My assistant preaches that to me every Friday."

"No one can tell you how to live your life, but it sounds

like you just haven't come to the right circumstances yet." Her tone is even, void of criticism.

"What are the right circumstances?" I'm forcing myself to sit still and not cross my arms in front of my chest. I don't need this woman to think I'm going into defense mode.

"I can't answer that for you. What I can say is, if you are even slightly self-aware, you will know."

I don't know how to respond. Life has always been singularly focused, nothing beyond taking care of my family. Nothing else has mattered. I am aware no one needs taking care of anymore, at least not in the way they needed years ago.

We're standing on the edge of a deeper conversation, not where I would normally go with a stranger, yet here I am.

"Ladies and gentlemen, we have begun our final descent into Buffalo. Please turn off all portable electronic devices and stow them until we have arrived at the gate. In preparation for landing, be certain your seat back is straight up and your seatbelt is fastened…"

We break our mutual stare at the same time. I pack away my laptop while she slips her sexy book into her black tote bag. Once we're settled against our seats, she takes a glimpse out the window and I take a glimpse at her. She meets my eyes in the reflection again, but this time she holds my gaze and gives me a sweet, closed lip smile, and I don't pretend I'm looking out the window. She diverts her attention to the approaching land below, but her smile doesn't fade.

Oddly, I'm savoring the last moments with my travel companion as we walk side by side on the jet bridge. As I originally thought, I'm much taller than she is which puts her at about five-foot-five, maybe an inch taller. This woman is stunning and that's not only my opinion; I see her turning heads when we walk the tiled floor towards baggage claim. It bothers me. I want to wrap an arm around her. Shield her.

Is this jealousy? Christ! I have never once considered myself the jealous type in my forty-two years on this planet.

"How long are you in town for?" I have to know.

"Two weeks. I'll have family time this weekend, some pre-Halloween fun with my niece, then I start teaching classes on Monday morning."

"What's your workload like? How many classes will you teach per day?"

"This isn't like working a nine-to-five job. I'll teach a short Intro to Meditation class at 8:00 a.m. on Monday. A silent mantra class later that morning, then a breathwork class right after."

"Sounds like you have this work-life balance down. Maybe I should take one of your classes to see what my sister is talking about."

"All my classes are completely booked, but if you come to the intro class, I'll make room for you."

I've built a thriving business over the last two decades. I know people. She's not selling me anything, just being kind with her offer. "Do you have a business card? A contact number?"

"I do."

She halts, I halt. Those Halloween fingernails disappear into her large tote bag, extracting a single glossy black card, and offers it to me. She has very pretty hands.

November Day. If her name wasn't printed below the elegant, blue butterfly artwork, I'd think she was teasing me.

It's at this moment I realize the introduction is coming at the end of our meeting instead of the start. This is so out of character for me.

"I'm Rhys Morgan."

I extend my right hand to her, but don't dare say her name for reasons I can't grasp. But when she takes my hand, the way her fingers slip over my palm, causes an unexpected tsunami through my blood.

"It was nice chatting with you, Rhys." My name sounds like sex in November's smoky sweet voice and I want nothing more than to hear it on repeat.

She releases my hand, grabs hold of the handle of her carry-on, and turns to walk away. I can't let her go yet.

"I have one last question I didn't get a chance to ask."

She turns back to me, leans in and studies my eyes for a beat. I have no idea what she's doing, but I like having her this close to me.

"Brilliant sapphire blue." Her voice is pure fucking smoke.

"What?" I'm still hung up on her closeness.

"That last question could be phrased as, what color are you attracted to in this moment?" November winks before walking away.

Fuck! Fuck! Fuck!

I'm too dumbstruck to reply. All I can do is watch her leggings-clad round ass and the sassy sway of her hips as she walks through the automatic security doors that lead to baggage claim.

Of course, I watch.

CHAPTER 2

November

"The tombstones are so real. I mean, not real, but they're not like the styrofoam ones that get blown away by the wind here. I can't wait to decorate tomorrow with the jack-o'-lanterns and skeletons. And the lights..."

I have no idea where I am.

I am unable to focus on my niece's Halloween chatter. I want to hear her ideas of how she wants to decorate the front yard, but it's dark out and I'm trying to get my bearings in this suburb of large, newly constructed homes. The family moved into a new house five months ago and this is the first time I'm seeing the new neighborhood. Once we exited the freeway, the thruway, nothing is familiar. And the more turns Alex makes, I don't know what direction is north, south, east or west.

"How many jack-o'-lanterns should we make?" Plum asks from the backseat of the 'still smells like it was just driven off the sales floor' SUV.

I pull my gaze from beyond my passenger side window and look over my shoulder at the ten-year-old girl who everyone calls my mini me. Although, when I look at Plum, I see my brother's darker eyes looking back at me.

"After we set up the cemetery, we'll have a better idea where the pumpkins could be placed."

"Plum has soccer practice in the morning, and Mark and I have a couple errands to run after drop off. I know the jetlag will keep you up, so have yourself a morning of leisure. After that, we kept the rest of the day free to decorate and maybe have a movie night. On Sunday, we'll have breakfast at the pancake house, then head out to the pumpkin farm. If it's not raining, we can do the hayride." Alex lays out the plans while keeping her eyes on the road.

"No rain allowed!" Plum's voice is a demand of Mother Nature.

"I wouldn't mind some rain." I sigh. *I miss weather.* "But I understand your plea and I want to have some pre-Halloween fun this weekend too."

"So far, no rain, but it's going to be cloudy all weekend," Alex informs us as she slows the SUV for the stop sign.

I look at my sister-in-law as she makes a left turn. My former sister-in-law? My friend? The marriage vow is, '...until death do us part.' I don't know what's the appropriate category for my brother's widow who has since remarried.

"How are you feeling?" I ask Alex.

"I feel great. Now that I'm out of my first trimester, I finally feel more like myself. My energy is back."

"And Mom isn't throwing up all over the place all the time," Plum inserts.

Alex glances at her Cheshire Cat daughter in the rearview mirror. "You make it sound as if there was vomit all over the house."

"There was that one morning when you couldn't make it to the bathroom. All over the hallway floor."

"That's enough from you, little girl," Alex scolds with a smile.

"Well, I'm glad you feel good now. You look fantastic." It's true. She looks bright and happy like she did on both her wedding days.

"Thanks. It's the pregnancy glow. So do you, by the way. Look fantastic that is, not pregnant. You were getting a lot of attention in the airport."

"What attention?" Plum's voice sounds puzzled.

"Auntie Novie turning the heads of men."

"Ew. Just stop, Mom."

"No one was turning heads," I singsong.

At a stop sign, Alex spares me a disapproving look, before making a right turn. "You never pay attention. I saw the tall man with black hair and the perfect amount of facial scruff ogling you."

Ah! The man I oddly couldn't help flirting with, but they don't need to know that.

I return my attention to a couple houses outside my window without really registering them. "Rhys was looking because we were seatmates and had decent conversation. Made the flight from Chicago go by fast."

Alex slows the SUV and pulls into an aesthetically lit driveway. "Interesting you know his name. Does Rhys live in Buffalo?"

As soon as she parks and the ignition is off, Plum is out of the backseat and running around the car to swing my door open for me.

"He does." That's all I answer, because I am more interested in where we are.

Plum makes a sweeping motion with her arm toward the giant, well, giant to an apartment dweller like me, two-story, modern craftsman as I step outside. "Welcome to our new house! I can't wait to show you my bedroom!"

Alex opens her door and steps outside. "Uh, Plum, I know you're excited, but didn't we discuss pouncing on Auntie Novie?"

Plum pouts. "I know." She slams my door shut once I'm out of the way.

I simultaneously hoist my travel tote onto my right shoulder while wrapping my left arm around Plum's narrow shoulders. The house exterior is large with a three-car garage and plenty of space between neighbors. Beautifully land-scaped as far as I can tell in the dark.

This house is very different from the starter home Roman and Alex shared.

Life really does go on.

"It's okay. We have time before dinner." I'm speaking to my niece, but my eyes catch the glint of light on glass as the front door opens.

Plum hugs me around my waist before relieving me of my tote. "I'll take this to your room."

"Thanks, my sweet."

Alex has opened the SUV's liftgate and is starting to reach for my carry-on.

"Alex, I'll handle the luggage," Mark shouts to her and hurries his gait down the steps.

Alex puts her hands up and backs away from the SUV, before snarking, "Yes, sir!"

Plum rushes past Mark. "Hi Dad!"

"Hi, Daughter!"

I swallow hard.

Dad.

This is not new. Plum has been calling Mark that for a few years, but it still stings. Probably because I'm not here enough to get used to it. When Alex and Mark married, Mark adopted Plum. They moved Day to her middle name in memory of my brother. And it made sense since Alex was taking Mark's last name of Phillips. Mark even asked my permission, and it broke me. He didn't have to ask, it was entirely Alex's decision, but he wanted to ask me because he is kind and considerate. Most important, he loves and treats Plum as his own.

"Hey, November! How was your flight?"

Mark leans down as I rise on my tiptoes to give him a quick, friendly hug. He's taller than Roman by a couple inches, but that's not the only difference.

If I had to vocalize it, I would say Alex chose a man that was the complete physical opposite of my brother. Roman had dark hair like mine, darker eyes, 5'10" and had the look of an athlete. Mark has sandy blond hair, light blue eyes, 6', and has the demeanor of a good looking, but geeky professor, which he is. A math professor.

"It was blissfully uneventful."

Alex kisses her husband on his cheek before side-eyeing me. "Maybe not from Los Angeles to Chicago, but Chicago to Buffalo is a whole other story. November met a man!"

"Mark, ignore her. Yes, I had a conversation with a man, but not in the way Alex is insinuating."

"Got it. You ladies better head indoors. It's getting colder out here."

"Let me at least grab my carry-on."

"Don't worry about it." Mark is already moving to the cargo space. "Alex honey, the lasagna should be ready in ten minutes. Salad is made and the table is set."

"Auntie Novie!" Plum shouts from the porch.

"I've been summoned."

Alex smiles. "You go ahead. Meet you at the dining table in ten."

"Will do."

I hurry along the warmly lit brick walkway and take my

niece's outstretched hand in mine, ready to be pulled along to wherever she wishes.

It's obvious Alex had me in mind when she decorated this guest bedroom. She knows I love the look of a sleigh bed with a thick comforter and pillows. This one is cherrywood dressed in autumn colored velvet and silky, smooth cotton sheets. It suits the house style. It's cozy, beautiful, elegance.

I should be buried under the covers, sound asleep after two a.m., but I'm currently curled up against the cold glass of the cushioned window seat, holding tight to a forest green silk throw pillow, and keeping the tears reeled in by watching the wind claim more leaves from the trees.

Alex and Mark are going above and beyond to make me feel comfortable in their home. And I'm putting on a smile and pretending to be relaxed to make them feel comfortable in their home. But the reality is, I don't know how I fit in here other than being the aunt who FaceTimes frequently, sends little unexpected gifts, and visits for Halloween. I've been invited for other holidays, but it's just Alex and Mark being kind and I don't want to intrude. So, I end up spending holidays with Genevieve.

Crap! I forgot to text Gen!

I stand and go over to the nightstand where my phone is charging. I sit on the edge of the bed and open the ongoing text thread and move my thumbs over the keyboard.

> I am so sorry I forgot to let you know I arrived!!!

> Shit! I am so sorry it's really late. If you're asleep, stay asleep.

Her answer is immediate.

> I checked your flight status. I knew you
> would be... busy. How are you doing?

> Fine. How was your date?

> Dismal. I think I'm going to take a hiatus
> from dating. I'm feeling done.

Instead of texting, I place an earbud into my right ear and call.

Genevieve picks up mid first ring. "Won't you wake up the fam?"

"Gen, this house is huge. We're all sleeping on the upper level, but my room is on the other side of the house facing the front. There's a library loft, a laundry room, the nursery, and who knows what between me and them. No one is going to hear me."

"I'm sure they put you in there to give you privacy."

"Oh, of course. I didn't mean anything untoward. You should see my room. Pretty much everything has been done for me."

"Untoward." Gen chuffs. "We have been watching too much *Bridgerton*."

"Perhaps."

I'm already feeling better talking with my best friend. I know how to ground myself, but sometimes a person who loves you and knows your life and real feelings does the trick.

"Tell me about your date."

"Nothing to tell."

"Really?"

"I think I need to hit pause. The apps. The endless string of first dates. Maybe I need to take a long break.

Maybe look for a new job while I'm at it. Complete change. I don't know."

Life has been rough for Genevieve over the last year. Her dad died. Her mom moved back to France to live with her mom's sister, Gen's aunt. She's the last of the four Torres siblings to live in Southern California. Her love life keeps circling the drain along with her dream of owning a bookstore. Retail space is expensive in Los Angeles for the size store she wants. And there are other all-romance bookstores in the vicinity that she feels guilty competing with. She gets paid extremely well for her high-level executive assistant position at an elite law firm, but it's not what she wants. Other than owning a bookstore, she doesn't know what to do.

"It's healthy for you to take a break and focus solely on yourself. Maybe take a long vacation. You have the time off banked. I know you have the money. Why don't we plan something together when I get back?"

"That makes me feel better. I could use a vacation. Ooooo! Let's do one of those river cruises through France that we always drool over. Maybe visit my mom."

"I'm all in."

My legs and arms are cold. Normally, I sleep naked, but I don't feel it's appropriate in a strange house. So, I'm wearing hot pink, jersey knit sleep shorts with a matching tank top. I slip into bed and pull the covers up to my chin. The sheets are cold, so I start to slide my legs against each other like a cricket to warm up.

Gen pauses before turning serious again. "How is everything going?"

"Fine." I let out a sigh. "Awkward. I expected as much, but it doesn't feel any better. I still don't know what to call Alex. Fortunately, I'm probably not going to have to introduce her to anyone while I'm here."

"Not even at the studio?"

"When we planned this, we both thought it best to keep things professional."

"No one needs to know your business if you don't want them to."

"Correct."

"Hey! It's almost three o'clock there. You better try to get some sleep. At least close your eyes and rest. Plum will be up early and want to have all your attention."

"She has soccer practice in the morning. Alex told me to sleep in if I want to. And it's nearly midnight there, missy."

"That's good. And it's not like I have anywhere to be tomorrow, missy. What are you doing tomorrow?"

"Plum and I are going to decorate the front yard. I don't think I bought enough of anything. I didn't think their front yard would be so big. Maybe we can go out and buy more."

"Don't stress it, Em. You're ultra-creative. You'll figure it out. Just have fun with your niece."

My eyelids feel heavy, my legs are warm, and I know I can sleep now.

"You're right. I'll work with what I have."

"Text if you need me. Anytime."

"Same to you. Good night."

"Good night."

Right after I set my phone and earbuds back on the nightstand, I let the sound of the wind in the trees lull me to sleep.

CHAPTER 3

November

A dozen jack-o'-lanterns.

I must be out of my mind.

Maybe it was the immersion of mind, body, and soul in the autumn experience today. The charming, well-maintained pumpkin farm complete with red barn and smaller outlying buildings trimmed in white. Hot beverages to hold to take the edge off the windy chill. The hayride under the canopy of orange, red, and gold leaves, the colors popping against the gray clouds beyond. The smell of freshly made apple cider donuts dusted with cinnamon sugar - the must-have during this glorious season.

Maybe it was the way Plum's eyes went wide and she cackled maniacally every time I loaded another pumpkin into the wheelbarrow after the four large ones already resting at the bottom. I could have stopped at the six, but when Plum suggested she run to get another wheelbarrow... Twelve pumpkins of varying sizes seemed like a good idea to keep us laughing together. Especially when she animatedly instructed what type of face we will carve into each pumpkin. Well, I will carve.

Alex and Mark don't understand the fun to be had from Halloween, so they awkwardly scooped out the guts of a few pumpkins and I carved. Plum penciled all the faces and helped pull out pumpkin innards and separate the seeds for roasting. Alex has always said Plum gets the Halloween gene from me.

I sent everyone to bed around nine o'clock; they all have to be up early for work and school. Mark was the last to go upstairs. I think he felt he has to keep me entertained or felt bad for leaving me to deal with the pumpkin mess. He is a truly nice guy. I assured him this is fun for me and he finally went to bed. I have to be up early too for class, but jetlag is still holding me firm in its grip, and I hate leaving a job undone.

The truth is, as much fun as it is making spectacular memories with my niece, my only remaining blood relative who I love with my whole heart, I needed a break from being on. To just breathe and turn my brain on low volume.

It's after ten now. I'm chewing the last bite of my fourth donut of the day, wishing I had bought another dozen, and admiring the face of my last jack-o'-lantern. I like the wisps of hair I carved into this stout pumpkin and I know exactly where I will place it outside.

A sweatshirt is not enough to keep the cold night wind of Western New York from sapping the warmth of a native Southern California girl, but I love how the wind adds another layer of thrill to this time of year. There is nothing like autumn in the northeast, especially during Halloween, and I soak it in every year I am here.

I have no idea where I got my love of Halloween from. My mom, who preferred Thanksgiving over Halloween, used to take me and Roman to the movies so she could avoid the whole trick-or-treating thing. We would go to the store and buy two candies each because it was cheaper than at the movie theater, and Mom would slip the candy in her handbag for safekeeping until we were seated and the theater was dark. That was our Halloween each year until Roman was in high school and allowed to go out with friends. I thought Mom would take me to the movies, but she didn't, and I usually spent the night in my bedroom reading by flashlight. Perhaps my Halloween fanaticism came from wanting what I couldn't have.

I cut across the front lawn to the base of a medium-size red maple tree that has stubbornly withstood the wind and still holding on to the majority of its leaves. It is stunning in its blazing red glory during daylight, darker hued in the night. Instead of wrapping the trunk and branches with strings of fairy lights, Plum and I drove to the closest hardware store and bought a small spotlight to stake in the ground to illuminate the tree and the display before it.

Next to a tall tombstone that reads *Welcome to the Graveyard*, a skeleton stands with its back against the tree trunk and holds the leash of a skeleton dog with glowing red eyes. After positioning the last jack-o'-lantern by the tombstone, I pull my hands into the sleeves of my violet sweatshirt to warm them, then walk to the sidewalk to survey what Plum and I created.

Genevieve was right. I did work with what I had and I can't help smiling to myself for a job well done.

I pull my cell phone from the thigh pocket of my black leggings and proceed to snap a few photos and take a quick video of the cemetery. The jack-o'-lanterns aren't lit, but I'll set the faux candle timers tomorrow at sunset. As freezing as I am, I slowly shuffle across the lawn, my sneakered feet shuffling through leaves strewn across the lawn, while sending a text of some photos from today to Gen, then hurry up the steps and through the front door.

Once inside, I realize how freezing my face, ears, and

limbs are. Quickly, I turn off the downstairs lights, double-check the door locks, then head upstairs to the guest bedroom. My cell phone pings just as I close the door.

> Plum is adorable! Looks like a fun day. You must be going to bed by now. Talk tomorrow?

> Lots of fun! Talk tomorrow.

I do have other text messages and emails waiting for me, but nothing that can't wait until the morning. There is a text from a number I don't recognize, but the first two lines have my heart trumpeting "Reveille".

> Hi November! This is Rhys. If the offer stands, I'd like to attend your 8 am class tomorrow. Let me know location details. Thank you.

He sent this message three hours ago. I don't need to account for my time to a stranger, but I don't want him to think I'm ignoring him. So, I pull up the same video sent to Gen and attach it to the text I type, but hesitate tapping the send button. It is so late to be sending what is essentially a business text. It takes a long moment to decide to tap the green button.

> Hi Rhys! Sorry for the late response. I've been elbow deep in pumpkin guts.

I worry my bottom lip with my teeth waiting to see typing indicators, but none come. It is late. Maybe I should send another text with class details that he will see in the morning. If not, maybe he can attend another class.

After sending A New Day's address on Wehrle Drive along with a text confirming he is welcome to join, I place my phone on the bed and proceed to undress for my shower. I'm down to my bra and leggings when my phone pings. I grab it, my fingers nor any other part of my body feeling cold anymore.

> Thanks for the info! You've been busy.

> My niece and I decorated and carved pumpkins this weekend. I just finished.

He really doesn't need to know any of that. And I'm suddenly aware I am nearly undressed while texting. He can't see me, but it still feels indecent.

> I don't know if you meant it to be, but there's a haunting elegance to the decorations.

I scroll up to study the video I sent. He's right. It wasn't my intent, but the whole cemetery scene is not gross nor scary; it is elegantly haunting. Eight resin tombstones, faux floral pieces in black and deep shades of purples, purple fairy lights wound through the trees and bushes, a few adult-sized skeletons staged just so, some ghosts we made from white tulle, and the jack-o'-lanterns.

> I see what you mean.

> You have an eye for this. Do you go all out for all holidays?

> Thank you. Just Halloween and Christmas. Do you decorate?

> I haven't decorated for a holiday in a very long time and when I did, not like that.

I chew on that bit of information. Does he not like holidays? Or just not decorating? Is there a reason why? I can't ask that over text nor is it my business.

> That's no fun.

I sent that text too fast. I'm teasing, but he doesn't know that.

That's probably accurate. Anyone who knows me would say I'm more work than play.

What to say? What to say? What to say?

> Maybe you are more play than you think. You are playing hooky from work tomorrow to take my class I assume.

Part of the morning.

> We all have to start somewhere. See you tomorrow!

Good night, November.

I gently place my phone on the nightstand and realize I have been standing in a dark room with only the glow of the screen to see anything. I connect the phone to the charging cord, then pad to the ensuite bathroom to shower. I need to calm myself. I need some sleep. I need to stop feeling so excited to see Rhys Morgan again.

CHAPTER 4
Rhys

I googled her.

As soon as I got home from the airport on Friday, before I unpacked my suitcase, I googled November Day. Instead of tackling emails and getting a head start on some reports as planned, I wanted to see what kind of work she does. Do I completely understand it all? No. Am I impressed at what she has built for herself? Extremely.

We may work in different industries, but I know what it takes to create a successful business, and that is exactly what November has done for herself over the last ten years. By her online presence alone, I can tell she is well-respected in her industry. She had touched upon working 'corporate' during our in-flight conversation, but that was a modest statement. We are talking about the formation of employee wellness programs for several Fortune 500 companies.

I'm embarrassed I thought she didn't know how to sell herself. She doesn't need to. There comes a turning point in success when you know you have made a name for yourself because people seek you out; you no longer need to shout from the rooftops to sell what you're offering. November is at that level and I admire her for it.

In my search, I also discovered she is thirty-four-years-old. Eight years younger than I am. By the look of her, I thought she was younger. I didn't think, no, I hoped not that much younger. I have never dated a woman, slept with a woman, more than a few years difference, in either direction, since the beginning of my sexual history. Regardless of her age, it's not like I will be dating nor sleeping with November. *Yet...* No, I can't entertain the idea because if she turns out to be as great as I think she may be, she will be gone in less than two weeks.

When I woke up on Saturday morning, I thought I had put my curiosity for my intriguing seatmate behind me. I had spent hours the night before reading what I could find on November without utilizing the kind of access I have for a deep dive. I didn't want to feel like a complete creep. But she kept resurfacing in my mind during my Saturday routine of working out, running errands, and getting work done for Monday. Replays of conversation highlights. Her audacity of giving me a sex scene to read. The unusual shade of her beautiful brown eyes. The high wattage of her wide smile.

Fucking annoying.

My Saturday ended with me at an independent bookstore buying a copy of *The Gods of What We Take for Granted*, then spending too many hours consuming as many chapters as I could. When was the last time I got sucked into a book like this? Never. I almost canceled my attendance at Sunday family brunch just so I could plow through more chapters, but I knew Carys would make me miserable come Monday for blowing them off.

By Sunday evening, I knew I had to see November again and didn't hesitate texting her.

Now, here I am.

For the past ten minutes, I have been sitting in my car outside A New Day, wondering what I am doing here. I parked far enough from the single story building's windows to not be seen. If November happens to spot me, I don't want her to think I'm losing my nerve. I am not that kind of man, but she doesn't know me. And that's the question of the day, isn't it? Do I want her to know me?

I get out of my car and take the short walk to the studio's entrance as I ponder that question, and another. Why do I want to know more about her? Yes, she is beautiful and interesting, but it's not like I could date her. She doesn't live here, not even close, and long distance is not how I envision a relationship for myself. Not that I have entertained the idea of a relationship in the last year. More like lost hope in having a real relationship in the last several years; the type of loving and honest partnership that my mom and dad had when they were alive.

And I am not going into this class thinking about asking November on a date. No. I just want to see if everything I know about this woman is real. That's what I keep telling myself, at least.

There is more activity within the studio than I thought there would be and 'studio' is a small word for the facility A New Day is. It's not the typical look of a gym with its light bamboo flooring, ivory walls with crown molding, and sage cushions on storage benches. No overly loud music. No harsh lighting. And I think I smell sandalwood and lemongrass.

Looks like an exercise class has just ended with the clients, mostly women, rising from their - what are those? Some type of flat, padded contraption with pulleys I have never seen. Definitely not any kind of equipment I have in my home gym.

I turn my attention to a woman with medium-length,

honey blonde hair standing at the reception desk, her hands moving quickly to tidy the surface. She is definitely the woman with the little girl that met November at the airport.

"Good morning," she greets me with a genuine smile, and a head tilt as if I'm familiar to her too. "May I help you?"

"Good morning. I know the eight o'clock meditation class is full, but November said she could fit me in."

"Rhys!"

As if me speaking her name willed her into existence, November appears in an adjacent doorway. She is more beautiful than my memory led me to believe.

The comings and goings of the surrounding people become insignificant as November steps into the open reception area. Her big eyes and smile are equally expressive, surprise and triumph washing over her fresh face. Whatever she is feeling, I will take it, as long as she continues to smile at me like that. That sound of the custom-made slot machine just for me.

"Good to see you, November."

I am actively keeping my eyes trained on hers even though they want to peruse all of her.

"Good to see you too."

If I blinked, I would have missed it, but her eyes did give me a lightning quick up and down, and I can feel my mouth grin a little wider.

"You must be the man November met on the plane."

I force my eyes to turn their attention to who I think is November's sister-in-law.

"Alex Phillips, this is Rhys Morgan," November introduces. "Alex owns A New Day."

I extend my hand to Alex, who has dark green eyes that borderline hazel, and is about an inch taller than November. "It's nice to meet you."

"Rhys and I talked meditation on the plane, and I guess he is interested enough to test out the intro class. I know the class is full, but I said I would squeeze him in."

"I hope it's not an imposition," I say to Alex. Having her here is a good buffer from me wanting to monopolize November's time.

"Not at all. When we originally scheduled the classes, we didn't know how many slots to open, so we started modestly. There is plenty of room for you."

"Thank you. Do I pay for the class here?" I begin to reach into the pocket of my hoodie to extract my credit card.

"Consider this a complimentary class."

"Oh, no. I insist on paying."

Alex puts her hands up to indicate she will not be taking payment. "Not for this class. If you decide to take future classes, you can pay for those at the friends and family rate."

By Alex's friendly yet firm tone, I know there is no room for debate and return my card to its pocket. "I appreciate your generosity."

"Enjoy the class."

A gentle tug of my sweatshirt sleeve pulls my focus, and I look down to see November release the navy fabric as she takes a step back toward the door she appeared from.

"Come on. The class is about to begin."

I follow. And once her head has turned away, I allow myself the perusal I was dying for moments earlier.

Her long, thick hair is up in a high, bouncy ponytail, just as silky looking as I remember. She is wearing a long sleeved, black, off-the-shoulder athletic top that tapers to her waist, black joggers that hug her hips and ass in a way I should not be thinking about, and black toe socks with the word 'LOVE' printed in white across the top of each foot. I normally don't consider colors on women, but November wears black extremely well. Even better is the lightly sun-

35

kissed skin of her shoulder and neck that I am itching to touch.

Coming here was a bad idea.

I tear my eyes away to scan the warmly lit, high-ceilinged room. There are several clients sitting on cushioned square mats in neat rows on the shiny plank floor. All swivel their heads to take a look at the new guy walking in with the instructor.

November gestures to a long bench against a wall with shoe storage underneath. "You can take your shoes off over there." She then points to a forest green cushion. "And I saved you a place in the back row because... you are so tall."

I'm pretty sure she was going to say it will be less awkward for me and she would be right. "Good thinking. Thanks."

"I have to start class now." She slides the pocket door shut and the sound is a signal for everyone's conversations to wind down.

I toe off my sneakers and bend to pick them up. "Go ahead. I'll be fine."

"I know you will."

She winks. She actually winks at me and I feel the jolt of that little flirty move ricochet through my body. I have to will my eyes to look away to find an empty cube for my sneakers. But, once I take my seat, cross-legged, my eyes are able to watch her freely - she is the instructor after all – and my brain soaks up every beautiful detail.

"Good morning, everyone," November speaks in a soothing tone, yet loud enough to gain everyone's attention as she navigates her way through the participants to the short riser at the front. "I'm November Day and I couldn't be more excited to bring my brand of meditation to Buffa-lo." She takes a seat at the edge of the riser, socked feet on the floor. "How is everyone doing today?"

There are plenty of 'fine' responses. I don't respond at all.

"The 'fine' of polite society." Her smile exudes ease and warmth and capability. "Fine is a good, acceptable answer when you're talking with a stranger or acquaintance, or maybe you're in a rush to get somewhere or do something. Fine is fine. But is fine really good to tell yourself? Not if it's not the truth. Or maybe we don't know how we're feeling in the moment. That's okay. No one can tell you how to feel."

Her posture is straight with relaxed shoulders, talking with graceful hand movements. Not a knee bounce or nervous twitch to be seen. Not a hint of boredom or arrogance in her voice even though she has probably taught this class thousands of times over the years.

"A great way to check in with yourself is through breath." She pauses. "How difficult is it for you to take a deep breath? I mean the type of breath that pushes your stomach out. No worries if you don't know the answer. We're going to test it out."

She picks up a small remote control and dims the lights, but I can still see her in the soft glow. She sets the remote down, then glances around the room.

"I love how this room looks like this. All cozy and warm."

She receives a roll of low, nervous chuckles that cease as quickly as they began.

"I am going to lead you in a technique called box breathing. Everyone, close your eyes." Her voice becomes low and smoky and it is the sexiest thing I have ever heard. I feel it through my clothes, vibrating across my skin.

How am I going to get through this with that voice?

I can't close my eyes. I don't want to lose sight of her.

"We are going to slowly and deeply inhale to a count of four. Hold the breath for a count of four. Exhale for four.

37

Then rest for four. We're going to do this for four rounds. After, we'll discuss, but first, let's all start by loosening up by inhaling and exhaling one deep breath."

She looks directly at me, and it may be dimly lit, but I can still see the curve of her wide smile and each word as she mouths 'close your eyes.'

Caught, I obey.

"Great. Now, let's begin."

I hear that smile of hers.

While I tie my shoelaces, I listen to November speak with a few clients and wave goodbye to others. Her students compliment her, ask questions. When I'm done, I stand from the white storage bench and catch her eye to motion I'll be waiting outside. She nods discreetly and I exit.

At the end of class, November had brightened the room from dim to a half brightness, so when her students exit, the light of the rest of the facility isn't blinding, therefore, not infringing on the relaxed state of mind the class instilled. I notice excellent service details like this. The things you don't notice, yet notice. Touchpoints. She is extremely good at what she does.

Where Alex stood before, there is a tall, twenty-something woman with nearly white blonde hair wearing a black studio logo sweatshirt assisting clients at the counter. I pick up a brochure and step out of her sightline while I wait for November. The brochure is of excellent quality and the information seems complete, including prices of services.

The last student, a man about ten years younger than I am, steps out of the meditation room with November. He is visibly smitten. I don't blame him, but I don't like it. She remains friendly, yet professional, keeping an appropriate distance and her body doesn't turn towards him. Good sign. I still don't like it.

November gives me a little wave and it catches the man's eye. He glances at me, sizing me up. Maybe it's my body language, maybe I'm glaring at him, but he gets what I'm silently communicating. She's with me.

But she's not.

I couldn't be more relieved when November says her polite goodbye and turns to me with her true, full smile.

"See anything interesting in that brochure?"

"Is there really a swimming pool housed here?"

"Yes, but don't fill your mind with a massive, Olympic-sized thing. There are three small pools in a large room, used for a variety of exercise classes and therapies. But you can reserve one, when available, for laps using the wave function. It's like running on a treadmill, you're in full motion, but not going anywhere."

I fold the brochure in half and place it in my hoodie pocket as I take a real look around at what is visible. "From here, I would never guess this facility is as large as it is. You want your clients not to feel overwhelmed."

She narrows her sparkling eyes at me, a little smirk tugging at the corners of her mouth. "You catch on quick."

I don't want to leave. I want to stay here with this woman and see more of her reactions. Understand how her mind works. Make her keep smiling at me. For me.

"Do you have time for coffee?" The words come out without any thought.

Her smile wavers and her eyes cast downward. I understand it as an immediate no. I am a complete idiot. I can't believe read her all wrong.

"I should really hang around here until my next class just in case they need me for anything."

November is so open; her whole face expresses her reluctance. Her unspoken apology. And I am trying to keep my demeanor in check, but disappointment is burning through me.

"That's perfectly fine." Poor word choice. The usage of 'fine' recalls what she explained in class. I have not felt this out of control in decades. "I did enjoy your class. Please thank Alex again for her generosity."

She laces her fingers together tightly in front of her body. "You're very welcome, and I'll tell her."

My smile doesn't feel natural, but I do it anyway. "Goodbye, November."

I turn away to sever the awkwardness before she can say anything further. Once outside, the coolness of the breeze is a welcome touch to my warm face. I don't hesitate getting to my car.

"Why did I ask her to coffee?" I mumble to myself. *I'm a fool, that's why.*

I asked her out even though this couldn't go anywhere. I know that. She is leaving in less than two weeks. She knows that. Of course, she would turn me down.

That was a dumb move, Rhys. Now, you can't even take another one of her classes just to see her again.

Just as I reach the driver's side door, I am aware of her.

"I have to be back in an hour. Is that okay?"

I turn toward that addicting voice.

November halts a few feet in front of my car. I take in the look of her. Blushing cheeks. Teeth chewing on her bottom lip. Strands of her ponytail lifting on the breeze as if it wants to take a souvenir of her. No jacket. Her sneakers are untied as if she hurried to slip them on and could easily slip them off again if I say no.

My lips twitch. As if I could say no, but I say nothing at all. Instead, I walk to the passenger side to open the door for her and she hurries to take her seat.

There is another smile of hers for me to collect.

CHAPTER 5

November

"**I**s it strange I can feel the giddiness vibrating off you?"

I can only laugh in response to Rhys' question.

The closest coffee shop from the studio is less than five minutes away and an absolute winner in my book, even though I haven't tasted the coffee yet. It could taste like tar, yet it would have my vote. This place is absolutely decked out for Halloween. Strings of orange lights trim windows and doorways and the beamed ceiling throughout. Several black fabric witch hats hang from the ceiling amongst honeycomb tissue pumpkins. An orange and black card-board letter garland spelling *HAPPY HALLOWEEN* hangs across the red brick wall behind the counter, anchored by a large cardboard skeleton at each end.

"Did you bring me here knowing they decorated like this?" I eye Rhys suspiciously, but I don't dare look too long. He is too handsome with his too black hair and too blue eyes and too defined bone structure that can't be hidden behind the well-groomed dusting of facial hair. Too intense. Too much to look at.

"No. Just a lucky morning." Okay, he does look just as surprised as I am.

Rhys places his large hand on my lower back to give me a gentle nudge, guiding me out of the entry to allow patrons to exit. If you asked me to describe one single item of one person who passed us, I couldn't. My pinpoint focus is on the warmth seeping through my sweatshirt and radiating throughout my body from one touch. Barely a touch.

"Lucky me." My voice comes out thick like syrup.

With Rhys close behind, I zigzag around a display of bags of whole bean coffee, and a small table of autumn themed gift items until we arrive at the end of the ordering line. It is now I realize how busy this place is. The length of the line. The occupied wooden tables and cozier couches and armchairs. The baristas call out to 'Niki' and 'Sean' and 'Mary' and 'Ken' that their orders are ready for pick up. The near constant sound of grinding coffee beans and steam and frothing milk. Prime coffee time.

"There's not much seating available and more people are coming inside. Do you want to find somewhere for us to sit while I order?" asks Rhys.

"Good idea. Any preference where?"

"Wherever you feel most comfortable is fine with me. What would you like me to order for you?"

"A large latte with whole milk and a few dashes of cinnamon, please. No sweetener."

"Anything to eat?"

"No, thank you."

An image flashes in my brain. If we were a couple, I would give Rhys a kiss on the cheek as I cross in front of him before he advances to the cashier.

A couple. A kiss.

I keep my feet moving toward the seating area as I attempt to make sense of that thought. This does not feel awkward. What felt awkward is the moment I declined having coffee with Rhys back at the studio. Someplace inside me felt panicked that I didn't go with him. I couldn't slide into my sneakers fast enough, forget tying them. I knew if I went to my locker for my jacket, he would be gone.

To my left, I spot two women in business attire vacate saddle brown, leather club chairs in the corner and I make a beeline to claim them. It may not be private, but at least it is furthest away from the crowd at the service counter.

I sit and realize I have nothing with me. No handbag. No phone. I never told Alex where I was going. No money. I'll have to buy his coffee next time. *Next time?* I'm not in Buffalo for very long and here I am assuming there will be a next time.

Rhys is standing by the pick-up counter, feet shoulder width apart, arms folded across his broad chest, owning his space and completely unbothered by the people around him. He is gorgeous, and everyone is aware. I am too far away, but by the shy smile the female barista gives to Rhys as he picks up our order, I can guess she is blushing. I get it, I'm surprised my cheeks don't flame red hot every time he looks at me. Just like he is right now as he walks to where I'm seated.

He hands me my latte in a white lidded paper cup with a cardboard sleeve.

"Thank you." I hold my cup; its heat is welcome to my chilly hands. "What did you order?"

"You're welcome." He reclines against the back of his chair. "I decided to try what you're having. I don't like sweet coffee drinks either and the cinnamon sounded good."

His legs are so long. His knees are nearly touching mine, and I am feeling quite fine with having him so close.

"I love cinnamon. Gobs of it. At home, I go through

bottles of cinnamon so fast, I always have a backup on hand."

"A rare November favorite? Noted." He takes a sniff of his coffee before sampling the flavor.

I know he just called me out for saying I don't have favorites during our first conversation. He thinks he's so slick. But, internally, I am beating back a smile for his subtle jab.

"Did you finish your book yet?"

It takes me a few seconds to understand what he is referring to, then I smile. "I have been so busy, I only read five more chapters."

"The book is highly entertaining,"

"Yes, that chapter is highly entertaining." I snort.

Rhys' full smile is glinting sapphire eyes, popping dimples, and pearly whites. I can see the boy he used to be, and if I had known him all those years ago, I would have been the little girl crushing hard on the cute boy.

I have to take a sip of my slightly too hot latte to anchor myself.

"No. I mean, yes, that chapter is, but I'm talking about the entire book. Riveting story. I couldn't put it down." He takes a longer drink from his cup.

I freeze. *Wait!* He read *The Gods of What We Take for Granted*?

"You read the book. When did you read the book?"

He finishes swallowing before answering. "I bought it on Saturday. Stayed up late because I couldn't put it down, then almost canceled Sunday plans to continue reading."

"Did you finish it?"

"I have about ten chapters left."

"I can't believe you bought the book." I shake my head.

"I was intrigued."

Of course, he's referring to the book, yet his pointed stare right into my eyes has me feeling... captivating.

I clear my throat. "When we both finish, we'll have to discuss."

"Looking forward to it."

The coffee must be doing the trick because I am feeling all kinds of warm.

Must be the coffee.

"I forgot to ask. How did you find the meditation class? I know it was mostly discussion, but I always appreciate feedback from newcomers."

"It was interesting."

"Oh, no! Interesting is the polite way of saying 'not for me.'"

"That's not true!" He laughs. "It was very informative, but I don't have enough experience with it to make a solid opinion."

"Okay, that's fair."

"How did you become a wellness coach?"

"Through my mom. She was her generation's version of a wellness coach. She was always into meditation, so I grew up with some knowledge. She slowly took college courses and became a nutritionist and a yoga slash meditation instructor. I was a sophomore in high school when I led my first meditation. My theater teacher liked to have a short meditation at the beginning of her classes to focus the students. One day, she asked if anyone would like to try leading the class and I was the only one to raise their hand. I loved it! She even allowed the students to give me feedback and they loved it, and the teacher had me lead meditation every class after that. A meditation instructor was born!"

"That's not all you do. I looked at your website."

Rhys takes another long drink. I think he may be almost done with his coffee.

"No, it's not. Over the years, I added services here and there until I realized there was a market for people wanting workplans for feeling their best, so I connect the client to resources. I like jigsaw puzzles and making these plans is a wellness jigsaw puzzle. Then one of my clients wanted to do the same thing for the employees at the company she owned. More companies followed; my business kept growing."

"And you teach meditation on the side." That smile of his is magnetic.

"Very on the side." I chuckle. "Alex wanted to introduce meditation to Buffalo, to her clients, and see if it is something they're interested in. She asked if I would teach classes this week and I thought it would be fun. I don't get to do that often."

"Well, I may not know meditation, but I do know you are excellent in front of an audience."

"Why, thank you!" I place my hand over my heart in a mocking fashion, then giggle. "Honestly, I highly recommend everyone take an acting class. That theater education I had in high school is priceless."

"That's a topic worth exploring, but..." Rhys stretches out his sweatshirt-clad arm to uncover his watch and checks the time. "I had a feeling it was close to when I have to get you back. We have ten minutes."

"That was way too fast," I whine. "I didn't have the chance to ask anything about you. I know..." I mull it over a bit. "I know nothing other than you travel for work and you seem like a nice guy."

"I think most people would say I'm a nice guy." He smirks, but offers nothing else and shifts forward in his seat to stand.

I stand too and look to grab my belongings, but all I have is a lukewarm, half-drunk latte to carry. As expected, Rhys finished his drink and discards the cup in the trashcan at the exit before holding the door open for me to pass through.

Outside is still crisp and breezy, but I welcome the chilly air to cool off, feeling overly warm from the coffee and, I'll admit, the company.

Rhys slows his SUV to a smooth stop in front of the studio entrance, sets the car in park, turns off the ignition, then glances at me as he opens his door.

"I'll get the door for you." He steps out and shuts his door.

The short car ride back to the studio was quiet in the way two people don't feel the need to fill the silence to grasp at a connection. It feels easy, us together. I have had fast connections before, like with Genevieve and Alex, but never with a man. Why am I questioning it? Is it because this ease is with a man for the first time?

My door opens as I click the seatbelt release and step outside. Rhys shuts the door as soon as I am clear.

"Thank you for the coffee. I'm glad I changed my mind."

Rhys takes a step closer to me. Not directly in my space, but enough to keep a private conversation private from clients meandering by.

"Why did you change your mind?"

My lips part before my brain has to form any scrap of an answer. All I can do is be honest.

"I felt it would be a mistake not to go."

His gaze goes to some unseen point across the parking lot as he slowly nods his head in understanding. Then his eyes return to mine.

"I know your plans to visit your family did not entail

going on a date with a man you barely know, but if you have any time at all to go to dinner with me this week. Tomorrow? Wednesday? I don't know, November..."

Do I explode into millions of particles of sparkly light? It definitely feels that way.

"Unfortunately, dinner is out. With Halloween on Thursday, I have projects planned with Plum in the evenings leading up. But I can do lunch tomorrow at noon if you can fit me into your schedule."

As I speak, I think I can interpret Rhys' emotions going from hopeful to disappointment to relief even though his facial features never falter. His eyes! The shift there is so slight, yet there. Or I could be imagining something I want to see there.

"Lunch tomorrow works for me. Where should I pick you up?"

I know I'm grinning wider than I should be, but so is he.

"Right here. I have classes to teach in the morning, but I'll be done in plenty of time."

"Great!" He tilts his head toward the studio door. "You better go inside. You have to be cold."

Am I?

I feel nothing externally, and everything internally bursting.

"See you tomorrow, Rhys."

I turn toward the studio door, and I am completely aware there is a smidge more sway in my hips as I walk away.

CHAPTER 6

Rhys

The presence sensor in my SUV activates the steel garage door of a nondescript, four-story, brick building, and I slowly proceed into the climate-controlled interior. I bought this building by the waterfront as soon as I moved back to Buffalo; it had been long abandoned, but the bones were still good. It took over two years of exacting renovations to shape nothing into something I am immensely proud of. For the first three years of my business, I didn't need a building to work from. I was the sole employee of Morgan Security and worked from home, which was perfect for navigating the parenting of two teenagers going through the stages of grief.

I had the capital from my half of the data storage company I started with a college roommate. The buyout was lucrative enough to cover my building and renovation costs, buy a nice house for me and my siblings to live in, pay for high school and college expenses for my sister and brother, and get my current business off the ground. I will always be grateful for that starter company. Without it, my siblings and I would not have what we do today.

Since it's late morning, I park in a space close to the garage door for easy exit at the end of the work day. Other than two disabled and a few guest spaces by the elevator, I don't believe in assigned parking, much to my brother's chagrin. If I am founder and CEO, and I don't care where I park, Gareth can suck it!

When I reach the ballistic glass elevator vestibule, I scan my hand in the reader for the locks to disengage and allow my access to the waiting elevator. Is this for show? Yes and no. Do we need ballistic glass? Probably not. Do I want random people wandering through my facility? Absolutely not. Does this display impress our clients who visit us, put their minds at ease, and demonstrate the possibilities we can provide for them? Definitely. Yet, because of the plans we hold and services we provide for companies and private people all over the world, the real security we utilize here is not for prying eyes. Our technology is protected within a sophisticated vault system, and for our own use.

Morgan Security doesn't advertise for business; we don't need to. Business comes our way via word of mouth, and we vet our potential clients extensively to make sure the people we work with are on the right side of legal. We have never been served a search warrant and I intend to keep it that way. The majority of my life has been devoted to building my company into the success it is. Why would I want to throw it all away for dirty deeds? For kicks? Self-sabotage? Take away my life's work and I wouldn't be left with much. An empty house. An empty building.

When the elevator doors open and I step onto the second floor, it's relatively quiet with the exception of muffled talking sounds coming from the large, glass-walled conference room to my far right. As I walk pass, I take a look and see Carys watching me from the head of the table as she speaks to those in attendance. I give a slight raise of my hand in hello; she returns it with a discreet nod. The other conference room and the media room I pass are vacant, but I notice the secondary computer lab is in use by a small group of programmers.

My office is located opposite the elevator at the far end of the building. It is the only office on this floor and I prefer it that way. The only other permanent person here is my executive assistant, Sophie Stryjewski. I used to feel bad that she might be lonely down here, but she assures me time and again that she gets more work done being down here. The third-floor breakroom awaits when she wants to gossip, then leave it behind when she has her fill.

I place the gift card I bought at the coffee shop on Sophie's ergonomic desk before she can look up from one of her computer monitors. She raises an eyebrow; she is really good at non-verbal communication.

"A thank you for the trouble of rescheduling my morning last minute." I take a deep breath in pause before landing the blow. "And for clearing my schedule tomorrow from 11:30 a.m. until 2:00 p.m. And, good morning, by the way."

I make my getaway into the open door of my office, but did I really escape that easily? If the low hum of Sophie's electric wheelchair entering my office is any indication, that is a definite no.

Sophie swings the door closed behind her. The resulting waft of air ruffles the ends of her sleek silver bob.

"Who is she?" She navigates as close to my desk as possible before making a full stop.

I place my key fob and wallet in my top desk drawer. "She, who?"

Her sigh is pure irritation. "You're dressed like you just came from the gym, but I know you haven't been exercising.

So, you were somewhere I haven't figured out yet, then went to coffee."

"Maybe I wanted some time to myself. I think I've earned it," I tease.

She ignores my feeble reasoning like I knew she would. "You had me reschedule your morning, and now, tomorrow afternoon. If it were business, you would have told me. If it were a medical issue, you wouldn't have that goofy grin on your face."

I chuckle. She is not wrong. She rarely is.

Sophie narrows her light brown eyes and continues, "AND, I don't think I have ever seen this side of you. I've known you for over ten years, no, over eleven years, and I have NEVER seen you with that smile."

Check and mate. I take a seat in my desk chair, lean back and lower my guard.

I have entrusted Sophie with many secrets that have never come back to haunt me. Each one of her birthdays, I hold my breath that this might be the birthday she talks retirement. She hasn't yet, but I do know she and her husband have decided their current teenage, foster-turned-adopted son will be the last child they raise. Once he graduates from high school and enters college, retirement is a real possibility, and I will lament that day as much as I will wish her well.

"Yes, I had coffee with a woman I met on the plane from Chicago." I feel my smile fade. "She's not from here."

"You like her." I hate how soft Sophie's voice is right now.

"From the little time I have spent with her..." I don't or can't say it. "But she lives clear across the country."

"So?"

"So, I don't think I am built for long distance."

She waves her hand at me like my statement is the most absurd thing she has heard.

"That's neither here nor there. You met this woman only Friday and you're already worried about a relationship. Rhys, rein it in. Try getting to know her during the time you have. Don't think so far ahead." Her sly smile appears, along with that all-knowing glint in her eyes. "Although, if you're already jumping to thoughts of a relationship, this woman must be pretty special."

An insistent knock sounds through the large, high-ceilinged office, and I already know who is on the other side of the door. Who both are. I am saved from responding to Sophie, but who knows what the pair on the other side of the door will bring.

Sophie rolls her eyes before turning her wheelchair around to exit.

"Come in!" I shout.

My siblings enter, Carys first, followed by Gareth.

Anyone can tell we are siblings. Identical black hair, shade of blue eyes, similar facial features. We are all tall, even Carys is an inch shy of six foot. My brother and sister are thirty-two-year-old twins, ten years younger than I am, but sometimes, I feel much older.

"Behave yourselves, children," Sophie warns as she exits, but leaves the door open.

"Why are you dressed like that?" Carys questions as she joins Gareth on the contemporary leather couch, easing her six months pregnant body down using the armrest to support herself.

I pull the brochure out of my pocket and unfold it before walking over to hand it to Carys.

"I think the more important question is, who are you fucking?" Gareth asks, sharp eyes analyzing me for a tell.

Carys punches Gareth hard on his bicep.

"Ow!"

He's not joking – Carys is strong. I taught her how to throw a punch when she was a teenager. Ah! The call from the principal's office when she laid out Tommy Leland for grabbing her ass. I was proud she defended herself, then threatened to rain down hell if they didn't punish that little fucker for sexual misconduct.

"Don't be crass!" Carys takes the brochure from me, opens and scans it. "What is this? Oh! This looks interesting."

Gareth rubs his arm as he peers over her shoulder.

"I heard about the facility and decided to take a look this morning. Carys, I know you wanted to give something extra to the employees, in addition to the year-end bonuses and the holiday time off. Something health focused. Maybe we can tailor a company membership."

"Why haven't I heard of this place? This is more my cup of tea than yours. Where did you hear about it?"

They don't need to know the details. "Someone on my Friday flight was talking about it."

"That's random, but I'm happy for the information. And you got a good vibe?"

"I did." *And from November.* "Check out the website and tell me what you think. I have to change my clothes for a conference call now."

Gareth stands first, then lends his hand to assist Carys in standing. They have always had the closest bond. Tommy Leland's car was keyed, and the tires were slashed, but there was no evidence of who had done it and the twins each had alibis. I have my suspicions, but Gareth never fessed up.

Although I have a good relationship with them, our age difference sets us apart. They were young when I went away to college. I came home for holidays and the summer months, and would take them on short day trips to ride the mountain coaster in Ellicottville or do Cave of the Winds in Niagara Falls or shuttle them to rowing classes to give my mom a break. Every time I was home, I felt the need to breathe life into bonding with them all over again. It was worth it.

Gareth extracts his cell phone from his pants pocket and scans the notification. "You canceled lunch tomorrow?"

Carys whips her head around at me. "Why are you canceling lunch with us?"

"Seriously, who are you fucking?"

There is no punch from Carys this time. She waits for my answer as well.

I walk to my closet and select a pair of pants and a dress shirt from the stash I keep at work.

"No one!" It is true. "Now leave, so I can change and get on with my day."

My siblings give me identical side-eye as they exit, whispering to each other.

"And leave Sophie alone!" She won't say anything, but I do not want them bothering her.

The door slams shut in answer.

Locked away in my ensuite bathroom, I strip out of my gym clothes. I should be thinking about the phone calls I need to make, emails to write, and the build report I need to put the final touches on, but all I can think of is where I want to take November to lunch.

CHAPTER 7
November

"The kitchen still smells like cooking caramel." Alex, dressed in the cozy pumpkin print flannel pajamas I brought for her, makes her way through the kitchen to the dining room where I have set up shop. "I wish there was a way to bottle it up. Candles just don't capture that buttery vanilla scent like the real deal."

I am grateful for the large table in this room. Plum and I needed a space to cut and wrap the four large baking sheets of vanilla caramel we cooked yesterday. As soon as Plum got home from school and finished her homework, we began the lesson of how to cut the caramel into bite-size pieces and wrap them. Finally, we created gift bags. Several caramel candies each in a black and clear striped cellophane treat bag, tied with the purple ribbon embossed with glittery black spider webbing we found at a craft store. The final touch was gluing these rhinestone spiders to the center of each bow. To my delight, the gift bags look smashing!

"Shouldn't you be going to sleep now?" I ask as I glue one final spider to a bag.

"In a few minutes." Alex picks up one bag and admires

it. "I swear, I wouldn't know how to do Halloween if you weren't around. The kids in Plum's class are going to go nuts over these."

"We made extra to bring to soccer practice tomorrow, and some for the neighbors. Plum will run them over to their houses after school on Wednesday, if that's okay with you."

"Of course. I hope you saved some caramel for us."

"There's a bowl by the refrigerator and I stuffed a freezer bag and placed it in the freezer."

"Best. Sister. Ever." Alex does a little dance in place, then stops abruptly. "Speaking of soccer, tomorrow is my early day because of soccer. I know you have lunch with Rhys and I'll be gone from the studio by the time you return."

"I'll have Rhys drop me off here."

"Do you have your house key? No one will be home at that time."

"I do."

Alex bites her lips together as she bobs her head. She's hesitating.

"Alex?"

"I didn't say it earlier today because I think I was shocked over your coffee with Rhys and your lunch date tomorrow. I'm happy for you. It's been a while since you last dated. It almost felt like you had given up."

"It has been a while, but I consider myself not completely closed off to finding someone. Regardless, nothing will pan out with Rhys, but I can enjoy a date with him."

Alex's face twists in confusion. "Why wouldn't it pan out?"

"Because he lives here and I live in LA."

"At the end of your two weeks here, if you and Rhys are still into each other, you could figure something out."

I stand to start cleaning up the table. "I like Rhys so far and I am sure I will still like him when I leave, but sustaining a long-distance relationship when two people barely know each other... Does that really set us up for success? I can't seem to find a man who cares enough to want to know me when I live in the same city as them. Believe me when I say I've tried."

What I don't say is: even when my shitty ass father left my mom and his children, never to be seen or heard from again, I had the best love role models in Alex and my brother. I saw their love, felt their love, for years. I saw the way they looked at each other. How Roman took care of Alex, and the way she took care of him. I saw what they created from that love in Plum. The life they built together. Although their love ended in tragedy, Roman loved Alex so completely, she knew he would want her to continue to live her best life.

Nothing I have experienced with the men I've dated comes close. I refuse to settle after witnessing the best kind of love.

Alex places the lids on the plastic totes going to Plum's classroom and soccer practice. "Aren't you lonely in Los Angeles? November, you are fortunate in you can work from anywhere in the world."

"Los Angeles is my home. The only one I've ever known. I don't always love LA, but I have my restaurants and stores and fun things to do there."

"Yes, you have your fun things, but when you're not working, you're pretty much a homebody. I see your Bookstagram. I know how much you read."

I smirk at the Bookstagram comment. "I won't deny that, but it is nice to know that when I want to go out into the city, all the places are waiting for me. And don't forget, I have Genevieve."

"I love Genevieve. She is a great friend for you. She is your family." Alex places a hand on her baby bump and sighs. "I just want more for you. If anyone can make a long-distance relationship work, you can. You have always been devoted to the people you care about. I would love to see you turn that care to a romantic relationship."

I give her a little dismissive nod in response, then change the subject. "Where should I store the caramel totes?"

Her frustration dissipates. "Just leave them there for now. I'll have Mark place them in the car tomorrow."

I walk around the table as she turns off the dining room light, then the kitchen lights as we pass through in weighted silence.

At the top of the stairs, Alex turns to hug me tight and I welcome it. When we part, Alex grasps my shoulders.

"One last thing: I love you. I know things have changed drastically in the last few years, but that will never change. You are my sister and I love you. I felt the need to tell you that."

I blink back the sting of tears. Alex and Plum and Genevieve are all the family I have in the world right now. She has no idea how much I needed to hear that from her.

"I love you too."

Alex studies me for a few seconds before releasing me. She yawns. "What are you going to wear for your date tomorrow?"

"No new conversations. We need to go to bed."

"You're no fun, but also right. Good night, November."

"Good night."

After I am showered, moisturized and clad in sleepwear, I slip into bed. Instead of catching up with *The Gods of*

What We Take for Granted, I choose to text Genevieve first.

> Available for a chat?

> Give me a sec.

Less than a minute later, Gen is ringing me through FaceTime and I answer. From the little bit of background, I can see Gen is sitting on her navy velvet sofa. She is makeup free and her long ringlets are pulled into a thick bun on her head; looks like she just finished washing her face which she always does when she gets home from work.

"Hey you! How are you?" I ask.

"Same ole, same ole. How about you? How was teaching? You haven't done that in a minute."

"It was fun. I think today's classes were very well-received, but we'll see what happens at the end of the week."

"And your weekend?"

"Plum and I made caramel yesterday, and I thought of you."

"I am so jealous right now!"

"You'll have your hot buttered rum caramel during Christmastime."

"Still."

"Soooooo, I have something to share with you." If I can hear the hesitancy in my voice, I know Gen can.

"Soooooo, tell me," she mimics.

"I have a lunch date tomorrow," I blurt out.

She looks as if the screen has frozen, but then her golden-brown eyes shift side to side, then back to me.

"Not what I was expecting at all. Did you meet someone at the studio?"

"No."

I start from the beginning. I spill to her all about giving Rhys the sex scene to read, our conversation on the plane, the meditation class, coffee, and him asking me out to lunch since dinner wasn't an option because of Halloween. When I finish, I take a couple deep breaths.

Gen blinks, then blinks again, before speaking. "First of all, that is one hell of a meet cute. Second, you have a pair on you for giving him that scene to read."

"Clearly." I snort.

"Third, for you to go on a second date..."

"First date. I don't consider going to coffee as our first date since it was more of a spontaneous thing. A 'let's chat for a few minutes' thing."

She rolls her eyes. "Whatever. You're seeing the man a second time."

"Technically, a third time."

"Stop it, November! You are spiraling! Bring it down a few notches."

She's not wrong. After my conversation with Alex this evening, I am well aware I dismissed what she said about having a long-distance relationship, but the real issue is having a relationship at all. It has been a couple years since my last relationship, if you can call it that, and it only lasted a few months.

"Tomorrow feels like an official 'I like you, you like me, let's see what happens next' thing. A real beginning."

Gen nods. "Yeah, it is. And I can tell you like him, even if you say you barely know him. You like Rhys."

"I like Rhys."

"And the man sounds dreamy the way you describe him. If you can snap a pic, send it to me. I want to see what the fuss is about."

"Maybe not tomorrow."

"Maybe not tomorrow."

We both settle into quiet for a moment.

"Gen, what happens at the end of my two weeks if I like him more?"

"No. We are not going to think that far ahead. You are going to put that out of your mind and enjoy your date. Lean into it."

"You're right."

"Always!"

We both laugh at that.

"Time for bed." I look at my beautiful friend. "Thank you for talking this through with me."

"I am always here for you. And I expect a full report tomorrow."

"I'll call you tomorrow night."

"Love you, babe."

"Love you back."

CHAPTER 8

Rhys

After several consecutive days of gray skies, the sun is poking through puffy white clouds this afternoon. Bright sunshine and crisp air. A breeze rustles tree branches, and sends leaves in all the colors of fall tumbling along the pavement outside A New Day. I couldn't have asked for better weather for the date I planned for November.

I am going on a date.

Spending time with her yesterday, watching her, talking with her; she has now taken up residency in my brain. Who am I kidding? She is all I have thought about since I parted ways with her at the airport. I think it is finally hitting me: this is a date with a woman who completely knocks me out. Yet, I can't grasp how it could go anywhere. Can it? Even if we can overcome the physical distance, there is our age difference. Although not a crazy number of years between us, she is only two years older than Carys and Gareth. Does she want marriage? Children? We would have to live in the same city. How attached is she to Los Angeles?

I shut it down and quiet the frenzy, and remember my conversation with Sophie about not getting ahead of myself.

One moment at a time.

The clock on the dashboard that I have been trying not to obsess over lets me know I have ten minutes remaining until the agreed upon meet time. I can text her now.

> I'm here. Take your time.

It doesn't take long to receive a response that she is on her way. I like that she didn't hesitate to respond. Makes me think she is just as excited as I am to see each other. We texted a bit this morning, mainly me reaching out to confirm lunch. She asked if I could drive her to Alex's house after our date; she would order a ride share if I had to get back to the office. As if I would make her order a car. Besides, all I want is to prolong my time with her. I know this even before our date has begun.

My eyes catch on November exiting the studio.

God! She's gorgeous!

The first thing I notice is her hair. She is wearing it down and doesn't seem to mind when the breeze tosses locks about her shoulders. My eyes roam downward to take in the rest of her. Formfitting, camel-colored crewneck sweater; a flirty, pleated, brown plaid skirt that reaches down to the middle of her thighs, thankfully, clad in camel-colored tights; and high-heeled ankle boots. Very date ready, and reducing my insides to mush.

I step out of my SUV to greet her. "Hi!"

When she reaches me, she stops. "Nice to see you again."

Her smile is the widest I have seen so far and it is devastating in the best possible way. If I hug her, touch her, I will not want to let her go. Fortunately, she reaches into her leather tote bag for something crinkly sounding.

She holds out a beautifully wrapped bag of what looks like candy and I grasp it from the top where I won't make contact with her skin.

"Thank you. The wrapping is definitely you – elegantly haunting like the front yard decorations." I inspect the contents of the bag through the clear stripes. "Is this caramel?"

She laughs and I know she liked my elegantly haunting comment.

"I taught Plum to make caramel the other day."

"You made this from scratch?"

"I have been making caramel for many years. I usually make it at Christmastime in flavors like hot buttered rum and gingerbread. But Plum is old enough to learn and it was fun showing her how. She really liked cooking the caramel, not so much the wrapping part."

"Thank you. This is really special." My eyes hold her gaze.

Her voice comes out a bit higher than normal. "It's nothing."

She looks down at the ground. I embarrassed her, but she doesn't understand how deep the act of this gift is penetrating into my chest. At some point while she was making the caramel, she was thinking of me when she didn't have to.

I lean down in an attempt to catch her eyes with mine.

"I mean it. Thank you for thinking of me."

"You're welcome." Her voice is soft, but I'm certain she knows my gratitude is real.

I straighten to my full height. "Are you hungry?"

"Famished."

I move to the passenger side door and open it for her. "Then let's get you fed."

There are many restaurants in Buffalo that serve great food, but I chose this particular one in Delaware Park for the lake view. The majority of the park's mature trees still cling to their autumn leaves, painting the landscape in fiery color against the azure sky canvas. With the sun shining and mild temperature, November and I opt to have our lunch at an outdoor table closest to the railing to enjoy the spectacular scenery.

November orders a hot chicken breast, apple and brie sandwich; I am in the mood for the French Dip. We decide to split each sandwich and share since we both liked the sound of each.

Love a good plan when it falls into place!

"It's been a while since I've been to this side of the park. Last year, Plum had a fun run on the other side near the zoo. We had to be at the park so early that morning, but it was a good time, especially the breakfast afterward at a restaurant on Hertel Avenue. I think most of the run participants ended up at that restaurant."

"Sounds like you have a close relationship with your niece."

November studies me for a brief moment, her eyes narrowing, arms crossing in front of her chest. "Oh no you don't." Her voice goes low. "There will be no talking about me until you start coughing up some information about yourself."

I have to laugh because I feel caught. *She's adorable.*

"Fair. What would you like to know?" My guess, she will ask what I do for a living.

"Which family members are you closest with?"

She is different. Why am I surprised when our first meeting was so unexpected?

Dates in the last ten years usually entail questions about my business. No. To be accurate, the questions were not about what I do, more around the topic of how much money I have, in an indirect way...sometimes direct. Honestly, there haven't been many other types of questions posed to me. Don't get me wrong, I like the idea of taking care of the woman I love, who genuinely loves me. What I don't want is to be a human bank account. Hence, why my attempts at romantic relationships have become fewer and fewer.

"Carys and Gareth are my only real family. And I consider my assistant, Sophie, to be more family than employee. I would compare her to a nosy aunt, but her nosiness comes from the heart." Saying that makes me smile because I have never put into words what Sophie means to me on a personal level. "We have some distant relatives scattered across the US and abroad, but no one we maintain a connection with."

"I understand that. I come from a very small family too." Her eyes cast downward to the table, perhaps preparing what to ask next. "And your parents? If you don't mind me asking."

Kind, compassionate eyes look back at me now and I know November is the type of person that does not do anything surface level. She wants deep. She wants real. She would rather keep her circle small than have anything superficial in her life. I understand that desire very well.

"After I graduated from college, I moved to Manhattan for business. I was there almost two years before I received the phone call from the Buffalo Police Department that my mom and dad were killed in a car accident. A drunk driver speeding down the wrong side of the street. Carys and Gareth were almost fourteen at the time. I remember it was the summer before they started high school. They needed me and I left the city."

The extent of a traumatic time in my life reduced to

essentially a paragraph. She doesn't need to know the minute details on a fine day like today.

November extends her hand to cover mine on the table.

"I am so sorry to hear about your loss."

"It was a long time ago, nearly twenty years." I can barely look into her eyes; the emotion there is overwhelming me.

"Grief is a weird thing. It knows no time and will rear its ugly head when you least expect it. Five years. Ten years. Twenty. It can zing you any time it feels like it."

I turn my hand over to hold hers, palm-to-palm. My hand is so much larger than hers that my fingers can wrap around her wrist from this angle, my thumb smoothing over her silky skin. It is my first time touching her and, of course, it would be different in the sense that this is not a sexual touch, but one of comfort and connection.

"You know grief." My tone is gentle, more so than I have ever heard it.

"My mother, almost eleven years ago from pancreatic cancer. From the time she was diagnosed to the time of her death, it was less than six months. I was twenty-three at the time. Roman was twenty-seven and had been married to Alex for several years already. If I didn't have them..."

She casts her eyes to the table, not able to look at me before speaking of what's next, but I swear I feel a faint tremor in her hand.

"Then my brother... Six years ago. A rock climbing accident. Plum is my only living blood relative. That I know of."

My hand gives hers a squeeze in an automatic response. Certain puzzle pieces are snapping together, but the one piece that clicks first is: Alex's current husband is not November's brother as I assumed.

"November, I am so sorry..."

She pulls her hand away from mine and it instantly feels

wrong not to be touching her, but a large plate has been set in front of her and another in front of me.

"Can I get you anything else?" our college-aged food server asks.

November gives me a little shake of her head, but only looks at her plate.

"No, thank you," I speak for both of us.

"Enjoy your lunch." She speeds away to wherever she came from.

If I had to guess, November is reeling her emotions in as she quietly places her cloth napkin in her lap. I don't want her to. I want this side of her, this vulnerability she showed so easily to me because she feels safe. I want to be her safe place. I am feeling off-kilter myself, but this is what I have been craving for so long.

What I would do to hold her right now!

"This looks delicious," she begins. Her mood shifting right before my eyes. "You know how to pick food establishments, don't you? The coffee shop you took me to was very nice."

She methodically picks up her half of the sandwich, making sure nothing slides out, then takes a careful bite. Thin wisps of steam rise from the chicken into the cool air. On her first chew, she hums her delight and it is now one of my favorite sounds.

"I think the view here is far superior." I pick up my own sandwich, but don't eat it yet. I need to make sure she is okay.

She swallows. Because her hands are full, she gestures with a tilt of her head toward the expanse of natural beauty to her right. "Yes, that is pretty gorgeous, but did you even see the ceiling decorations at the coffee shop?"

She teases me, and now I can eat.

~

The moment I open the restaurant door for November to exit, I feel the air has become breezier. The sun is still shining bright, but the big, white, puffy clouds are moving quickly to their next destination. Who knows what tomorrow will bring?

November stops at the end of the narrow walkway to take in a final look at the lake. She inhales the fresh air.

"It is beautiful here. I have always loved how Buffalo has so many different bodies of water around. The lakes. The rivers. The creeks. Even that waterfall on Main Street in Williamsville. A waterfall right in the middle of town, practically on top of a busy street." She shakes her head at the absurd idea. "And autumn is the very best time of year to be here. At least in my opinion. Alex would argue that summer is the best, but I think she's a California sun girl at heart."

"Would you like to walk a bit?" I ask with an encouraging tone.

She turns her face up to see me better. "Do you have time?"

"Plenty of time."

Yes, I have to return to work after I drop her off. Yes, I have tasks waiting for my attention back at the office. Yes, I am positive my brother and/or sister have been looking for me and pestering Sophie for information. Yet, I plan to milk every second of my time with November.

I offer her my arm to hold on to as we take the stairs down to the paved walkway around the lake, and the joyful relief I feel that she hasn't let go once on flat ground is something I have never felt with a woman.

"Thank you for lunch, and sharing meals. Both sandwiches were good, but I think mine was the better choice." She's kidding and not at the same time.

We begin our stroll to our right, heading down a path between a grove of maple trees and other foliage I couldn't identify if my life depended on it.

"You're welcome. And, in all honesty, I think I liked yours more too."

"I do know food."

"That's a bold statement."

"And I stand by it."

"Do you have many go-to restaurants in LA?" I hate that I asked that question. I hate the reminder that she doesn't live here.

"I do, but I don't really eat out a lot. I am one of those rarities in LA who love to cook and do frequently. Do you know how to cook?" she asks, glancing up to see my face.

"I have a feeling if I tell you I know how to cook, you will have expectations I will never live up to."

Her laughter makes me feel proud of myself.

"My cooking is mediocre at best," I continue. "I haven't cooked anything in a long time either. I have prepared meals delivered to my house for dinners during the week. Lunch is nearly always out somewhere. Breakfast is usually something simple."

"How... depressing." She faux frowns.

It's my turn to laugh. "What can I say? I live a stereotypical bachelor life when it comes to food."

We come to a little clearing under a few trees at the lake's edge. November stops and I halt with her.

"Look at all the geese!" She points, then releases her hand from my arm to take a couple steps closer to the water for a better view.

"They'll hang out here for another week or so, then fly south."

I'm not looking at the geese. Why would I when I have this woman all to myself? She is breathtaking to me. Her hair reaching nearly to her waist in back is dark and milk chocolate colors in the sunlight. The curve of her tight body from her shoulders to the taper of her waist, then flowing outward to her hips; a perfect hourglass.

She twists at her waist to look over her shoulder at me. Her expression is not one I have seen on her face before. She looks... shy, and my heart becomes a puddle. I feel the gravitational pull and I will not deny myself those steps to be close to her.

My hand goes to her waist, a gentle touch, barely resting my fingers there.

"Is this, okay?" My voice is sandpaper.

November nods, and turns her body to face mine.

The air between us changes to something thick, like a cool wind turned heavy with heat, through my lungs, my blood. This stretched out moment of my vision bouncing between her sparkling eyes reflecting the sun and those delectable cherry glossed lips I want to devour. Her mouth. The thoughts and ideas and emotions that come forth via words and sounds through that mouth.

I swallow, my voice barely audible. "I may lose my fucking mind if I don't kiss you right now."

Her one assured step into my space is all the permission I need.

The hand on her waist moves to her back to pull her close. My other moves up to the side of her neck and continues on to where it has been itching to be since I met her, burying itself in that lush hair.

She tilts her head back, and I lean in.

My nose grazes her velvety cheek, breathing in her warm vanilla and cashmere scent. I leave barely a kiss there and she inhales jaggedly as her hand grasps the front of my dress shirt. My lips move to the corner of her sweet mouth and I am done testing the waters. I dive in.

Her plush lips match me in their want and she gives of herself all that I need. I lick the seam of her lips, and she welcomes me in. Her tongue caresses my own in such a seductive manner, it coaxes my brain to want unspeakable things. Her arms wrap around my neck, pulling herself flush against me and I feel my body go hard... all over.

Before I lose complete control in public and fuck her against the closest tree trunk, I break the kiss. My forehead rests against hers as I gasp for a full breath, my heart pounding as if I just sprinted around this lake.

"Tell me I can see you again." I am a desperate man.

Her fingertips play with the back of my hair where it meets the collar of my shirt, and I am a madman for what I want to do to her here, now.

"I would be highly disappointed if you didn't."

CHAPTER 9

November

W e kissed. We kissed. We kissed...
Those two words have been on repeat in my head since Rhys took my hand in his as we strolled back to his car. And during the drive to my family's house, when we planned our next date.

Rhys has to fly to Manhattan for a meeting tomorrow, but will return same day. Thursday is Halloween and that is reserved for Plum. So, Friday dinner it is. And through that entire conversation, I continued to think it.

We kissed. We kissed. We kissed...

And, oh, I want more.

Rhys slowly pulls into the driveway, eases his foot down on the brake pedal to stop at the walkway leading to the front door, then places the car in park. He raises my hand he has been holding to his lips to place a kiss on top before returning my hand to my lap. When he steps outside, my eyes track his handsome self as he comes around to my side.

The chant changes in my head.

Kiss him. Kiss him. Kiss him...

The sky is no longer as bright and blue as when we were

at the lake. The rays of sunlight poke through here and there, trying to help prolong the rush of a best day, but the rain clouds are moving in because it is time to say goodbye. I love rain, but I am on the sun's side this time.

When I step outside, the wind whips my hair around and I have to sweep the stray strands from my face as Rhys closes the door behind me. He wastes zero time wrapping his arms around my waist, pulling me against his firm body into something much more than a hug. He buries his face into my neck, breathing me in, savoring my skin there with a press of his lips.

He murmurs, "I can't believe I have to let you go when I've only just had a taste."

I am a warm puddle of goo.

No one is home yet and I am grateful. All I need right now is a little time to sit alone with the highlights of our date, which is all of it, and my feelings. I march upstairs and into my bedroom to change my clothes. There are no plans tonight with Halloween tomorrow, so I can get as cozy as I want, which means soft joggers, sweatshirt, and fuzzy jack-o'-lantern socks. Last, I check my phone because I know Genevieve texted around when she thought my date might be over.

It's a busy day, but had to check in.

How was it?

More than I could have dreamed.

Talk tonight?

Working late. I'll call as soon as I leave.

I shove my phone in my thigh pocket, and head back downstairs to turn on the indoor Halloween decorations not on a timer. We will hang out in the family room tonight and watch a family friendly Halloween movie after Plum finishes her homework. Dinner is already prepared, a big pot of chicken noodle soup I made yesterday that just needs to be reheated. The soup will be perfect because it has started to pour buckets outside.

I hope Rhys made it to work before the rain hit.

That man has quickly become a second nature thought in my mind. I am trying so hard to stay in the present and only think how fantastic spending time with him has been, yet, this creeping dread of an expiration date is testing the elasticity of my good feelings bubble. As much as I want to ignore it, I do have to go home.

I hear the kitchen door to the garage open. Alex and Plum are home and I didn't even hear the car tires slosh up the driveway.

"Take your cleats and socks off and leave them here." I hear Alex instruct Plum. "You might as well get in the shower now and put on your pajamas. We're not going anywhere in this rain. And if you knock out your homework before dinner, we can jump right into movie night."

I step into the kitchen to make them aware I'm home. "How was soccer?"

Alex startles a little.

"Sorry. You're home earlier than I expected. Did you get rained out?"

"Yep!" Plum exclaims as she makes an ugly face at her

81

mucked-up cleats. "This was our last outdoor practice. All our games and practices will be inside starting next week."

Plum is sopping wet, but Alex is dry, and she notices my blatant comparison.

"Mom usually waits in the car. Parents aren't allowed to watch practices."

"Why?"

Plum shrugs. "I'm going to take a shower. I feel icky." She hurries out of the kitchen.

When we can hear her running up the stairs, Alex whispers, "The coaches don't appreciate some of the meddling, overbearing parents."

"Got it." I nod once.

"Anyway, forget soccer! Tell me EVERYTHING! I've been dying to know!"

I have known Alex my entire adult life, and a couple of my teenage years. Roman and Alex were college sweethearts, and when I look at our relationship through that lens, I don't know how I could have doubted my closeness with her. We have no secrets, and I am not about to start now.

"I don't think I've ever had a better date."

Alex bounces on the balls of her feet a few times, then grabs my arms to give me a little shake. I didn't know she was so invested in my love life.

"Where did you go?"

"A restaurant at Delaware Park. The food is great. I want to take you, Mark, and Plum there for brunch on Sunday. Is that okay?"

"Yeah, yeah, yeah. Then what happened?"

"It was such a beautiful day, with the sun shining and the trees so gorgeous, we went for a walk by the lake."

"Oh my God! You kissed!" She shakes me again, slightly harder this time.

I laugh at her excitement. "How did you know?"

"You have a glow. It's not the sex glow, but it's a 'that fine man can kiss like a god' glow."

This time I snort, but she's not wrong.

"Yes, that fine man can kiss like a god," I admit.

"When are you seeing him again? I'm assuming there will be another date. Please tell me there's another date."

"He is out of town tomorrow for business and with Halloween in there, we made plans for Friday night dinner. I know you're going to the Halloween party at the neighbor's house, so I thought it would be okay."

"Em, it is completely fine. With all the kids at the party, I am sorry to inform you, Plum won't even know you're not there. Besides, I want you to go out and have a great time with Rhys." Her expression turns cunning. "And don't feel the need to rush home."

"Alex, I am not going to walk of shame it here with my ten-year-old niece in the house who wakes up early."

"Friday will be a late night, so she'll be sleeping a little later than usual."

"Still a no."

"Oh, come on! Don't you want to get naked with that man? I know he wants to get naked with you."

"How do you know that?" I feel my face scrunch in confusion.

"I know it has been a while, if ever, since you've seen a man who is seriously into you, but you have to see the hunger in his eyes when he looks at you. I was only around you two for a few minutes and I saw it."

My mind goes back to our kiss. I did see it. I felt it. I recognized it because I felt the same.

"I don't want to plan anything. If it happens, it happens."

"What are you going to wear? Maybe I have something in my closet that would fit you, but you have way bigger boobs. Maybe we can do some quick shopping on Friday morning since we're not working. Maybe buy more than just for one date."

"Let's browse your closet first. You have great clothes."

"No, let's shop," Alex whines. "Plum will be at school. Mark at work. It will be just us. I love my daughter and husband with my whole heart, but I need an adult girl day."

My heart softens at that statement. I haven't thought of it that way. It has been too long.

"Why don't we take Plum to breakfast, drop her off at school, then you and I can head down to East Aurora. I like that little clothing boutique there. We can shop and have lunch and be back in time to pick up Plum."

"It's a date!"

Alex is so excited for us to have girl time with me and it warms my heart.

"It's a date."

When I turn off the bathroom light and step into my dark bedroom, my attention is drawn to the window seat. Rain drops splatter against the glass preventing me from seeing beyond a couple feet outside. Perfect sleeping weather. No need for the rain sounds app tonight, but I do reach for my cell phone on the nightstand to switch the morning alarm on.

Instant butterflies. The texts from Rhys must have arrived while I was showering.

> Sophie loved your caramels.
>
> I shared three, then had to hide my bag from her because she stole three more.

Contain it as I try, my grin pulls the corners of my lips so tight. I don't remember the last time I smiled like this.

> Feeling warm and fuzzy inside.

What would you feel if I told you I loved them more?

> Jealous much?

I don't know. Never felt like this before.

I would not be surprised to see my body floating right now. My thumbs hover over the screen's keyboard not knowing what to text in response. This crush... I mull that over for a split second. Yes. I do have a crush on Rhys.

How could I not?

> Are you crushing on me, Mr. Morgan?

My heart pounds against my chest when his answer is immediate.

I most definitely am, Ms. Day.

Am I brave enough? My thumbs fly through seven characters.

> Me too.

Good night, Ms. Day.

> Sweet dreams, Mr. Morgan.

...of you.

The squealing radiating from within my chest is not conducive to drifting off to sleep, but I cannot rein in the brimming excitement over something new and good and full of possibility.

Possibility. Something that may happen. Or may not. Is the glass half full or half empty?

As I tuck myself into bed, I wonder.

CHAPTER 10
Rhys

It's dry outside now, but I'm monitoring the dark clouds above, wondering when the rain will drop today. Hopefully, after my plane takes off. I need to attend that meeting to close a very lucrative business deal. One that means extra fat bonuses for my employees this Christmas. I have the very best workforce and I want to maintain it. Money is not the only factor to keep my employees happy, but it goes a long way.

Are you at work?

It dawns on me that November might not have her phone on her. When we went to coffee, I noticed she wasn't carrying anything, so maybe she stores her belongings while working. If she doesn't respond in a minute, I will go inside the studio.

I am. Why?

> Do you have two minutes to come outside?

On my way.

The brightness of her smile turns high the moment she sees me leaning against the hood of my Mercedes sedan. Her long, high braid swishes behind her as she practically skips to where I am parked. She is happy to see me and how good that makes me feel is indescribable.

"New car?" she inquires.

"Old car. I took the SUV in for maintenance. I'll pick it up in the morning."

She stands between my legs, within reach, but not entirely where I want her.

"Shouldn't you be at the airport?" She addresses me with a quizzical brow.

I reach for the hem of her violet hoodie and tug her closer.

"I am on my way, but I had to see you and bring you this." I lean to the side so she can see the large latte cup behind me.

A little surprised gasp escapes her lips and my blood heats. I like that sound very much and I'll have to think of other ways to lure it out.

She leans in to reach around me for the cup, but I sit straight again, blocking her. My hand moves to her hip to hold her in place. Her eyes meet mine, holding my gaze, pretty pink lips parting. She makes her move by completely entering my space, her arms gliding over my shoulders until they are entwined behind my neck. There is no hesitation when she kisses me hotly on the mouth and it is exactly what I need from her right now.

I'm trying to be good, trying not to slip my hands

where they don't belong, but I can't help myself. I wrap the end of her braid once around my fist and pull, not tight, but enough for her to feel it and she shivers against me.

She fucking shivers!

I feel the nip she gives me on my bottom lip and that sting of pleasure goes right to my dick. I am truly thankful I have many hours before my meeting to clear away the haze that caused in my brain.

What am I doing?

I think she can read my mind, or maybe she registers the lessening of my tight grip on her hip, because she breaks the kiss.

"Why do we do this in public?" She giggles.

I'm laughing while my eyes scan the parking lot, but no one is around to see us. "I have no idea, November. You pull something a little wild out of me. This is not my normal."

"Maybe I bring the exhibitionist out of you."

"Or maybe I bring it out of you." I reach behind me to pick up the latte and hand it to her.

"Thank you for this. And planting that kiss on me."

Reluctantly, I stand. "You started it."

She lifts the cup to her lips and takes a sip, not commenting at all.

When she's done swallowing, I give her a kiss more suitable for public, tasting cinnamon and milk and chocolaty espresso on her lips. It tastes so good, feels so good, I kiss her one more time.

"Text me when you land both ways, so I know you're safe."

"I will." One more kiss, and I really need to leave even though I do not want to.

November steps backward, out of the car's pathway, as I walk to the driver's side and force myself to get in. She watches me pull away, giving me a little wave, and my heart aches that she didn't want me to leave either.

~

No rain yet.

I stare out the window of my first-class seat, waiting for my brother to join me. Gareth always prefers to wait until the last minute to board a plane. Flight time to LaGuardia is only an hour and a half, but Gareth likes to walk around and not be cooped up on a plane when he doesn't have to be. Fortunate for him, having an assigned seat allows him that option.

He appears to be the very last person to board, flirting right back with the flight attendants. It is not lost on anyone that Gareth is a pretty boy, and a bit of a playboy. Who am I kidding? A lot of a playboy and he relishes in his reputation. At age thirty-two with money to spare and a fun-loving spirit, he plays right into it. I don't understand his lifestyle because it has never been interesting to me, but at least he makes it very clear with the women he's involved with that he's not looking for anything permanent. I instructed him long ago, as our father had instructed me as a teenager, he needs to be open and honest with his intentions, and always use a condom.

My concern is he will never get past this stage in his life. Don't get me wrong, Gareth is very serious when he works. Law suits him. He is extremely good at his job. If he was a slacker, brother or not, he would not be representing Morgan Security. Gareth wants to succeed in his career and for my company. He may be young, but he is quickly building a name for himself. I often wonder if he will move on at some point. More like, when.

He loves Manhattan and all it has to offer. I will be

returning to Buffalo after our business meeting, but he will stay through the remainder of the week and weekend. Right there shows what drastically different stages we are in our lives. He loves the big city life and he could go far in his career if he moved there. I know, I did that once to soar. For me, the energy of the city fed my ambition and motivation. And if he does choose to go, I not only have to be ready for it, I have to make sure he knows it's okay for him to live the life he needs to.

Gareth drops himself into the aisle seat next to me carrying a bottle of Dr. Pepper, a bottle of water, and a tube of mint Mentos. When he flies, he is nothing but a creature of habit. Since he was a kid, he buys the same items for every flight. The weird thing is, he never drinks Dr. Pepper or any soda for that matter at home or at a restaurant or hockey game. Nor does he buy Mentos any other time. It has always been these three items on every flight, and he has never explained why.

"We beat the rain," he comments as cracks open the Dr. Pepper bottle lid and takes a sip.

"We're not in the air yet."

One of the flight attendants Gareth was flirting with closes and secures the door.

"Everything is going our way today." He peels open the Mentos and offers me one, but I shake my head in refusal. He takes one out and pops it into his mouth.

"I like your positive attitude." I pull out my cell phone to switch it to airplane mode.

"Has nothing to do with positivity. It's a done deal. I saw them drooling over what we have to offer. They want us." Gareth powers down his phone completely, then places it and the bottle of water in his messenger bag under the seat in front of him. "Carys and I have been talking about you."

"Good or bad or indifferent?"

I glance out the window to see the world go by in reverse and half listen to the safety instructions spoken over the intercom.

"Carys thinks it's good. I'm indifferent."

I don't need to answer, because he will just talk anyway. Whereas I learn the essence of a person through observation, he learns through what they say. Gareth loves to talk.

"We are ninety-four-point-two percent sure you're seeing someone. I think you're just getting laid on the regular, but Carys thinks it's more than that."

The plane taxis the runway and I continue to watch out the window and ignore Gareth. This is going to feel like the longest flight.

"Shit. Is Carys right? I hate when she's right. Who is the mystery woman?"

We are picking up speed and Gareth is ruining takeoff for me. I love to fly, and takeoff is the best part.

"I need to know who it is, Rhys. You and I socialize in the same circles, and the last thing I want is to be somewhere you have -"

My head whips around to face my little brother, and by the devious grin on his mouth, he received the reaction he was seeking.

Damn! He's too good at that.

He continues, "Now that I have your full attention, do you want to tell me what's going on with you? And your lady...friend...thing?" He pops another Mentos into his mouth.

"There's nothing to tell. And we don't socialize in the same circles."

"That's right, you don't socialize at all."

"Why are you even interested in my love life?

His eyes widen. "Love? I didn't say anything about you being in love. Are you in love?"

"I am not in love. You know very well what I mean. You're just being an asshole."

"Yes, I am an asshole, and I have no problem admitting it. But who else are you going to talk with? I am your brother and the closest thing to a real friend you have. It's not like I'm going to tell anyone." He takes two large swallows of soda and I know that has to burn.

"What about Carys?"

He winces from the soda burn, not from mentioning Carys. "I don't have to tell her anything. She's my twin, we share brainwaves or some shit. Somehow, she just knows without words being spoken. A Jedi thing. For all we know, she can hear this conversation in her head."

I have to chuckle over the Star Wars reference. Yes, Carys is very Jedi mind trick.

"Let's discuss this afternoon's meeting." I really don't want to talk about my love life right now.

"There's nothing to discuss. We've gone over it too many times for what it is. As I said, this is a done deal. Let's get back to you and, what's her name?"

"I'm not telling you her name so you can look her up."

"Fair. You can tell me what the problem is, because I can tell by your protectiveness of her, you are into her, but you don't seem..." He mulls it over for several seconds as his eyes, the mirror image of my own, study me. "Is excited the word I'm looking for?"

Well, Gareth just hit the nail on the head. I am into November; there is no question about it. The more I see her, talk to her, think about her, I know I am in way over my head in such a short amount of time. There can't possibly be a future for us, so, no, I am not entirely thrilled that I only have another week to make the most of my time with her, and I'm stuck on an airplane that is taking me away when I should be... What? Clinging?

"She doesn't live in Buffalo." My words come out almost as a mumble.

"Where does she live?" He screws the cap back on the soda bottle, then bends down to place it in his bag, switching it for the water bottle.

On an exhale, I answer, "Los Angeles."

Gareth sits upright and nods, understanding my problem now. "Wait. How did you even meet her? When did you meet her? It couldn't have been that long ago if she doesn't live here."

"Friday. I met her on the plane from Chicago. She's visiting family." I'm not going into her meditation classes or any other details he can sleuth with.

"If she has family here, then ask her to extend her stay to get to know each other more."

He makes it sound so simple, but it's not. My life is here and hers is clear across the country. Even if we decided to do long distance. How often would we really see each other? When is the expiration date for us living apart? Would we be setting us up for failure? I have never had a long-distance relationship before. Never had any long-term relationships before. My confidence in doing this right is lackluster, and my fear of losing her is rising exponentially after our lunch date.

"I can't ask her to put her life on hold like that. We barely know each other. And even if she did stay a few more days, then what? A relationship through FaceTime and texts, and maybe seeing each other for a few days here and there. It doesn't solve the fact that I'm here and she will be there and where does that leave us in the long haul?"

My brother studies me hard while he slowly chews his most recent piece of candy. I think he has consumed the entire tube already. All I can smell in the air around me is mint.

"Well, then it's obviously not that serious of a thing and it will be easy to say your goodbyes at the end of her visit. If you've already made up your mind that nothing can come from this, I don't know why you're stressing." Gareth unbuckles his seatbelt and holds up the crumpled blue, white, and silver candy wrapper. "I'm going to go throw this out, see who's up for flirting, and when I get back, be in a better mood. Turn that frown upside down."

That's a phrase our mother used to say when we were pouting over something silly, like not being able to eat ice cream for dinner. I wonder if Gareth even realizes he used it.

He gets up and does exactly what he said, knowing damn well he turned my thoughts about a relationship with November upside down.

∾

Fun fact: I don't like suit jackets. I like ties even less, therefore, the last time I wore a tie is when I walked Carys down the aisle, and I only did so at her request. I do wear a jacket when called for and a business meeting such as this is one of those occasions.

Irritation is crawling along my skin and it isn't because of the tailored jacket. There has been something off since the moment the receptionist escorted us into this modern, expensively decorated conference room and it was empty. Gareth and I are not early; we are right on time. This smells like a 'you need me more than I need you' moment, but I take it in stride. The fact of the matter is, Morgan Security doesn't need Fourthwrite's business. I'm here and I might as well see how this plays out.

To kill time, Gareth and I check our emails and texts. I lean back in my leather chair and keep my focus on my cell phone even when I hear people approaching the door. If they want a pissing contest...

The next odd thing is when Fourthwrite's founders, Jon and Don, identical twin brothers – you just can't make this shit up – enter the room. There is no apology for their lateness, and no introductions of the slew of people entering the room after them like subjects following their kings. This is too many people for a simple signing of a completely hammered out contract and the shaking of hands. Gareth and I take up two seats at the table, the remaining twelve are occupied by, supposedly, Fourthwrite personnel, but I can't shake the feeling something not good is headed my way. If they are trying to intimidate me for whatever reason they have up their sleeves, it is obvious they don't know anything about me.

I am proud of my brother because he has definitely caught on and cuts right to the chase. "Gentlemen, it's a pleasure to see you all again." He makes a pointed look around the table. "Although, there are definitely more here that I have never met before, and not an attorney in sight. What game are we playing here today, gentlemen? There are too many players for Monopoly, but I guess we can play teams. Prepare yourself, I was really good at Monopoly as a kid."

I chuckle. I can't help myself after hearing his opener. "Gareth is not lying. He beat me most of the time."

"But you slaughtered me at Battleship."

My smile is pure pride, but not for the memory. Yes, Gareth is a Monopoly genius. That much is true. Gareth complimenting me on my skills in Battleship is a bold-faced lie. We never played Battleship. Never even owned the game.

Gareth just sent me a message about going to war.

And the look on Jon and Don's identical faces is priceless. Two kids with their hands caught in the cookie jar.

They are so young, not much older than I was when I left Manhattan and started Morgan Security. When I first met the duo, they seemed okay and they passed my vetting process, but something has changed in the last couple months and it's more than just the overabundance of money they quickly made if this conference room is proof of that.

There is nervous tittering around the table, but the two forty-something men, sitting to my far left, wearing dark suits with ties, leaning forward with their elbows on the table, are not laughing. Definitely sizing me up. And I am nearly one hundred percent sure they are not employees of Fourthwrite.

"Jon, Don..."

I hear the hint of mocking in Gareth's voice and almost kick him under the table. Almost.

"Questions? Comments? Concerns?" he continues. "Or is this your way of calling the deal off?"

This rattles the twins. Yes, Gareth is very good at provoking the response he desires.

Jon is the first to speak up. "No!" He shoots some knowing look to his brother, who shoots some knowing look to the unknown men at the end of the table. "We wanted to renegotiate the price of some of the job scope. I believe there is potential to lower the cost of the discovery mission your tech crew will conduct for leaks and weaknesses in our systems."

Don chimes in. "My brother and I also wanted to ask if the results report was even necessary when you are just going to fix the problem areas. Would that reduce the cost?"

"Those costs have already been negotiated and are final." Gareth's tone has changed from the dramatic to all professionalism. "You're not paying for mediocre service. You're paying for the best."

The two men who have been trying to mindfuck me with their glares during this meeting shift in their seats in response to Gareth stating our service is best, and I now know we have competitors in the room. That's who these fuckers are. At some point, I am positive I will find out why they are at the table. Am I worried? Not even close. There isn't another company out there that can do what mine can. If Fourthwrite decides to go another direction, I will not lose sleep.

Gareth continues, "Providing a lesser service jeopardizes the reputation of Morgan Security. This isn't a cafeteria plan. The scope of work in the contract is akin to rule of law in how we execute our work."

Jon and Don look to me, but my only response is to stay relaxed in my chair and not say a word. I check the time on my cell phone, then keep my face expressionless as I look up.

"Could we have the day to think about it?" Don sheepishly asks.

"Rhys has a return flight to catch. If I don't hear from you tonight to cancel, I will be here at eight o'clock tomorrow morning to have the contract signed. I think that's fair."

With that, I stand. As Gareth stands, I look to the competitors. "Have a good day, gentlemen."

We step outside onto the wet sidewalk of Park Avenue, and move toward the curb. I already called our driver who should arrive in a few minutes depending on where he parked himself to wait for us.

"That was wild." Gareth is smiling with pure amusement.

"Your Battleship reference was pretty brilliant."

"Sometimes I surprise myself. Do you think they'll sign?

"Did you notice there were competitors in the room?"

Gareth looks perplexed, then dawning realization takes

over. "The two uptight guys. How do you know they're competitors?"

"They had a few tells."

"If Jon and Don are smart, and that's a coin toss, they'll sign and quickly discover it was the best decision they made all year. I don't know why they would want to go cheap when it comes to protecting their intellectual property."

"My guess is they've been given some misinformation that another company can do the same work for cheaper."

"If they do sign, what will you do with the hefty payday?"

"Double the employee bonuses. It has been a stellar year for us."

"We keep growing because of their good work and dedication. What else?"

"Buy some really expensive tech Asher has been raving about."

"I would listen to him. He knows his shit."

"Do some updates to the building."

"I don't see how you could improve it, but knock yourself out."

"Add funds to our foundation."

"Sounds good."

A very light sprinkling of rain dots our coats and hair as we wait. Too light to warrant seeking shelter. Yet it smells like more to come; the hovering clouds above are a deep charcoal gray.

"Do you need me to stick around? I can change my flight."

"Why? Do you want to join me in some Halloween debauchery?"

I don't need to respond to his sarcasm, but I do notice when he looks away.

"Rhys, you know I can handle business. I plan on

ordering room service and working in my hotel suite tonight. I will be fresh as a daisy at tomorrow's meeting. No need to babysit me."

Gareth doesn't show it, but I think I hurt his feelings. Being, essentially, his parent through grief and his teen years, I had to pay close attention to the signs. Carys was much more open about what she was feeling and thinking, still is. But my brother hid by throwing himself into excelling in school, and girls. I see him doing a version of that now with work. Carys reminds me time to time that I am not only his big brother, but someone he admires.

"Brother, I have complete faith in your abilities. I meant, if you can think of any reason for me to stick around, I will stay. I would never question your work ethic."

He clears his throat. "I foresee zero problems. Whether they sign or not."

"What are you going to do with your bonus? It's going to be huge."

"I was thinking about that. I come to the city often enough to buy something here. Nothing ridiculous, but it might be nice."

I run my hand through my damp hair. Here it is. This is what I thought might come.

"You thinking about moving here?" My voice remains steady, regardless of how unsteady I'm feeling.

"Move? As in permanently?"

"It's okay if you want to. I wouldn't blame you for seeing where this city can take you."

"Why would I want to do that?"

"Aren't you bored? It can't be all that interesting for you in a small city."

"You think I'm bored?" He sounds shocked that I would say such a thing.

"I don't know. You keep everything close to the vest."

"Then let me be crystal clear. I love my job and the work we do. I actually enjoy working with my siblings; I get to annoy Carys on the daily."

I have to laugh at that because Gareth really does love to poke the bear. Carys is the only woman I know who will dish it back to him, though Sophie jumps in sometimes if he's being extra dickish. He thrives on the fight. Probably why he does the pro bono work for small businesses. He enjoys fighting for the underdog.

"And before you ask, no, I don't feel beholden to you," he remarks.

That was my other thought of why he stays with my company. I never asked, but always wondered if he felt obligated because of what I gave up to finish the job our parents began in raising my siblings. It was not something I viewed as a burden. I did not think that then and definitely not now.

We both see the black town car with our driver, Billy, pulling toward the curb.

"Besides, half the fun is everyone underestimating the pretty boy lawyer from Buffalo." Gareth looks up at the skyscrapers surrounding us, maybe imagining what it would be like to work from an office high above this impressive and powerful city. "They never know what hit them."

First thing I do when the airplane's wheels make contact with the ground is pull out my cell phone and do as November requested for the second time today.

Landed.

Welcome home!

Seeing those words from her makes me wish I was going home to her. She was waiting to hear from me and every cell in my body feels wanted in a way I have never felt. November knows nothing about my business or my finances; she cares about me as a human being.

> Thank you!

> Will you be at the studio in the morning?

Teaching three classes, then Alex and I will head out.

> I'll bring you another latte and wish you a happy Halloween.

You're spoiling me.

> You deserve to be spoiled.

> I will see you in the morning.

Good night, Rhys!

> Sweet dreams!

...of you!

An arrow hitting its mark. My heart.

CHAPTER 11
November

My costume is a bit over the top compared to the other employees at work this morning. More like, I am in costume and they are wearing clothes in a Halloween theme. The witch costume I assembled is actually simple. I found a long, black, off-the-shoulders Renaissance-style dress online, black stockings to keep my legs warm, and black Victorian reproduction boots with a low heel. The centerpiece of the ensemble is the gorgeous, wide-brim, velveteen witch hat with a bent tip and swathed with black satin ribbon and tulle, and deep burgundy faux roses.

Posing in the mirrored wall of the Pilates studio, I snap three photos with my cell phone camera. Quickly, I select the best, attach it to a text, and ship it off to Genevieve to wish her a happy Halloween. We rarely spend Halloweens together, but she always wants to see what I am wearing and if she attends a party, I want to see her costume.

"Taking a pic to send Rhys? You should, you look stunning," Alex comments, having stalked up behind me to peer over my shoulder. She is wearing a black maternity sweatshirt with an orange jack-o-lantern face right where her baby bump is located, and cute black leggings with jack-o-lanterns printed all over. I am thrilled she made an effort.

"No, I'm wishing Genevieve a happy Halloween. Rhys will get to see my costume in person. He is stopping by any minute."

"Well, isn't that sweet! He couldn't wait until tomorrow to see you."

I check my dress and hat in the mirror one more time before turning to face Alex.

I smile. "It's Halloween and I'm in such a great mood, I won't even attempt to negate your statement because, I think, it's true. Rhys implied as much, whether or not it was just flirting. And I am looking forward to seeing him. How is that for honesty?"

Alex stares, before bursting into laughter. "Thank you for that! And I know how much you love Halloween, but I think the good mood is more about Rhys. You know, you could ask him to join us for dinner and trick-or-treating."

My phone pings. It is way too early for a response from Genevieve, so it could only be one other person. When I look at the phone screen, I swear my heart roars his name. *Rhys!*

I'm here.

On my way.

"I am seeing Rhys now and tomorrow night. No need for him to be amongst the Halloween chaos when it's not his thing."

"Just thought you might want to maximize your time together. Let him see this side of you. See him in a new environment."

"He is about to get a healthy dose of this side of me right now." My hands gesture to my dress and my hat. "I'll be back."

On my way past the front desk, I grab two bags of caramels from the large wicker basket I brought in this morning for anyone who wants to take one. Unfortunately, I don't have pockets in this dress, so I hold both cellophane bags from the top with my fingers on one hand, and open the door with the other. When I am through the door, I hide one bag in the folds of my dress and allow the other to be seen in my other hand.

It rained pretty hard last night, and with the wind joining in the havoc, the tree branches are nearly stripped clean, their boldly colored leaves strewn thickly on the ground destined to wither and be raked. Very little sunshine is to be seen and the clouds look like they are sticking around. It is my fear that it will storm earlier than forecasted tonight and trick-or-treat will be canceled. I do have alternate plans just in case. I will not allow weather to ruin Halloween.

Rhys looks hot as hell dressed in all black, standing with his feet shoulder width apart, hands tucked into the pockets of his pants. The deep onyx of his dress shirt perfectly matches his hair. He looks movie star handsome, standing in front of his glossy black SUV. If I suspend reality for a few seconds, I can see him as the sexy, rich warlock in a TV series, and I am completely into the look.

"Wow!" he calls out as he eyes me up and down. "I knew you put a spell on me!"

"The way you look right now, I can say the same about you."

He looks down at his clothes, then back at me. "I am dressed for another day at the office."

I stop in front of him, but stay out of arm's reach. "You

can let me imagine you dressed in all black for Halloween just for me."

His smile is wide, his eyes brightening, and I love that I can bring that out in him. He spots the bag of caramel as I had hoped.

"Is that for me?"

"No, it's for Sophie."

Rhys fakes a frown.

That's when I hold up the second bag. "This one is for you."

"Now who's spoiling whom?" He takes both bags from me and admires the ribbon with a gentle touch of his fingertips. There is an odd smirk on his lips, as if he's keeping a secret.

He carefully places the bags on the car hood, then takes a step forward to wrap one arm around my waist to pull me close. His gaze follows the line of one bare shoulder, across my collarbones, and ending at my other shoulder before lingering at my lips. He allows his fingers to twine through a lock of my loose hair.

"You are stunning, my little witch." His voice is smooth as velvet. "Elegantly haunting."

I am overwhelmed by his compliment. Rhys likes me being me, and it is one more reason my heart is in so much trouble at the end of the next seven days.

A breeze blows through and ruffles both of our hair, playing with us, teasing us to get on with it. But Rhys takes a step back.

"Before I get carried away, I have something for you."

He takes my hand in his and leads me to the passenger side door.

"My latte!"

After opening the door and placing the bags of caramel

on the leather seat, Rhys turns to face me, handing out to me... not my latte.

I stare at the stack of three books tied together like a present with the same spiderweb ribbon I placed on the first bag of caramel I gave him.

Half of my brain is stunned; half is greedy for the books.

"For me?" My voice sounds small and high, not like my own, but I have never been surprised like this before. Perhaps this is its sound when I am absolutely flabbergasted.

'When I was at LaGuardia, on my way home, I stopped in a bookstore to pick up the second book in *The Gods* series and saw a display of witchy romances. At least, that's what the sign stated. I hope you haven't read them."

Finally, I take the thoughtful gift from his hands, the titles barely registering, but I see the ribbon he used, he kept, not knowing he would be buying these books for me in the near future. He held onto the ribbon instead of throwing it out.

The prickle behind my eyes is new for receiving a gift and I continue to look down at the books to try to regain control. This gift is so much more than Rhys realizes. I have dated men for far longer and none of them have cared to see me beyond a pretty face. *Arm candy.* Yes, one man actually called me that.

Rhys sees me.

I swallow hard. "It doesn't matter if I read them fifty-five times. I love them. Thank you."

Rhys must hear the emotion in my voice, because he gently lifts my chin up with his index finger to examine my face. His brilliant blue eyes are a swirl of emotions going by too fast to read. I feel his thumb swipe softly against my bottom lip, his eyes now following the movement.

He dips under the wide brim of my witch hat as I tilt my head back to allow him as much access to me as he desires.

His lips are warm and eager, matching mine in need. I feel his tongue beg for invitation, and I allow it inside to entwine with my own.

"This makes total sense to me now."

The voice startles us. We break the kiss at the same time and turn toward the female voice.

I recognize the pregnant woman from yesterday's meditation class. I offered her to sit on the riser with me so it would be easier to sit and stand for her.

"What are you doing here?" Rhys' voice is tinged with annoyance, as his hazy expression clears.

The woman walks closer now that we stopped kissing, her eyes sparkling bright, and mouth grinning wildly. "I took November's class yesterday. I loved it so much, here I am again."

Rhys takes a sharp inhale through his nose. "November, this is my sister, Carys."

Why didn't I see it yesterday? Tall. Jet black hair. Sapphire eyes. Her facial features are slightly softer than Rhys' chiseled ones, but there is no doubt this woman is a close relative.

"It's nice to meet you, Carys." I extend my right hand to her and she is overjoyed to shake it as Rhys looks on.

"It is extremely nice to formally meet you, November. I love your costume!" She cackles. "You have definitely bewitched my brother."

"Carys." Rhys' grumble is a low warning.

She rolls her eyes at her brother. "I am going inside to check in." She reaches for the books and relieves them from my grasp. "I'll take these inside for you. You can kiss hands-free now."

"Carys."

She ignores her brother and heads down the walk to the

studio's entrance. I can still hear her giddy laugh when she opens the door.

Rhys places his hands on my naked shoulders, his thumbs stroking my skin absentmindedly as he speaks. Each smooth touch heating my skin in a way I have never felt before.

"Please know, I would have told you if I knew Carys would be here."

"Rhys, don't worry about it. I'm fine. I don't know Carys at all, but she seemed pretty fine with it."

"Oh, she is more than fine with this and I am positive I'll hear all about how fine it is at work today."

I laugh at his annoyance, which makes him smile because he knows I am truly okay.

He pulls me back into the warmth of his embrace. I hadn't realized I was cold.

"Happy Halloween," he whispers against my lips.

"Happy Halloween."

I pick up the kiss where we left off, but this time, I can wrap my arms around him and run my fingers through his soft, thick hair.

Thank you, Carys.

After I allowed Rhys to take a picture of me in my costume, he handed me my latte with one last lingering kiss. On my shoulder. On my neck. On my lips.

Heaven!

When I step inside the studio, I see Carys chatting excitedly with an equally excited Alex. When I approach, they suspiciously stop talking.

"Carys, do you know my sister-in-law, Alex?"

"We met yesterday when she was here," Alex answers.

"We were comparing pregnancy notes. I didn't know Carys is Rhys' sister. Small world."

There's a vibe going on here that I can't place my finger on yet. "It is a small world."

"How did you meet my brother?" Carys asks me as she begins to unwrap a caramel from the bag she claimed for herself.

I guess I should have expected questions, and I have no idea how much Rhys wants me to share. Wouldn't he have given me some direction if he cared? "We met Friday. On our flight to Buffalo."

"I was there!" Alex interjects. "I mean, not on the plane, but at the airport, picking up November. I saw the way your brother was looking at my sister."

Oh, Alex!

"Do tell." Carys knows she just struck gold.

"They were sitting together. I didn't know they talked the entire flight, but I saw the way Rhys' eyes followed her at baggage claim."

I am so glad I never shared the details of that conversation with Alex.

"If the way they were kissing outside is any indication, my brother is really into your sister. I haven't seen Rhys with anyone like that since he was in high school. He hasn't seriously dated anyone in ages. I knew something was going on with him. My brother, Gareth, and I were talking about the change in Rhys."

Carys' tidbit of information interests me, but I don't want them talking like I'm not here. And it feels wrong to hear about Rhys from anyone other than Rhys. I want to know him through him.

"Okay! I think Carys and I need to head to class. We have less than two minutes."

There. End of conversation.

Carys walks away with me, but speaks to Alex over her shoulder. "Let's exchange numbers after."

"Absolutely! I'll find you after class."

Rhys and I are in so much trouble.

~

The black cloak I bought came in handy this chilly Halloween night, but I left my witch hat at home since the wicked weather decided to wreak mayhem on trick-or-treating. Twenty minutes in, it started to sprinkle. Plum and I toughed it out - what's a little sprinkle of water when there is Halloween fun to be had? Forty minutes in and it started to rain, but still nothing to deter us Day Girls from our goal of collecting mass amounts of candy. Fifty-two minutes and we were running home, soaked to the bone, and laughing like hyenas all the way.

Fortunately, I had the cloak to save the candy from ruin. Even better? I had the forethought to buy bags of candy and stash handfuls around the house for a Haunted Halloween Hunt. After showers and putting on cozy pajamas, we turned off all the house lights, and Plum, flashlight in hand, went on a hunt while I told her if she was hot or cold. I really hope I remember where all the hiding places are; it was an excessive amount of candy.

When I thought all had been found, and Plum's large tote bag was overflowing, all of us hunkered down in the family room for a timed round of Boooo-opoly while *The Nightmare Before Christmas* played in the background, and eating our fill of an array of chocolate (Alex and Mark mainly, and me hoarding all the Midnight Milky Ways), Sour Patch Kids (me trading orange and cherry for Plum's lemon and lime), Laffy Taffy (no one likes banana!), Swedish

Fish (all of us), and Skittles (love them! But why does purple always taste like perfume to me?).

Most important, Plum's Halloween wasn't spoiled by the rainstorm that has now become everything you want for a spooky night. Cracking thunder. Flashes of lightning. Sometimes the lightning takes the shape of crooked hands reaching across the dark clouded night. The wind bending trees and rattling windows, both seeming to withstand breaking. Weather like this is rarely experienced in Los Angeles, and I am glued to the window seat in my bedroom, my eyes going dry not wanting to miss any of it.

How can my family sleep through this? Candy coma?

Resting on the cushion in front of my bare crossed legs, the screen of my cell phone illuminates with an incoming text.

I hope the rain didn't ruin your Halloween.

Thinking of you.

Those last three words - the pounding of my heart could rival the thunder.

The rain killed our trick-or-treating, but nothing could ruin Halloween.

Do I dare?

Love that for me!

I watch for text bubbles when a call rings through. Rhys is calling me!

I take a deep breath before answering. "Hello."

"I just realized it's after ten. I'm sorry if it's too late to call." Rhys does sound sorry.

"I'm lucky if I ever fall asleep before eleven. But right

now, I am glued to the window watching Mother Nature in action."

"Do you enjoy storms?"

"I am fascinated by all kinds of weather. In Los Angeles, we have sunshine, for insanely long stretches between having anything resembling rain. Oh! There is May Gray and June Gloom. What's happening outside my window right now is exhilarating."

As if to exclamation point my sentiment, a bolt of lightning strikes down as if Zeus flung it himself, and my inhale is quick and sharp.

"Are you okay over there?" Rhys's voice is a smile.

"Perfectly enchanted. How are you faring wherever you are?"

"I am home, reading in bed."

I like the sound of that very much and can picture it clearly in my head.

"How far are you in book two?"

"I'd say a quarter through. Have you finished book one yet?"

"Almost. I am surprised I haven't yet. The book is so good, but other things have been vying for my attention."

"You've been busy. By the way, Sophie said thank you for the caramels. She stole my bag too. And Carys said I need to keep you around if only for the caramel."

"Using me for my caramel. It's the story of my life," I joke.

"You have other talents."

I know Rhys is not talking about anything sexual, but I can't keep my brain from going there. Especially knowing how he kisses; I wouldn't mind going there. With that thought, my skin is warm and tingling everywhere.

"Carys and Alex exchanged numbers," I croak out, then clear my throat.

"Carys said how nice it is to have a new pregnant friend who has done this before. How excited she is to get to know you too."

"You do realize they're plotting."

There's a pause on Rhys' end before he quietly asks, "Would you mind?"

Would I mind?

"I think I mind feeling forced into doing something. I don't mind them becoming friends and fangirling over you and me spending time together."

"Agreed." He's smiling again, and that makes me feel giddy.

"So, how should I dress for our dinner date?" I really do need to know for tomorrow's shopping excursion.

"I liked what you wore for our lunch date."

"Thank you, but where we are going, is it the same type of attire or dressier?"

"November, you are gorgeous in anything you wear."

There's a little jig going on inside my body. "You are very charming, but not helpful."

His laugh is rich and deep, and infectious, tickling a giggle out of me.

"We are going to a nice restaurant with a view of the city and Lake Erie."

"There you go. Was that so hard? What time will you be coming to collect me?"

"Seven. Our reservation is for seven-thirty."

"I'll see you at seven."

"Good night, my little witch."

"Sweet dreams, Rhys."

"Of you."

Thunder. Lightning. Sighing.

CHAPTER 12
Rhys

T he overnight change from October to November brought colder night air, the calling card of winter just around the corner. Last night's Halloween storm brought debris in the form of downed branches, trees, and some powerlines. I left my house earlier than originally planned just in case I had to backtrack and find a new route as I did when heading to work this morning.

Being late to pick up November for our date is not an option. Any time spent with her feels important, but there is something about this date that feels more so. Is it because this is our first evening date? It could be just because I respect people's time, but I'd be lying to myself. I know she has become important to me at an alarmingly fast rate. I am not entirely ready to process that fact, but I also recognize my time with her is limited.

When I pull into the driveway, I'm about ten minutes early, and November's family is exiting the front door, descending the porch stairs. She had mentioned they were going to a neighborhood party tonight, and by the number of cars parked on the street, people ambling by, and the sound of Halloween-themed music on the breeze, the party is close.

"Alex, good to see you!" I call out as I shut my car door.

"Nice to see you too! Come meet my family."

As soon as I am within reach, I extend my right hand to Mark Phillips. Even if I didn't already know that Mark is not November's brother, seeing him now, I would guess Mark is of no blood relation from how completely different they look from each other.

"Nice to meet you, Mark. Rhys Morgan."

"Good to finally put a face to a name." He shakes my hand firmly, but not unfriendly the way men sometimes do when they don't trust one another. He releases my hand, then rests it on the young girl's shoulder. "This is our daughter, Plum."

I turn to November's 'only living blood relative' and she is a smaller, cookie-cutter image of her aunt with the exception of the eye color and shape. Plum's eyes look nearly as dark as the night sky to her aunt's reddish brown. I wonder if Plum's eyes are her father's. I wonder if November recognizes him each time she looks at her precious niece.

"It's a pleasure to meet you, Plum." I give her hand a quick shake as she seems shy. "Your aunt talks about you quite a bit. All good things."

"She does? Like what?"

"What an excellent soccer player you are. How much you love Halloween. And you now know how to make caramel, which is very delicious."

Plum beams, then tilts her head to the side and I sense a question coming on.

"Are you Auntie Novie's boyfriend?"

That's a question I did not see coming.

Mark, thankfully, steps in. "Plum, we don't want to be late for the party. Let's go, Daughter."

When I look to Alex, she is beaming as well. "Yes! We need to get going and Rhys needs not to be late." She begins to walk away, but turns back to me. "You should join us for brunch on Sunday, Rhys. We are going to that restaurant you took November to lunch."

"Thank you for the invitation, but I have a standing brunch with my siblings on Sundays. Gareth is out of town, but my sister and her husband will be expecting me."

"Carys? Carys is great! I'll text her an invite as well. Good food, new friends. It'll be fun! November can give you the details."

"You already spoke to her about this?"

"We just talked about it and she's on board."

November's warning of our sisters plotting comes to the front of my mind.

"I'll talk it over with November."

"Great! Have fun tonight!"

"All of you too."

I turn toward the porch steps as an excited Plum pulls her parents away.

Shortly after I ring the doorbell, November appears on the other side of the leaded and beveled glass front door. Just the blurred image of her through the glass makes my heart race, but there is nothing like seeing her in the flesh once the door is open. She is the most beautiful woman I have ever seen. Her smile is dazzling starlight in the night, and I think I stop breathing because that smile is excitement over seeing me. And I love how she doesn't even try to hide it.

"Hello, Rhys." Her voice is smooth, smoky honey.

Before answering, I unashamedly allow my eyes to drink her in, starting with the long, loose curls of her dark hair, to the short, ivory-colored sweaterdress that hugs her hourglass shape in a tempting way, to taupe over-the-knee, high-heeled boots. On my way back up, my eyes catch on to the bare skin of her thighs and my mind wanders to what she could be wearing under that dress.

"Rhys?"

Her teasing tone snaps me back to her eyes, to her wicked smile, and I want to eat her up.

She steps back from the open door to allow me entry, and I move in close, wrapping my arms around her waist and lean in to nuzzle her neck. If she's not shy about expressing herself, why should I be?

I want her.

I breathe in the spicy scent of her. She switched her perfume to something suited to nighttime, something dark and rich with a hint of cherry and cinnamon. Instantly addicting.

"You are stunning," I whisper the words into the skin just below her ear, and I am rewarded with her arms wrapping around my shoulders, pulling me closer.

"Thank you," she whispers back.

I place my hands on her hips and slowly extract myself from her body before I discover exactly what's under this dress, and my dick demands we stay in. There will be no sex tonight. The last thing I want is for November to think I just want to fuck her and forget her.

"Are you ready to go?" I have yet to remove my hands from her hips though.

"Ready." She takes a couple steps out of my grasp to grab a small clutch off the marble console table by the front door.

"Do you have a coat?"

"I'm quite warm in this dress and these boots." She gestures with a flourish from her torso to her feet.

My pointed gaze narrows in on her naked thighs.

She steps around me and out the open door we forgot to close. "No worries. I can't imagine feeling cold around you."

Suddenly, it feels like a hot summer day, and I know exactly what she's talking about.

~

During our drive to the downtown waterfront area, we discuss Sunday brunch and agree it will be harmless for our families to mingle, fun even. I ask November about her day, knowing she spent time with her sister.

"As much as I've been loving my time with everyone together, it was nice to have some one-on-one time with Alex. We went to East Aurora and had lunch at this restaurant that makes the best wood-fired pizzas. We strolled down Main Street. I bought candles and a couple cute sweaters for Genevieve from a couple boutiques I like."

"I love wood-fired pizza. Would you be willing to go back with me?"

"You make it sound like taking you somewhere would be a chore."

To know she wants to be around me the way I want with her is something I will be thinking about all night.

"Maybe that should be our next date."

"Won't brunch on Sunday be our next date?" she asks.

"I consider that a get-together. Dates are just for you and me. Alone."

When I glance at her, she is looking out the window, but I don't fail to notice her wide smile in the glass reflection.

I also don't fail to notice the college-aged valets ogling my date and practically falling over each other to help her out of the car. My expression must be scathing because the boys are quick to look elsewhere. It is amazing how oblivious November is to their attention; if she notices, she's not letting on. But I place a possessive hand at the small of her back, guide her inside the hotel lobby, and keep it there so no one else gets any ideas.

It is equally unnerving and stupidly prideful to see heads turn in November's presence. Men and women in the elevator, the customers as we pass the crowded bar, all the dinner guests seated at white clothed dinner tables. November may be a beautiful woman, but this is different. She glows. She is the sun and everyone else is plants and flowers following the sunlight.

I am exactly like them, but I want to be the closest to her warmth, her light.

The hostess shows us to the table I requested at the floor-to-ceiling window table with the view of the marina lit up for the night, and I pull out November's high-back chair for her, catching a waft of that sexy scent of hers as she sits. I have been to this restaurant many times before, usually with family, sometimes for business, never a date. And as I take my seat across from her, I cannot see myself here on a date with any other woman.

Our server appears at our table to take our drink order. When November mentions having champagne, it sounds equally good to me, and I feel like celebrating.

"Would you like to share a bottle?" I ask.

"Why not?"

I scan our options listed on the wine menu, then speak to our server. "A bottle of the Krug Brut Rosé, please."

"I will prepare your bottle and return shortly," the young man states with a smile, knowing that if he continues to play his cards right, he is in for a huge tip tonight.

"How was your day? Now that I think of it, I have no idea what you do." She guffaws, placing a hand over her face.

"Don't be embarrassed for not asking? I actually like that what I do to earn money is not a priority."

She lowers her hands to her lap. "Why? Isn't your job important to you?"

"It's very important to me."

"So, it's not okay for me to skip something so important to you."

"In this case, it is." I take a long look at November biting into her plush lower lip and I want to reach across the table to smooth over that bite with my thumb, but continue instead. "My job can be a problem for me. More like, my finances. People who know me, or know of me, equate me to money. I learned early on in my career, that money is a blessing and a curse."

The expression on November's face turns from quizzical brow to the release of understanding as she slowly nods.

"And that career is?" She stretches the 'is' in attempt to lighten my mood.

"Security." I chuckle.

She rolls her hand in gesture to give her more information, but we are interrupted by our bottle service. Once our glasses are full, and I ask for five minutes alone since we haven't even glanced at our menus, our server flits away.

I raise my flute of tiny beads trailing upwards in rosy liquid, and November smiles sweetly as she raises hers.

"I have had the best week in a very long time and I am one thousand percent certain it is because of you, November. I can only wish for more."

Her smile wavers for a millisecond, but it registers somewhere in my heart because we both know 'more' is only a wish. In less than a week, she will be on an airplane, headed back to her home. Her life.

My own smile wavers.

"Then, here's to good days ahead," she says softly, her smile holding.

Our glasses meet in the middle with a light clink. An

effervescent kiss. A reminder to stay present with this beautiful woman who is burrowing into my chest.

We do have a conversation about my work over our steak dinners.

Is it strange that I enjoy watching November eat? Strange to me.

I tell her about the business I started with my college roommate, moving to Manhattan, then returning to Buffalo after my parents died.

"How did you manage to start a new business while taking care of two kids?" she asks before taking a bite of herb covered potato.

"It was a tremendous help that Carys and Gareth were young teenagers and not little kids. I was able to accomplish a lot while they attended school, while they did their homework, and after they went to sleep. They liked to be busy during the summertime, taking rowing and sailing classes, college prep classes, Carys liked to paint, Gareth toyed with a variety of sports, we all had regular therapy appointments, and I was their chauffeur. Working from the car is pretty easy."

She stares at me. "That's a lot."

"I got them through high school with their sanity intact, and that's what I'm most proud of."

"I'm sure your parents would be proud too."

My throat is tight hearing those words, and I force a sip of water down, having switched after two glasses of champagne.

She continues while pushing tiny roasted potatoes on her plate with her fork. "That first year after Roman died, I lived with Alex to help her take care of Plum. We went through the suffering and healing together, and it gave Alex time to figure out life without her husband. I often think about my brother in context of how he sees Alex and Mark raising his daughter. I'm sure he feels proud, relieved maybe, seeing his daughter happy and healthy and loved."

My hand reaches across the table for hers. She gently releases her fork to the plate's edge, then allows me to guide her hand toward me. I lean in to place a light kiss to the top of her fingers, then smooth that spot over with my thumb as if I can sink every feeling I have, yet cannot speak of, into her skin.

"He is, November. He is."

One dinner, one conversation, and I feel entirely too close to this warm and caring woman. Exposed. Flayed wide for her to take whatever she desires from me and I would be grateful for it. She will take my heart all the way across the country and I will never get it back. My whole life, I have played it safe with my heart, knowing damn well that it can be lost any moment in time. Yet the idea of November keeping my heart with her wherever she is in the world should terrify me, but I can't seem to care.

CHAPTER 13

November

S aturday was a much-needed lungful of the freshest air, and simultaneously felt like wading through hip height wet sand, agonizingly slow. After our dinner date, I needed a break from the intense emotions I felt seeping into my soul. Being careless with my heart is not something I am used to, but that is all I want to be with Rhys and it makes no logical sense.

When Alex asked how the date was, I told her about the restaurant and some conversation highlights, nothing too heavy. I knew I couldn't talk about my feelings because she's biased and wants me to be with Rhys. Alex wouldn't mind me uprooting my life in LA to be close to the family. She was actually surprised I came home at a reasonable time; she was curious as to why I didn't spend the night with Rhys. My answer was it is too soon for that, when, honestly, if I had spent the night with him, I don't think I could recover from it. Yet, oh, how I want to.

Still, I need to talk my feelings out and call Genevieve. When she answers, my immediate thought is she might be biased in wanting me to stay in Los Angeles, but she is surprisingly diplomatic.

"Em, I have known you many years, and I think I know you very well. You haven't laid your heart on the line in at least half the time we have known each other. And when you did, honestly, your whole heart wasn't invested. I get why. Alex and Roman loved each other with their whole hearts, and you saw the beauty in that love. You also witnessed Alex's near destruction when your brother died. Yet, you could take a lesson from Alex's experience. She mourned her devastating loss, and was lucky to find love again, if your description of her life with Mark is true."

I couldn't speak around the lump in my throat if I tried, which gives Gen all the permission she needs to continue.

She sighs. "Babe, you and I both understand there are no guarantees in life. People come in and out of our lives for a reason or a season. Some do stick around, though. You just need to decide how much of a risk you're willing to take. I certainly can't tell you, and as much as Alex would like to, she can't either. This is your life. Your heart. Do what feels right to you."

Genevieve makes complete sense to me, but I still needed time away from Rhys and my complicated feelings. Luckily, Saturday was a busy day with Plum's soccer game in the morning (Her team won and she scored two goals!), breakfast out, then we enjoyed a full afternoon at a fall festival. We were all exhausted by dusk. Although Rhys and I texted throughout the day, I was still able to empty my spiraling mind, and have fun with my family. Create special memories with my niece. Isn't that the entire reason I'm in Buffalo?

When Sunday brunch rolls around, I feel refreshed and open once again. My family and I meet Rhys and his family at Delaware Park, arriving close to the same time. After introductions are made, Rhys took a moment to say a semi-private hello with a sweet kiss to my cheek, nothing like the hot hello he gave me on Friday night. I am not complaining about the sweet kiss, especially after he tucked me into his side as we walked into the busy restaurant, but the hot hello was fire!

I give my name to the hostess and as we wait, Rhys stands behind me and wraps his arms around my waist, and I understand, he missed me. All those complicated feelings I raked away yesterday like fallen leaves on the lawn come blowing back in. I missed him too, and it was just one day.

Plum, dressed in a purple sweater close in shade to my own and a matching high braid, emphasizing the mini me look, stands before Rhys and me, her arms folded across her chest.

"Mr. Morgan, you never did answer my question."

"Rhys. You can call me Rhys. What question is that?"

"Are you Auntie Novie's boyfriend?"

Alex steps up and answers her daughter instead. "As good as a question as that might be, Plum, this is new to all of us and not a question that you should be asking."

Plum looks a little embarrassed, so I pull her into a hug. Rhys pulls his arms away so I can embrace my niece fully and rub her back. Try as I might to ignore the looks and whispers between Alex and Carys, I know both are elated at Plum's question, and the PDA Rhys and I give each other.

Fortunately, we are saved by our table being ready. When we sit outside near heat lamps, Plum chooses to sit between me and Rhys, which quietly surprises all of us. Turns out, Plum and Rhys have things in common. Rhys played a variety of sports as a kid including soccer; he was also the same age as Plum when Carys and Gareth were born, so she asked advice on how to be a good big sister and she was absolutely fascinated Carys has a twin brother.

"You had a baby brother and a baby sister?" Plum's eyebrows are as far up her forehead as they can go.

"I did," he replies.

"I am soooooo glad Mom is only having one baby. I don't know how I would handle twins. You're a pro. Will you please be my big sibling teacher?" She sounds exhausted already.

We all stifle laughs.

"I'd be happy to give you any advice I can to help."

Rhys looks honored to be asked and my heart is pumping wildly in my chest.

"I really appreciate it." Plum picks up her fork and takes a stab of pancake.

She even ordered what Rhys is having: blueberry pancakes with a side of bacon.

Enchanting. That's what this whole scene around the brunch table is, enchanting. Everyone seamlessly fitting together as if we have all known each other forever. A skit from a beloved family TV show. It is eyeball rolling, sickeningly sweet, yet fills my heart full of what ifs. I see it and tamp down my smile because I shouldn't be bowled over by one brunch.

When I glance up at Rhys, I know he sees it all, too. Yet he is not fighting back a smile, no, his expression is much more serious. And that sound in my head is an alarm, a warning bell ringing loud and clear.

CHAPTER 14

Rhys

During brunch, Carys blindsided me by asking November to broker a relationship between Morgan Security and A New Day for our employees. Carys loves the services the facility offers and its location. She and I had agreed to approach November with the idea, but I had no clue Carys was going to lay it out there today. It's fine, and necessary to get the ball rolling while November is still in town, but she could have given me a head's up.

November agreed to meet with us tomorrow afternoon at my office and we kept the business talk to a minimum. Alex was invited to attend the meeting, but she has parent-teacher conferences in the afternoon, and trusts November to organize a plan since this is her wheelhouse. I am happy to work with November, to have her at the office tomorrow, to spend time with her in a new way. What I am not excited for is to see a new facet to this woman that I know will sink me deeper into my feelings for her.

At brunch, witnessing how easily our families blend together, and the pleasant commonalities I have with Plum,

I felt overwhelmed. As good as it is, I could feel it slipping through my fingers. Not even five full days from now and November will be gone.

Fuck unfair!

I hold November's hand in mine, a little too tightly, as we all exit the restaurant. The scene around the lake looks drastically different from when we were last here. The trees, once aflame with autumn color, are now stripped bare by the Halloween storm, and I feel just as bare.

Alex touches November's arm to attract her attention, and we both turn toward Alex in unison.

"Em, if you want to go with Rhys, it's fine. We're just going to go home and get ready for the week ahead. Plum has homework to do and a bedroom to tidy. You go have fun."

Alex walks away to say her goodbyes to Carys and her husband, Gregory, as if it's a done deal, but maybe November should go home anyway.

I turn November to face me and take both her hands into mine. I kiss the top of each as I pull her in close. When both her hands are wrapped in mine against my chest, I keep my voice low for no one else to hear.

"You should go home with your family and spend time with them."

Her face remains immobile, but her eyes are crestfallen. I am the worst person in the world right now, but I continue to try to do what's best for both of us.

I try to explain. "I know Alex said they're just doing day-to-day stuff, but you could still spend time with Plum."

November doesn't say anything, but nods in agreement as her teeth sink into her bottom lip. I release one of her hands to press my thumb to that soft lip to set it free, then give her a chaste kiss to that same spot.

"I will see you tomorrow, okay?" I can't bear the physical contact anymore, the change in her demeanor, and let her other hand free as she nods once again.

She pastes a smile to her lips as she hugs Carys and Gregory goodbye, then leaves with Plum and Mark and a questioning Alex. All I want is to run after her and take another walk around the lake with her. Kiss her the way I want to kiss her. Be alone with her.

Keep her.

Carys must see it written all over my face. She states, "Here I thought you were a smart man. The smartest, actually."

The snark. I cross my arms in front of my chest, and turn what I know is a scowl on my face to my sister. I am in no mood for her judgement and my tone reflects such.

"Tell me, Carys, what, in your infinite wisdom, would you have me do?"

Now, her tone reflects she is no mood for me.

"Rhys, I get that you think November is going home this week, never to be seen or heard from again. That bullshit is nothing but self-sabotage."

"She is leaving! What am I supposed to do, ask her to move here? If she hasn't since her family has lived here, why would she move for me?"

Carys gives me a hard, frustrated expression. "No, I don't expect her to move here after knowing you only a week or two. I will tell you this, though. In the past two hours, I have seen a whole other side to you. Affectionate. Adoring. Smitten. Not even two weeks and November has brought out in you something you have never experienced in longer relationships. You have options, but only you can figure out whether or not to give yourself a chance at something life-changing in the best possible way."

She gives me a quick kiss on my cheek, then turns to walk back to her husband, who knows better than to interfere with siblings sniping at each other, yet keeps a sharp eye on his wife to make sure it is nothing more.

My eyes focus on the bare trees populating the park. They might not look entirely beautiful or majestic right now, yet they will when covered in ice and snow, when the cherry blossoms bloom and others full of buds ready to burst open, the lush green leaves of summer, and, again, to blazing autumn color. The cycle of tree life.

I want November to see all of it... with me.

The Sunday routine has been tossed aside in favor of me trying to see through the mountain before I begin the climb. For hours. My brain is exhausted from flicking the switch from 'won't work' to 'how can we make it work.' Now, standing on my back patio, watching the sun set, I know only one thing.

I am an idiot.

Hours wasted thinking about what ifs rather than hours spent with the woman I have been obsessing over all day. All I know for sure is, I may have limited time with November, but I am going to spend as much of it with her as she will allow.

I fish my phone out of my jeans back pocket and open a fresh text box.

> I know this is last minute, but if you don't already have dinner plans, will you allow me to take you out tonight?

> Or out for dessert?

Ellipsis. No ellipsis. Ellipsis.

How about dessert for dinner?

I can be there in less than twenty minutes, but I will wait if you need more time.

I'm ready now.

On my way.

When I pull into the driveway fourteen minutes later, I see November stand from the cushioned armchair she was sitting in on the wraparound porch. Once I am out of my SUV, she is walking toward me in the breeze. We are magnets coming together, clinging to each other. We both know the hourglass will not hold back the sand.

I am an idiot.

This is how we should have spent the last handful of hours. Her body tucked into mine, and me holding her tight, my forehead resting against hers.

"I am so sorry. I should not have pushed you away when all I want is to be near you."

She snuggles in a little closer. "I'm just happy you came to your senses."

I don't want to let her go, but I promised her dessert. So, I release her and open the passenger side door. There's a smugness inside my chest over having her back in my car. I close her door and rush to get into my seat.

"What would you like for our dessert dinner? Cake? Pie? Donuts? Ice cream?"

She clicks in her seatbelt. "Do you have ice cream at home?"

My smile is overly wide, an unfamiliar stretch in my cheeks I haven't felt in a long while. Regardless of the weather or season, I always have ice cream in the freezer. In my home.

"As a matter-of-fact, I do."

∼

I try to see my house through fresh eyes, as November views it. The middle automatic garage door opens to reveal my black sedan parked to our left, and as we pull in to park, the garage door closes behind us. To our right is a well-organized storage system including two wall racks holding a blue, single-person kayak and a black mountain bike. Everything in its place and clean.

"Do you kayak or is that just decoration to impress... people?" she teases.

"I do kayak, although I didn't get on the water as much as I would have liked this past summer. The bike, on the other hand, seems more like decoration now. I don't know the last time I took it off the rack."

She doesn't wait for me to open her door and steps out of the SUV the same time I do. Once we are standing together at the door to the house interior, I address the other part of her question.

"As for 'people,' I have never had another woman here."

My gaze holds hers as I watch what I said sink in. It is important she understands that having her here is something I don't take lightly. She doesn't say anything, but gives me a barely-there nod. I only turn away to disengage the fingerprint lock on the door handle, then hold the door open for her.

"Very high tech." She smirks as she steps inside.

As soon as I close the door behind us, the lock engages. I point to a windowed second door off the mudroom we're standing in, before kicking off my sneakers and bending to place them in an empty cubby.

"That leads to the side yard where the garbage and recycle cans are stored. The glass on the door is ballistic; it would be difficult to break in there."

November sits on the black bench to pull off her shiny black rainboots, then places them neatly in a taller cubby.

She stands. "Are all the windows in your house ballistic?"

"No. Just the ones on exterior doors. The windows are breakable in case of an emergency, but all have manual locking mechanisms. There are also wide-coverage cameras on the property."

"So, no running naked outside."

I shake my head. "If that's your thing, the cameras shouldn't deter you."

"It's much too cold for me to do that now, but maybe in the summer."

She's teasing me, but her mention of summer, however it might be in jest, makes me pause at the thought of her here next year.

I follow her down the short hallway to the kitchen, pointing out the door to the walk-in pantry and another to the smaller cleaning supply closet.

"Wow!" November gasps as her eyes scan my kitchen. "This is just... Wow!"

Her violet manicured fingers trail along the quartz countertops, the dual oven Viking range, the large side-by-side Sub-Zero refrigerator, freezer and wine storage, then stopping at the far end to pop open the large appliance garage housing a Vitamix and a four-slice toaster. Before closing the door, she throws me a glance I can't quite interpret, but I'm enjoying her perusal of my kitchen. She doesn't open anymore doors, but her eyes are full of longing that I wish were on me.

She begins her stroll back my way, eyebrow raised in mocking gesture. Her lips roll together to hold back a smile, a laugh. She's making fun of me without saying a word.

I chuckle, and she knows her point has been made.

With that, I move to the freezer and eyeball what flavors of ice cream I have in stock. "What would you like? Peanut Butter Chocolate? Pistachio? Black Raspberry Truffle?"

"Oh! Black Raspberry! Black Raspberry!"

The childlike excitement over ice cream is unexpected and makes me roar with laughter. "Could be any cuter?"

I grab two pints of the same flavor, shut the freezer door with my elbow, then grab two spoons from a nearby drawer.

"What can I say? Ice cream brings the cuteness out of me."

"No, you are always cute." I quickly kiss the tip of her nose as she comically bats her eyelashes at me. "Where would you like to sit? I could turn on the fireplace in the living room or make a fire outside."

"Let's just sit here at the counter, so I can drool over my dream kitchen."

I pull one of the six British Tan leather stools out for her to sit, place a pint and spoon in front of her, and know I'm forgetting something, but it's been a long time since I had any guests in my home. Then I remember.

"Would you like something to drink? I can open a bottle of wine or champagne. Water? I'm a decent bartender if the drink doesn't have too many ingredients, but I do know how to use the espresso machine pretty well." I'm rambling. I'm nervous. I'm never nervous.

"Rhys?"

"Yes?"

"Thank you for offering, but nothing for now."

Finally, I take the stool on her right, and proceed to open my pint of ice cream, soothed by the first taste of rich berry flavor.

"I feel bad for only feeding you ice cream for dinner. I can heat one of the meals in the refrigerator if you want something more substantial."

"More substantial than ice cream? Please. If I could, I would eat ice cream for breakfast, lunch and dinner." She nudges my bicep with her shoulder. "Besides, I'm the one who suggested dessert for dinner."

We eat a few bites in companionable silence and I sneak looks at her doing what she said she would, drool over my kitchen, well, sans drool. I can almost see her imagination picturing herself making her caramel at my stove. I want that so much it hurts my heart. I am desperate to think of something else.

"Where did your name come from? I can't imagine November being a family name, but I could be wrong."

"It is the month I was conceived."

I choke out a laugh at her deadpan delivery of the joke, but I quickly realize it is not a joke.

"And your brother?" It slipped out, and I realize too late that asking something so simple could bring pain.

"Roman?" Her face brightens and my muscles relax. "Roman was named after the place he was conceived."

"Wait. Rome?"

"My parents, with their own brand of humor and sentimentality, vacationed in Italy, Rome specifically, approximately nine months before my brother was born."

I chuckle out, "Well, I like your name."

"I like your name too. And I am assuming with names like Rhys, Carys, and Gareth, you have Irish lineage?"

"All Irish. My father, James, was Irish American. He did

137

his junior year abroad at Trinity College in Dublin where he met my mother, Róisín, also in her junior year. My dad ended up transferring because he couldn't imagine leaving his love behind. They married after graduation, then moved to Boston first, then Buffalo."

"What a beautiful love story! Like something I would read in one of my romance novels."

Raising a spoonful of ice cream to my mouth, I ponder my father's decision to stay in Dublin to be with my mother. He loved her so much; he couldn't imagine his life without her.

"This isn't your childhood home, is it?"

Her question pulls me from thinking about more what ifs.

"No. When our parents died, Carys and Gareth had a difficult time adjusting to life in their home without our parents. My therapist didn't think it was a good idea at the time, but I would have done anything to help them in their grief and I had the money from the sale of my half of the original start-up I owned. I bought this house and placed our parents' home in trust, just in case Carys or Gareth wanted to move there eventually. Carys lives there now. She and Gregory renovated it soon after they married."

November places her spoon in her half-eaten pint, then rests her small hand on my bicep, tilting her head to make sure she can see my face. Her eyes are so soft in their assessment of me, I have to look away.

"I don't know if anyone has told you this, but you are a really good brother."

My chest aches. No one has said that to me. I know my brother and sister love me and are grateful our parents raised me to be responsible. I took the reins and tried to do what I thought our parents would want me to do.

I hear her stool push away and feel her before I see her

stand and slide her oversized sweater-clad body between the counter and me. She hugs me so tight. My whole body relaxes into her when I breathe in her warmth, the peace she's offering to me. The lump in my throat eases enough for me to whisper a 'thank you' in her ear. A kiss on the soft lobe, just below on her neck, the spot of lightly fragranced skin where her neck meets the loose neckline of cashmere. My lips linger, tasting her there with the lightest touch of my tongue, and my skin vibrates with the sound of her sigh.

My nose trails the length of her neck, my hand mimicking the motion up her back until my fingers are lost in her loose locks. I place my lips against her pulse, lightly sucking, wanting to mark her, feeling the tempo of her blood pick up its pace.

"Rhys..."

The sound of my name on November's breath is pure sex to my ears; I have to pull away to believe what I am hearing by examining her face. What I find in her dilating pupils, flush cheeks, and full parted lips - I am making her feel good. It is all I want, all I will ever want, if it means she will forever look at me with that bone-deep desire.

When my thumb gently swipes across her lower lip, her tongue darts out for a taste, to tempt. It works; that small sexual contact she initiated sparks across my skin like gunpowder speeding toward a keg of dynamite. I groan.

Fuck!

Our lips crash together, and she gives as good as she gets. We are at once gliding lips, tangled tongues, and nipping teeth. Handfuls of hair. Greedy, gripping hands under sweaters searching for skin.

She tastes sweet, like the berry ice cream we ate, and it makes my brain imagine licking her, like a dripping ice cream cone. My dick swells painfully hard against the zipper of my jeans.

When my hands meet the delicate lace of her bra, my thumbs circle the very tips of her nipples – she gasps, and my dick jumps. It is suddenly too hot in the house and my clothes feel too tight for my body. Without a second thought I pull away to yank my sweater with my undershirt over my head, and send it careening to the wood plank floor. When my sight is no longer obstructed by my clothes, I see November has followed my lead, magenta cashmere now piled on top of my navy wool and white cotton.

The lace I felt is black with, maybe, roses, but my sole focus is on her hard nipples poking through, begging to be soothed by my tongue. I oblige – licking and sucking one nipple into my mouth as far as the lace will permit while pinching and pulling the other. She moans low and smoky.

My hand grips her hip through the fabric of the leggings she wears, and they are in my way. I move my hand from her breast to the waistband and prepare to tug them off November's gorgeous body.

"I need these off," I plead my words against wet lace. "Please tell me I can take them off."

"Yes!" she hisses. "Fuck, yes!"

I grin at her eagerness and knock over my stool to drop to my knees. She jumps at the clatter against the floor, but I don't care; I will destroy my whole house for one taste of her pussy.

When I yank the waistband down her round ass, I am quick to notice she isn't wearing panties. My thumb reaches round to swipe against her pussy – soaked! Two tugs, her legs and feet are stripped bare, my hands making their way back up her shapely legs. November is all warm, velvety skin, and my eyes, my fingers, my lips, my teeth and tongue, want to become very familiar with every inch.

As my eyes cast upwards, I catch sight of her bra falling to the floor. She wants this as much as I do.

"Goddamn, you're pretty all over." My voice is rough with need.

She blushes, but doesn't look away. "And you're so damn sexy, I could scream."

My hand slides far enough toward the front of her pelvis to swipe my thumb through slick pussy lips. Her hips buck forward as she audibly sucks in her breath.

"Ember, if you feel like screaming at any time, don't hold back."

I am salivating for that pink, glistening pussy when I lean in for my first lick, and the flavor of her is sweet cream coating my tongue. Instant addiction. I dive deep, relentlessly licking and sucking, my hands gripping the globes of her ass to lock her in place.

My name is on repeat from up above. "Rhys! Fuck, Rhys! Please! Rhys! Make me come! Rhys! Yes!"

It is the sweetest music.

Her hands squeeze and pull at the hair on the back of head, her hips pressing forward for more friction. If more friction is what she wants... I scrape my teeth against her tight bud and she screams.

"That's my pretty girl."

My cock is screaming to be let out. My hand reaches down to unbutton my jeans and lower the zipper as much as I am able for just a little relief. It's not enough and I reach inside to squeeze my shaft hard over the briefs. My brain is in sensory overload: hearing her hard pants and mindless pleas; inhaling the spicy scent of her arousal; tasting the sweetness of her flavor on my tongue; feeling the scorching hot pain of my hard cock. This time I reach inside my briefs to allow myself two ironfisted strokes.

I groan against her swollen clit as I suck her hard and slide two fingers into her sweet mess. November grips my hair tight, just like the walls of her pussy around my fingers as she tips over the edge, comes on my tongue, my name bouncing off the hard surfaces of the kitchen.

Her legs shake, and I wrap my arm around her waist to hold her upright. The intensity of my mouth to get her off turns to soft licks, wringing out her orgasm.

When I stand, my girl is blissed out and blushed all over. The prettiest.

"That was... That was..." She's still mindless and breathy, and that's all the compliment I need.

I wrap my arms around her nakedness, scoop her up bridal-style before she can protest, and carry her to the front of the house and up the staircase.

I need her in my bed.

I have made up my mind.

I am keeping her.

CHAPTER 15

November

The upstairs hallway is a blur of dark wood and shades of white – all I see clearly is Rhys. Black pupils swallowing blue irises. Thick hair a mess from my hands. Swollen lips. Pulse jumping in his neck. Strong, naked shoulders and chest. I feel his hard muscles everywhere his body connects with mine as he carries me to, presumably, his bedroom.

He crosses the large owner's suite, then lays me across the soft, navy comforter of a king-sized bed. When he stands upright, he nods absentmindedly, his eyes full of heat, and I interpret the expression as him admiring the way I look on his bed.

I like what I see as well.

The absence of his body heat combined with the cool touch of the fabric beneath me, gives me focus to appreciate the magnificence of this man. My eyes drink their fill of well-defined muscles and a prominent bulge in his half-zipped jeans. He may not kayak and bike the way he used to, but he definitely takes care of himself in other ways I have yet to discover.

He bends, places his palms on the bed at the outer side of my thighs, and kisses the top of one knee, then the other. The top of my right thigh, the inside of the left, teasing my buzzing skin with his wet tongue and the scrape of his facial hair. As he takes his time crawling up my body, he leaves a trail of hot kisses that zing me to my core. A bite to my hip, a lick in between my breasts, my collarbone - I am throbbing between my thighs once more.

Whereas our kisses downstairs were passionate and frenzied, when his lips caress mine now it's sweet and exploring, not unlike a first kiss with someone you want to get to know on a deeper level. Yes, yes, I believe we both want that.

Rhys' tongue slides against the seam of my mouth, asking for permission, and I gladly part for him, my tongue curling against his in invitation. As he deepens the kiss, his wide body hovers over me, when all I want is to feel his weight covering me, to feel him enter me, fill me.

My hands reach around his back in an attempt to pull him down.

He breaks our kiss, his eyes searching mine. "Are you sure?"

"I want you, Rhys." I want this to be crystal clear. "I have an IUD and I haven't been with anyone since my last test, years ago."

He brushes my lips with his. "Same. Minus the IUD."

I laugh, and the smile he gives me: oh, my heart!

Still, Rhys hovers, like he is waiting for more permission, or for me to change my mind. But I want to be with this man. No. I need to be with this man. Something I have never felt with another. So, I give assurance as actions; hands smoothing over the smattering of soft, black hair over his pecs, working slowly down the firm muscle of his abs, then lower to scrape my nails through the soft dusting of his happy trail. I am watching this sensual journey, but

Rhys is watching my face, his hooded eyes never leave mine. Until...

My fingers clasp his zipper and pull it down the rest of the way, then I reach inside to tease his cock, hard as his granite countertops, with a featherlight touch. His hips rock forward and back, forward and back, searching for relief and release.

Honestly, I have no idea how he has been holding back all this time.

"Take them off me." His voice is hoarse, as if speaking for the first time after walking a day through the desert with nothing to drink.

I sit up to give him a deep French kiss as I burrow my fingers into the waistband of his jeans and boxer briefs, pulling the fabric down as far as I can from this angle, and he kicks off his clothes the remainder of the way.

I am obsessed!

His body is made of the planes and plateaus an artist would love to sculpt.

And that long, thick cock is already pointing toward my pussy all on its own. My fingertips brush the top of the head, spreading precum as I explore the feel of his smooth skin over marble.

I lick my lips.

Rhys lowers his forehead to mine, eyes shut tight, jaw ticking.

He rasps out, "Stroke me."

I shiver from the sound of his voice, and my pussy walls clench. I don't need the evidence; I know I'm drenched.

My hand encircles the head, my thumb takes its sweet time stroking the sensitive undershaft back and forth. When Rhys' hips jut forward, I stroke him, slowly, firmly, to the root.

"Tell me how you want me," I whisper.

His hot breath comes out in pants, its heat tickling my nipples, but he doesn't speak right away. He opens his darkened eyes and a hundred different ways to have me flash across them.

"Ass up." He sits back on his knees and helps me flip over onto my stomach. "I want to see all of you tonight."

As I scoot to my knees, my hair falls forward. The next thing I feel is Rhys' big, warm palm between my shoulder blades. At first, I think he will push me down, then I remember what he sees.

"Beautiful," I hear him breathe, more to himself than to me, as his fingers trace along my spine.

I've had my tattoo for years, and because I don't see it, sometimes I forget it's there, the only tattoo on my skin. A blue morpho butterfly, its wings spanning from shoulder blade to shoulder blade, shadowed with a 3D effect to look like it's taking flight.

Soon, Rhys' hands and lips move down my ribcage, my waist, the small of my back. When I lower to my elbows, he hums in appreciation of my ass, then I feel it. The wide head of his hot cock, sliding through my slick, getting himself wet. My ass pushes against him in needy response.

"You want me," he rumbles out.

"Yes!" I hiss.

He breaches my entrance an inch, sucking in air between his teeth. "Goddamn, you're tight."

He pushes in another inch. Another. And I don't think I can take him all the way if I am already feeling so full. I shift on my knees to widen my legs as he thrusts in further, gripping my hips as if to hold himself back from fucking me senseless too soon.

"Rhys, I don't know if –"

"You can, Ember." He slides almost all the way out

before sliding in further this time. "Look how well you're taking me already."

Rhys reaches a hand underneath me and I feel two fingers circle my clit firmly. My skin feels hot, and I am trying to take in a full breath as he takes me completely, hitting spots inside I didn't even know existed.

"Fuck! Fuck, Ember!" He is in all the way to the hilt, but remains still, even though I can feel him vibrating in anticipation. "Tell me I can... Tell me I can move."

"Move," I whimper.

The slide, the burn of him is delicious friction consuming my focus; I barely feel him graze his teeth along my shoulder. Barely feel my painfully tight nipples rub against the comforter I am fisting with both hands.

Rhys' rhythm escalates, thrusting harder, hitting me deeper. His fingers rubbing my clit in sync, and I am in pleasure overload. I cry out an unintelligible spill of words, my brain short-circuiting.

"That's it, Ember," he pants his hot words into my ear. "Come for me. Come all over my cock."

His body is slick with sweat crowding over mine, his swollen cock fucking me harder. It's too much. He's wrenching my orgasm out of me and my body will not resist. I come – HARD!

"Rhys!"

His hips drive hard, his pelvis slaps against my ass, as he chases his own orgasm while prolonging my own. He grunts and groans as liquid heat spills and pools deep inside me. He comes and comes, I come some more, until we are just a heaving, breathy mess. Boneless.

Nothing has felt this good to me ever.

Rhys pulls me in, snug against his body as we settle into each other. My head and arms tucked into his chest; our legs entwined. His fingers trail lazily up and down my spine as he buries his nose in my hair. I hear him breathe in the scent of my coconut oil shampoo as if it is the oxygen his lungs need to survive.

I am sated from far more orgasms than I have ever had in one night. He took care of me, making sure my pleasure came before his every time; something I have never experienced with another man. The warm washcloths he used after each session, cleaning me, soothing me. Always seeking permission before taking me again. Always finding what works for me.

This man.

"Stay."

How can one word make me so happy? I wonder if he can feel my smile against his skin.

"I can stay, but you'll have to take me back before Plum wakes up, which means early. I'm not going to walk in the door after a night of sex for my young niece to witness."

I feel Rhys' whole body still.

"No. That's not what I mean." His hand flexes against the small of my back. "Yes, I want you to spend the night with me, but I want all your nights."

My too relaxed brain has trouble grasping something it should understand from Rhys' vulnerable tone.

"Are you asking me to sleep here until I leave?"

"Yes, but in my scenario, you don't go home."

Now, it is my turn to still.

Stay?

I move my head back just enough to examine Rhys' face. There is nothing but sincerity written there as he searches mine for the response he is so hoping for.

My lips part to form words, but they take some seconds

to spill out. "What? Do you mean change my flight? Stay through the weekend?"

Rhys shakes his head. "That's too soon. I want you to cancel your flight and stay with me indefinitely."

I have to sit up for this conversation, so I untangle myself from his body, hoist myself onto my knees, and stare down at Rhys now lying on his back. I blink. Blink again.

"Rhys, I know the sex was good. Okay, fantastic, but -"

"No." He sits straight up, twists his body to face me, then covers my shoulders with his big, grounding hands. "I know what the optics look like; my timing is shit. Setting sex aside, I was already making my way to this conclusion. Sex between us is the best I ever had, but it is one item in a well of reasons we should give ourselves the chance to explore us in a relationship."

When he realizes I am stunned silent, he continues to plead his case. "I will do long distance if it is all you have to offer me and we will figure out those dynamics... I just think... If we give us time to be together, really be together..."

His tone is frantic, his gaze intense, so full of truth. My eyes drift downward to my hands for a break, but he slips a finger under my chin to hold my attention.

"Ember, please, tell me what you're thinking."

What do I think?

Rhys is right. The optics are sex influenced decisions, and it doesn't help matters that we are completely naked while having this talk. Yet, the sincerity in the depth of his eyes; I know in my heart he is forthcoming. This is something he wants. Still, we could both benefit from time to ourselves to think things through.

I take his hands into mine and give them as reassuring a squeeze as I can.

"I think we need a cooling off period. I think we should

get dressed and you drive me back to Alex's. We try to get some sleep, although, I don't know how that will be possible, and we lay it all out tomorrow."

Before I finish speaking, his whole face falls, the light in his eyes going dim. I lean forward and catch his lips with my own in an attempt to breathe the hope back into him.

"This is not a no, Rhys." My lips speak the gentle words against his mouth, then pull away to look him in the eye. "This is, let's talk this through in the light of day."

To my surprise, the drive back to Alex's house is not in total silence. The ride began that way, but when Rhys speaks, I know it's because he wants to dissolve any tension there may be between us. I want that too, but just didn't know what to say.

"Your tattoo is very beautiful. How long have you had it?"

"I was wondering if you would ask me about that."

"I would have earlier, but I was occupied with other things."

He really wants to fix things between us, but what he doesn't understand: there is nothing wrong to fix.

"About five years now. I got it on a whim. Not like I was drunk out of my mind kind of whim. More like I was sitting on the fence and one day I hopped off."

"Why a butterfly?"

Very few people know this story, because... I don't know, maybe they would think I'm delusional or silly. Luckily, very few people have seen my tattoo. Now, I wonder what Rhys will think about it.

"Before my mom died, she said she would visit me from time to time under the guise of a butterfly. I thought she was making an attempt to console me, but about a month after she died I began to see butterflies in the oddest places. Once, I was in my car at a stoplight and a butterfly came out of nowhere, fluttering in front of me just beyond my windshield until the light turned green and it flew away. Or talking about my mom would conjure a butterfly. Over time, the visits became fewer and fewer, so I decided to carry a butterfly with me wherever I go."

Rhys watches the road as he drives, and is quiet for several seconds before responding. He reaches across the console to take my hand is his, lacing his fingers with mine.

"Dragonflies." He pauses the equivalent of one breath. "For me, it was dragonflies. For weeks after my parents died, I would see dragonflies in pairs. It registered to me as an oddity, but I chalked it up to it being springtime. I didn't know."

Tears prick the back of my eyes. I cover our clasped hands with my free one. "How would you know unless you had someone like my mom to tell you? I wouldn't have known either."

"What do you think it all means?"

"I'm not sure. Maybe it's as simple as love can work wonders."

The remainder of the short ride is silent.

When Rhys parks in the driveway, I stay seated to allow him to open my door for me. The last thing I want is for him to think I'm rushing to get away. I know I hurt his feelings tonight, but I want him to really think about what he's proposing. I want him to be one hundred percent sure, not '...making my way to this conclusion.' Half a day apart might help him be sure. For me, I need to think without his naked body pressed against mine all night.

When I step out of the car, Rhys enfolds me into his arms, keeping me as close as possible. My whole body relaxes against his. Perhaps he has come around to the idea of time to be sure.

"What time should I pick you up for tomorrow's meeting? I'd like to give you a tour of my building beforehand."

"Plum is off from school tomorrow for parent-teacher conferences, and I'll hang out with her. Mark and Alex will be home to have lunch with us. Is one o'clock okay with you?"

"Perfect," he says against my temple, kissing me there, then my cheek. He kisses me as if it were his last.

I kiss him back as if it will lead to more.

As difficult as it is, I muster the will to extract my body from Rhys' embrace, and force myself to head up the walkway. It would be far too easy to stay in his arms until sunrise.

"Ember, I won't be changing my mind, if that's what you're thinking."

When I turn around, Rhys has his hands shoved in his jeans pockets as if keeping them there will prevent himself from coming after me.

"Ember." I taste the name like I have never said the word before. "No one has ever called me that before. You started that earlier tonight. Why?"

"Because you are igniting something inside me that I have never felt before."

I return to him. How could I not?

The smile-infused kiss I brush against his lips is innocent in comparison to what we have done to each other's bodies in the last few hours.

"Good night, Mr. Morgan."

"Sweet dreams, Ms. Day." He places a light kiss on my forehead and lets me go.

Before I get too far up the walkway for Rhys to hear me through the wind kicking up the leaves on the ground, I turn around.

"Of you."

Did he think I wouldn't say those last two words that have quickly become our thing? I don't know, yet the relief that washes over his body makes my heart ache.

Of course, everyone is sound asleep. It's after midnight when I tiptoe up the stairs and quietly shut my bedroom door. I might be located far away from the other bedrooms, but I am still mindful of common courtesies.

I fish my cell phone out of my handbag and hurriedly send a text as I flop onto my bed.

> I need to talk!

In less than a minute, Genevieve's FaceTime rings through. She looks red-faced and sweaty, and I know she stopped a late-night Peloton workout burning off excess energy to be there for me. I would do the same for her, and have over the years.

"Hey!" she pants out.

"Rhys asked me to stay."

"Awesome! Just send me your new flight info and I'll calendar your airport pick up."

"Okay. I see how you would interpret it that way. I did too. And we're both wrong." I blow out an exhale. "Rhys is asking for something more indefinite."

Gen's golden-brown eyes become shifty as her brain processes this new data.

I realize she may need more context.

"I am pretty sure the plan is for me to stay with him, basically, live with Rhys while navigating a possible relationship."

The cell phone image shakes a bit as Genevieve hops off her bike seat, then bounces slightly as she walks to, I presume, her kitchen. She doesn't speak yet, just pours herself a glass of cold water from the refrigerator before taking a seat at the counter.

"Okay. I've had some time with it," my best friend begins. "And I'm on board with Rhys' idea. I understand where he's coming from. The plus is, you can work from anywhere, so that doesn't matter. You have no pets or plants you need to rush back to. You just have to change your flight from LA to... Where is this teambuilding in December?"

"Florida. And thanks for reminding me about changing that flight."

"So, you've already made up your mind." She winks.

Genevieve is sneaky like that. I swear, she should have gone into psychology, become a therapist. She can pull anything out of anyone.

"Further context, Rhys brought this up not long after we had sex."

"Yeah, you should have led with that tidbit." She waggles her eyebrows. "How was the sex?"

"Mind-shattering. Leg quaking. Heart melting."

"Way to go Rhys! A man who knows how to give good orgasm."

"Plural. And I want more, but..." I sigh, going back to a serious tone. "Could this actually work?"

"Like the old saying goes, 'You'll never know until you try.'" It's her turn to sigh. "Em, if you have even the tiniest inkling coming from your heart, well... I know if it were me, I'd have to know. Don't you want to find out?"

My beautifully bighearted, beautifully wise, beautifully caring, best of all best friends.

"I do."

CHAPTER 16

Rhys

Half a day later and I am still fired up to plead my case for November agreeing to stay, but during our drive to the office, I know this is not the time for a serious conversation and to make plans. Instead, I am content to listen to the play-by-play of her morning with Plum, a morning spent baking. The result of which is stashed away in the large, linen-covered basket tray belted into the back seat. I have already attempted to sneak a peek, but that was met with a playful hand slap from November. But the smell of cinnamon and vanilla and sugar permeating my car interior is making me salivate and I am not above begging for a bite of whatever baked good she's willing to part with.

Or a bite of her, which is equally sweet tasting. The thought makes me shift in my seat, feeling the half chub in my pants.

I can't look at November or my dick will get harder. She may be completely covered in black knit fabric, but she's wearing a wrap top tucked into a tight pencil skirt, paired with black patent stilettos. If there was ever a test of my willpower, it's her in this outfit. No, not the outfit. I have had a taste of her. I know how she fucks. I am greedy to have her again.

I pull my SUV into the driveway of my building and wait until the door is fully open to proceed into the parking garage.

"This area is really interesting to look at. Very industrial. Kind of gritty. It's on the rise from the ashes, isn't it?" she asks.

The space I vacated to pick up November is still empty and I park.

"Kind of gritty was an understatement when I bought this building. There were only a couple factories operating across the river at the time. No other life. I didn't buy here because I thought the property value would increase. The area is interesting and I liked the idea of repurposing something old. Also, the price was a steal, although I paid dearly on the renovation."

She looks around the huge garage, full of employee vehicles. "I bet."

I get out of the car, open her door, then the backseat door to grab the tray of treats. This time I peek. There must be four kinds of cookies, slices of banana bread, and what looks like salted caramel brownies.

"Is that your caramel in brownies?" I ask after I close the backseat door.

We start walking toward the elevator vestibule, the only sounds are our voices and the clicking of her sexy as hell heels on buffed clean cement.

"Yes. I melted down the last of the candy with some cream, then swirled it into the brownie batter."

"I want one of those when we get to my office."

"No."

"No?" I glance at her as I shift the tray to one arm, and palm the security lock.

November watches all of it with intense interest.

I watch her fine ass as she passes me and through the door I hold open.

Am I salivating over brownies or her?

"I already saved a few for you in my tote bag, so don't touch those."

The elevator door opens and we step inside. If my hands were free, they would be all over her right now. Cameras be damned!

Instead, I settle for a kiss to her temple. "Thank you for thinking of me."

The door slides open and she steps off, nonchalant, as if she didn't just shoot an arrow through my heart with her kindness.

As we walk down the hall, I point out the features of this floor.

"It's so quiet. Where are all the employees?" Her eyes dart around, genuinely curious.

"This floor is mainly for meetings and collaborating; it houses my office. The floors above are livelier."

"Interesting you chose, essentially, the first floor for your office instead of the top floor. That's where the majority of CEOs situate themselves."

"I didn't see the point. I still have a nice view of the river."

We approach the open door of the small computer lab and I hear Gareth's voice. I stop. November stops.

I sigh. "As much as I would like to be alone with you, we should say hello."

She tilts her head to the side in question, but I just tilt my head toward the door in a 'follow me' gesture.

When we step inside the lab, Gareth's eyes immediately

laser in on November, and he does a head nod/shake combo. And I hear him breathe, "Damn, Rhys. Just, damn."

I scowl in my brother's direction and almost remove November from the room, but she has to meet him at some point.

Gareth grins, because he successfully poked the bear. He steps forward and offers his hand to November. "I'm sure you already know who I am, but I'll introduce myself anyway. Gareth Morgan."

She confidently takes his hand to shake, which he brings to his lips for a kiss, then he continues, "You must be my future sister-in-law."

November doesn't falter, sarcasm laces her upbeat voice. "Aren't you amusing?"

Gareth laughs, still holding her hand. "Oh, I like you, November."

I balance the basket of treats on one arm, while extracting November from my annoying little brother with the other, mouthing to him 'motherfucker' over her head, before I introduce her to the other man in the room, someone safe.

"This is Asher Adams. He is our technology consultant, an extra pair of genius eyes, and a long-time friend. Asher, this is November Day."

Asher, always polite and respectful, wearing the same passive expression I've come to expect from him, rises from his chair to shake November's outstretched hand.

"Nice to meet you, Ms. Day."

Her smile is bright. "Please, call me November."

He releases her hand, and states, "Asher," then retreats to his chair and his work.

November reaches into her tote bag, fiddles with something, then pulls out a single white paper napkin. She places the napkin on the desk beside Asher, then retrieves the tray from me, pulling the linen back and presenting the sweets to him.

"Would you like some? I made them myself."

Asher looks to me as if for permission, which I give with an encouraging nod.

"Is that banana bread?" He keeps his eyes focused on the tray.

"Yes. It's made with oat flour. Lots of banana, lots of cinnamon. Very moist."

Asher reaches in and carefully removes a slice, then places it on his napkin.

"Thank you." Asher barely looks up at her, but his voice is kind.

"You're very welcome."

I have always wondered about Asher and his life. He isn't talkative about the past, not talkative at all. In spite of whatever he has had to deal with, Asher is highly intelligent, responsible, hard-working, but keeps to himself.

My thoughts are interrupted by Gareth's voice.

"I'll have one of those brownies."

November replaces the linen covering, then picks up the tray, which I take from her hands.

"Maybe later." She faux close-lip smiles, then turns on her heels and out the door she goes.

Before I follow November, I chuckle at the dumbfounded expression on Gareth's face, and I don't miss the ghost of a smile on Asher as he chews a piece of banana bread.

When we are out of earshot of the computer lab, November speaks.

"Well, he's adorable." Her voice is even, but I don't like it.

I frown. "Gareth?"

"God, no! He is way too pretty and he knows it. Sorry. I know he's your baby brother and all, but I had to cut him down a peg."

We pass Sophie's desk, but she is nowhere to be seen. I open the door to my office and let November inside.

"Do you mean Asher?" I ask, placing the tray on the steel, industrial-style coffee table, then walk over to November who is standing before one large window, taking in the view.

"Clark Kent eyeglasses are a thing in romance novels, you know."

My hand reaches out to grip her hip, possessively, demanding her attention.

She looks down at my hand, then back to my face. "I didn't know you had a jealous streak."

I take a step closer, wanting to kiss that smirk right off her mouth.

"Only when you call another man adorable."

She folds her arms across her chest, shelving her breasts in the most tantalizing way.

"If you read as many romance novels as I do, when I character pops out of the page, you would take notice too."

My expression must be full of confusion, because her fingers clasp the lapel of my dress shirt and gives it a slight tug.

"Characters in books are like actors in movies. When you see an actor in real life, whether you're a fan or not, you acknowledge the sighting. Book characters are a bit different because you use your imagination based on the details the author provides. Therefore, when you see a person who represents a type of character, you have to take note."

I get close, really close, herding November until her back

connects with the window and she stops talking. I plant my palms against the cold glass just above her shoulders, caging her in.

She smirks again. "Does that explanation soothe your beast inside?"

I take a small step closer and bury my smile in the warmth of her neck. "I hope you're not into threesomes, because I won't share you."

"The Why Choose trope has never been my cup of tea."

She laughs and I kiss her mouth to capture the cheerful sound.

My hands grip her waist, but they want to do so much more to her body, and I stupidly left my office door open. Instead, I break our kiss, lacing my fingers together at the small of her back to keep them from doing unspeakable things to her. Her arms rest on top mine, hands relaxed on my biceps.

"I have no idea what this trope thing is about, but I will learn if you choose me."

"You and I have just begun, and I want to see how this..." She smiles and motions her index finger back and forth between our bodies. "Plays out."

My heart stutters.

Is she saying what I think she's saying?

"Tell me you're staying."

"Yes. I am staying in Buffalo with you."

I smile so hard it hurts, then hug her so tight, I have to immediately let go to not crush her. My hand finds hers and I lead her to take a seat on the leather couch. We sit close, turned as much as we can to face each other, legs touching.

"First, when would you like to move your things to my house?"

She thinks for a moment. "I want to tell my family first,

and I'll do that today. If it's okay with you, tomorrow after dinner. That will give me time to pack and get things in order."

"Just text me when you're ready to go."

"Okay. We should probably have a check-in date. A point not too far away when we decide..."

"If we're working or not." I finish her sentence. She nods. "The end of this month?"

"That's good."

I take her hands in mine, caressing the top with my thumbs. "I know this is sudden. We are at the beginning of getting to know each other and have a lot to figure out. I need you to know, I am in this one hundred percent. I want us to succeed and will work hard for us to get there."

"I'm with you, Rhys. I am not going into this half-heartedly. I have to see where we go from here. The thought of going back to Los Angeles... I just know I would kick myself for not taking the chance."

I can't answer. Not because I don't want to, but because I hear Sophie's wheelchair approaching.

"Let's talk more when we leave the office later."

November nods right before Sophie enters the open door.

Sophie stops in the middle of the room; her sole focus is my... *girlfriend*.

"Gosh! I knew you had to be gorgeous!"

"Oh, Sophie," I say under my breath.

November stands to greet my assistant, extending her hand when she reaches the wheelchair. "You must be the legendary Sophie."

Sophie covers their clasped right hands with her left. "No wonder Rhys is falling all over himself because of you."

"Actually, Soph, you are not wrong." I stand as I speak, walking over to wrap my arm around November's waist, then have a silent conversation with her about informing Sophie.

When November nods her head, I turn my head back to Sophie. "We have news."

"You're getting married!" Sophie whoops. "Show me the ring!"

"Who's getting married?" Carys enters.

"Called it!" Gareth follows close behind.

November buries her face in my chest, probably to hide her embarrassment.

"Stop! All of you stop!" I shout. "Everyone, take twenty steps backward in your conclusions. November and I are NOT engaged."

November hasn't looked up yet, and she is just too cute right now. I see her smiling against my shirt, and I don't hate that; although she's embarrassed, she's not protesting.

"You said you have news, and the way you two were looking at each other." Sophie's voice is pure annoyance.

"Sophie. What I was going to tell you is, November has agreed to stay in Buffalo -"

"Yes!" Carys claps.

"Please, everyone, hold your reactions until I'm done telling you exactly what is going on." When they seem settled, I continue, "Tomorrow night, November is moving in with me. We are going to take the remainder of this month to see where things go."

As I finish, November faces everyone, but I don't take my arm off her waist. This is a huge step for her, for both of us, and I want to send a clear message that I am in this with her.

"Carys, I would appreciate you not saying anything to Alex," November requests. "This is just now new, and I'm planning on telling her when I get home."

That hadn't occurred to me; I'm relieved she thought of it.

"Of course," Carys replies.

"Thank you." November steps away from me to give Carys a hug.

I can't quite explain what seeing that hug does to my heart. To see Carys care about the woman I... No, I can't say that. I can't jump so far ahead of myself. Not when November has just made this decision to test the waters.

"Has Rhys shown you around the building yet?" Carys asks.

"No, we just arrived," November answers.

"I'll give you the tour and we can begin a discussion about the benefits we want to offer our employees."

"Great. I brought baked goods for the employees. Where should I leave them?"

"I'll take them to the breakroom," Sophie offers. "You won't want to be around when the locusts descend. Free treats are very popular."

"Thank you."

November turns around to pick up the tray, but Gareth has gotten to it first and already snagging his brownie before handing the tray to Sophie. He knows better than to try to take the tray up to the breakroom himself. If Sophie says she will do something, she will. If she wants help, she is not shy to ask for it. Besides, I think she wants to gossip about my new girlfriend.

And when I look at my new girlfriend, she has her hands on her hips, glaring at my brother as he takes a huge, exaggerated bite of brownie.

Carys links her arm with November's to escort her out. "Come on, friend."

"Wait a minute." I lean in and give November a quick kiss on her lips. "See you later."

"See you later."

"You two are quite the match," Sophie singsongs before exiting with the tray.

Carys and November follow. November winks at me over her shoulder before she disappears out the door.

My eyes linger on the space where they were.

"You are so gone for her."

I glance at my brother who is happily eating his brownie. I know when dealing with Gareth, it's best to nip things in the bud.

"I am," I state evenly. "Were you reviewing Fourth-write's scope of work with Asher?"

"Your future wife is quite the baker." He polishes off the brownie before speaking again. "Yes. Now that the contract is signed and the deal is a go, Asher is getting to work in hacking their system to look for the holes. He's settling in to work through the rest of the day and I wouldn't be surprised if he works into the night. Once he gets started, it's difficult to pry him away."

"I'll have to stop in again and give him a quitting time."

"Just let him do his thing. He knows how to take care of himself. When he's tired, he'll go home."

"Still. I'll check in before I leave for the day. Order some dinner for him."

Gareth shrugs, accepting my plan. "So, you'll be shacking up with your lady friend. Who came up with that idea?"

"I asked her to stay."

"She didn't rope you into this plan?"

I could be annoyed, but I know Gareth is, in his way, looking out for me.

"Not at all. You will find November is nothing like the women who have tried to rope me in the past. If you give her a chance, I know you will like her."

"I already like her. She gave me crap, bakes a great brownie, and is very easy on the eyes."

I drag my hand down my face. "Gareth."

"Good as gold." He heads to the door, stops, and looks back to me. "I'm glad you're giving this a chance."

Gareth is gone before I can remark.

Me too.

CHAPTER 17

November

Alex and I sit across from each other at the refurbished antique desk in the small home office she and Mark share on the second floor. The office is one of the rooms that separate my bedroom from theirs. It is simply, yet tastefully decorated with an almost summery, beachy, Cape Cod style that is a direct contrast with the bracingly cold, autumn vibe going on today beyond the two windows behind my sister.

There are a few bookshelves against the walls to my right and left, full of books and vacation knickknacks. I recognize Roman on some shelves. His favorite science fiction novels, books I borrowed as a young girl that I barely understood, but eventually lead me to Romantasy as an adult. Decorative jars full of sea glass he liked to collect throughout his short lifetime. The large, imperfect vase he made during a pottery class he took Alex to on a date in college. I remember Roman telling me shortly after that date, he was going to marry Alexandria Henry. I knew from his magnificent smile and confident tone; my brother was head over heels and not kidding at all.

Fortunately, I had time alone while Alex sent Mark and Plum off to soccer practice, to calm my emotions after seeing the stuff my brother loved in this room. There are framed photos of Roman in Plum's bedroom, a small collage on one wall. Candid moments of Roman and Plum together, so she is reminded her father made time for her: he cherished his sweet and sassy daughter. I fully expected to see those pictures in Plum's room. Seeing my brother's stuff in here was a knife to the heart.

Six years. Eleven years. It never seems to stop hurting. I never stop missing them. The saying 'time heals all wounds' needs to be changed to 'time helps you manage.' Grief may lessen, but there's always a fissure just waiting to crack open when you least expect it. Even an eight-hundred-year dormant volcano can blow at any time.

We have been talking business for the last hour or so. I have updated Alex on my tour and meeting at Morgan Security and am now winding down. Funny thing is, I know I could have provided her this information in half the time, but I'm stalling getting to my news.

"Although they have forty-three employees now, they do plan to hire up to seven more over the next year, so A New Day would need to absorb, potentially, fifty new customers in addition to your anticipated clientele growth. Currently, sixty-five percent of their employees are men, but their new hires will most likely be women."

"How do they know that already?" Alex is listening while looking at the same data in an email I sent to her earlier.

"Carys told me. About ten years ago Morgan Security started offering full ride scholarships to S.T.E.M. girls entering the private high school Carys and Gareth attended."

"That is very generous." She looks at me now.

"Oh, that's not all. The scholarships extend into college, and graduate school, if the girls continue to meet the company's annual criteria. After graduation, if they choose to and qualify, those same girls who would be adults entering into the job market, are offered the opportunity to work for Morgan Security."

Alex pauses for a long while, digesting this staggering information, so I continue.

"The first two recipients of this line of scholarships will begin employment with Morgan next year. Carys told me the scholarships were Rhys' idea and, together, they created the program. The company has quite the charitable foundation for being a small company, mainly contributing to children's causes."

Her eyebrows raise in surprise. "Small company or not, it sounds like their business makes a whole lot of money to afford the scholarships alone."

"The meeting I had with Carys was an eye-opener. I mean, I had an idea that Rhys did well for himself, but he flies under the radar. I can tell Carys greatly admires her brother. She said that Rhys could easily be a billionaire, but he pours so much of the money Morgan Security and he himself earns into their foundation to spread the wealth."

"How does that make you feel?"

"I'm not sure. Living in Los Angeles and working with other CEOs, I've been around flashy wealth and quiet wealth. I've dated many men with money. Some felt that because they had more they could control me, as if. And I think about when my dad left my mom, she was ill-prepared and struggled because my dad held the purse strings. That's why she always taught Roman and me to be self-sufficient, especially me as her daughter."

I point to myself with both my index fingers to emphasize the lessons I sometimes resented because Roman wasn't being taught them, but I understand now that my mom was worried about her girl because of what she went through with my father. It wasn't lost on me that her anxiety heightened when I asked at what age I could start solo dating after I heard a few girls talking at school about their parents' rules. Mom was fair in offering up age sixteen, but because her life was so hard and I knew she was having a difficult time letting me grow up, I didn't start dating until I was eighteen. I liked boys from afar and lived vicariously through the love lives of other girls.

I continue, "Regardless, whatever Rhys has is none of my business, and has no bearing on me."

Or maybe it does. I'll be living with Rhys starting tomorrow night. I know nothing of his expenses and what I should contribute to. I have never lived with anyone before. Rhys and I are going to have to talk money whether I want to or not.

Money is exhausting.

I close my laptop, then drum my fingers a few times before I begin the other conversation I need to have with my sister.

"Actually, I have some news."

Alex closes her laptop now, and gives me her full attention. "Tell me."

"I'm not going home on Thursday."

"Are you extending your trip? Is this because of Rhys?" She is very perky in her hope.

"I am, and, yes. After dinner tomorrow, Rhys will pick me and my suitcases up, and I will be staying with him for a while."

That landed as I thought it would, I think. Her expression morphs from excitement to confusion to something in between.

"For how long?"

"The end of this month. We'll see how it goes then."

She begins to rub her belly. "Okay. I did not see that coming. I thought you might extend your stay another week. Maybe figure out the long-distance thing. I did not expect you to live with Rhys for a month."

"That makes two of us, but here we are."

"Okay. It's your decision, but I need you to know, you are welcome to stay with us for the month and date Rhys."

I smile, trying to relay some levity. "That's a good option, but we decided to go the immersive route."

"Okay."

Alex tends to say 'okay' a lot when she's nervous.

"Look, I don't know what the future holds for me and Rhys. Neither of us do. What we do know for sure is, we want to explore the what if. We don't want to be on different sides of the country and see each other every now and then. Call me crazy if you want. I see the potential of something good, no, something great coming from this trial."

"Okay. Okay. It's obvious you and Rhys are really into each other. This is huge, and I am just trying to wrap my brain around your plan. Don't get me wrong, I love the idea of you staying in Buffalo and seeing you more often, but I'm just a little nervous for you."

"If it makes you feel better, I'm nervous too. How do I explain?" I take a breath and allow myself to feel what's inside me. I place a palm against my chest, right over my heart. "There is this tug in my heart. And I feel like if I don't see where my heart is tugging me to, I'm going to regret it. Isn't life about getting to the end of it with the least number of regrets?"

Alex's smile starts slow, but it gets there.

She nods. "You made your point. And this all begins tomorrow night?"

"Yes. We thought the sooner the better."

"Well, then, let's tell Mark and Plum when they get home."

~

While Plum takes her after soccer shower, I select an outfit to wear tomorrow and set it aside, then pull out my suitcases. I start to pack my shoes and clothes from the closet, and think about what to say to my niece. How do you explain your love life choices to a ten-year-old? I know she will be happy I will be staying in Buffalo longer, but will she understand me living with Rhys? She's ten, not two. Does she have friends or know other kids who have parents or guardians in untraditional relationships?

"Auntie Novie?"

I guess I will soon find out.

My door is open, but she has learned to announce herself before entering into someone else's space.

"Come in!"

Plum's long, thick hair is barely toweled dry and she is wearing her pink and white striped pajamas with pink bereted Hello Kitty slippers. When she takes a few steps into my bedroom, she immediately spots the suitcases.

"You're leaving?" Her eyes are huge.

I rush over, take her hand and lead her to the bed where we have a seat together.

"Yes and no."

"I don't understand."

I smile to give her reassurance that everything is fine.

"My plan, so far, is to stay in Buffalo until the end of the month."

"But you're not staying with us?"

I take a deep breath, and dive in. "You know how Rhys and I have been dating?"

"Yeah."

"We decided that we like each other so much, that we want to see if a relationship will work between us. Since I live in LA and he lives here, we decided it would be best for us to spend as much time as we can together. In order to do that, I have decided to stay with Rhys for a while."

"Do you love each other?"

"Oh, my sweet, that is what Rhys and I are going to figure out."

Plum stares, eyes squinty, at a spot on the wall as she considers what I have explained to her.

"I think I understand, but I know I'm glad you'll be staying longer."

"If you have any questions, I'll try to answer them as best I can."

"Can I, maybe, sleep over one night soon?"

I take her hand in mine and give it a playful swing. "I will talk to Rhys and we will make some plans."

"Soon! I want to see Rhys' house and make sure everything is good."

I snort. "Of course."

The next twenty-four hours go quickly, probably because I keep myself overly busy with changing my Florida plane ticket and other work, laundry, packing, cleaning the guest bedroom, and texting with Genevieve and Rhys. Genevieve is being completely supportive. My mind occasionally drifts to how it will feel to not live in the same city as my best friend if I stay here permanently. I cannot allow my brain to go there, because it is too painful to consider.

Genevieve has always been my rock. Now, I am handing that title over to Rhys. If this relationship is supposed to work, isn't he supposed to be the person I rely on the most? And vice versa? Gen will always be my best friend, my sister from another mother, but Rhys and I are starting intimacy from the ground floor right now. I feel life shifting, and I'm not going to lie, it hurts. Change is hard, and this is only the beginning.

I texted Rhys at eight p.m. that I was ready to go, then Plum carried my tote bag downstairs, Mark carried my large suitcase, and I took one last look around the guest bedroom and turned off the light before taking my carry-on down the staircase to the front entry where Alex was just opening the door to let Rhys inside.

The moment Rhys' deep sapphire eyes see me, they search for anything that may be out of sorts, that I might have doubts, that I might be sad for leaving my family. Because of that concern, I feel everything is right in the world.

When I am near the bottom of the staircase, Rhys takes my carry-on from me, then leans in to place a hello kiss on my cheek.

"Is there anything else you need to bring downstairs?" he asks.

"No, this is everything."

"I'll help you take the luggage to your car," Mark states with no room for refusal.

I feel my eyes widen, but Rhys only winks in response that everything will be okay.

"Thanks, Mark," Rhys replies, and follows Mark out the door with my carry-on and tote bag in his hands.

From the very beginning, I have liked Mark, always thought of him as a good person for loving Alex and Plum as well as he does. There is nothing I can fault him for, and he has always treated me with kindness and respect.

Alex ended up telling Mark I am moving in with Rhys while I was telling Plum. Alex didn't tell me exactly what she said to her husband, but I know he has concerns. Whatever he wants to discuss with Rhys outside is between the two of them. If Rhys chooses to share, great. If not, that's fine too. But Alex and I hang back a minute, giving the men a moment while listening to Plum hint around about a sleep-over at Rhys' house, giving each other knowing looks, before stepping outside just in time to see the men shaking hands.

On the walkway, I hug Mark goodbye first. "Thank you, Mark, for everything."

"You are always welcome back. Anytime." He speaks quietly, only for my ears, and I understand it to mean if things don't work out with Rhys, I have a place to escape to. Message received, loud and clear.

From Mark's arms, I go to Alex for a hug. When I glance to Rhys, he is standing with his hands in his jeans pockets, not really knowing what he's supposed to be doing. Or maybe he's wondering how he fits in this scenario. Something we will have to figure out, together.

"For purely selfish reasons, I'm really glad you're sticking around," Alex states, not quiet at all, and she receives a swift roll of laughter for it.

"Of course, you are," Mark comments as he wraps his arm around her waist as I release her.

Finally, Plum. I pull her into my arms and squeeze her tight. She's getting taller. Growing up. During this trip, I have caught flashes of the woman she will become. Although years away, I want to be around to witness her transition from child to teenager to woman. And I will be awestruck for it.

"Okay, my sweet," I say against the top of her soft,

freshly washed hair. "Rhys and I will see you at your soccer game on Saturday."

She squeezes me back, lets me go, then turns toward Rhys.

"Rhys?"

"Plum?" She has his complete attention.

"I'm counting on you to take care of Auntie Novie."

"Taking care of your aunt is my top priority."

She gives him a quick, unexpected hug goodbye, before joining her parents.

I stretch out my hand for Rhys to take into his, and we proceed to his SUV where the passenger side door is open, waiting to whisk me away to another one of my life's chapters.

"I love you." I wave to my family before sliding into my seat.

Rhys closes the door when I'm tucked inside, and I watch as Mark herds his family out of the cold night air, into the warmth of their home.

My only tether right now is to my instinct, that this feels right, and the only reason I'm not panicking. It could also be how Rhys holds my hand in his, the reassuring strokes of his thumb against my skin, and that ever-present tug in my heart.

When Rhys and I are barely out of the driveway and on the road to his home, my cell phone pings, announcing an incoming text. I use my free hand to pull my phone out of my tote, and glance at the text from Genevieve.

> Have you left yet?

I free my hand from Rhys' to text back.

> We are in the car now.

The phone rings, and I answer. "What's up? Aren't you at work?"

Genevieve's voice sounds oddly neutral. "Yes. I took a little break. Will you put me on speaker?"

I do as she asks. "You're on speaker."

"Great! Hi Rhys! I'm Genevieve Torres. I'm sure you have heard about me by now, but I thought I would introduce myself since you and my best friend will be spending a lot of time with each other." She sounds friendly enough.

Rhys smiles. "It's nice to meet you, Genevieve. November has told me about you. All good things. I wish we could have met for the first time in person."

"Yeah, me too." Gen still sounds friendly, but then, her voice drops an octave. I know that voice. It doesn't come out often, but when it does – look out!

"Rhys, from what I have heard about you, you seem like a smart man, a responsible man, a caring man even. All that is great, but not good enough. You do realize, I am entrusting you with the welfare of my very best friend, don't you?"

I am instantly tense, but when I examine Rhys' face, the corners of his lips lift in amusement.

"I do."

"Do you understand what being the caretaker of November's welfare entails?"

Rhys takes my hand in his again, giving it a squeeze, and I no longer feel like taking up nail biting as a nervous habit.

"Genevieve, I love how you want the best for your friend. In that, we are like-minded." Rhys is not joking; he is trying to put her at ease. I think he wants her to trust him, and knows trust is earned. "In time, I hope you will find me worthy."

There is silence on Gen's end, long enough to think the call might have dropped, then she speaks again.

"I will give you the benefit of the doubt, for now." Her voice has moved close to calm. "Please, Rhys, take care of my girl."

"That is my plan, my priority."

My heart somersaults hearing Rhys state those words, because I hear his truth. Everything he has shown to me so far, his words are backed by actions. I want to weep from the relief and excitement and Gen having my back and Rhys being the man he is.

That weight I was feeling at the beginning of our drive is now gone at the end.

CHAPTER 18

Rhys

When I came home from work yesterday, my day was not done. I walked through my house and listed everything I needed to do for November to feel welcome. So far tonight, we have checked several items off that list. The most important was to key her into the security locks, and demonstrate how to open and close the doors. I asked which car she would feel more comfortable driving, and when she said the sedan, I gave her the key fob to place wherever she wants. We took a thorough tour of the house, something we didn't get to when she was last here. I wrote down the Wi-Fi password along with the contact numbers for Carys, Gareth, Sophie, and a few others I thought she may need.

Last night, I made sure one of the medicine cabinets over the dual sink vanity was empty as well as the drawers on that side. I moved my out-of-season clothing into a spare bedroom closet, clearing out one complete side of my walk-in for November. She has plenty of space for her belongings; and I was able to bag clothing items I no longer wear to donate.

After we unpacked her, I took her luggage downstairs to the closet where I store my own. I may have overestimated how much space November would need; there are gaping sections with nothing hung, and several empty drawers. She and I lean against the built-in dresser drawers on my side and gawk at her side.

"Can't blame me for being overzealous." I shrug.

We laugh. The sound makes me ache to be as close to her as humanly possible. She is standing next to me, and it is still not close enough.

I wrap an arm around her waist, simultaneously pulling her body in front of me and sliding mine behind hers, tugging her back to my front, and hold her as we stare at the sparse closet space.

I love being here like this with her!

"You can bring your clothes back from wherever you hid them." Her hands cover mine where they are clasped on her belly.

"No. That side of the closet is yours to do with whatever you want. Besides, you will need some clothes for colder weather the deeper we go into November. Definitely a warmer coat, but we can hang that in the coat closet downstairs."

"Are you sure?"

I bury my face in her neck, placing a lingering kiss through her hair. "Positive."

Holding November feels too good. Too right. I am trying to behave. The last thing I want is for her to think I brought her to stay with me for a few weeks of easy access sex. Sex can wait a night. In that case, if I don't create some distance between myself and her warm, delicious body, my dick is going to get the wrong idea.

My hands move to November's waist to guide her

forward as I push my back off the drawers I was leaning against, take her hand and guide her out of the closet.

"Before we get ready for bed, which side of the bed would you like to claim?" I ask as I close the door behind us.

"The side of the bed is the only thing I don't care about when I sleep, so you choose."

My eyebrow raises. "The only thing? Is there something else you need? Extra pillows? Another blanket?"

She clasps her hands behind her back. "I have all kinds of sleep idiosyncrasies."

"Idiosyncrasies?" She is completely serious, but I can't help smile. "I'm intrigued. What possibly can those be?"

"You asked." She exhales dramatically, then gestures to the navy encased pillow she pulled out of her suitcase and tossed on the bed when unpacking. "I use silk pillowcases because they tend to stay cool during the night and don't leave indentations on my skin. And, when I sleep, I prefer the room to be ultra-dark, and cold."

"How cold?"

"Whenever I visited Roman and Alex here in winter, I would shut the heating vents to my bedroom and crack open the window."

"That's cold."

"Best sleep ever. I was buried under a very thick comforter though."

"Anything else?"

"Of course! I'm a side sleeper, moving side to side throughout the night, holding a pillow so I don't slip my hands under my cheek and leave weird finger imprints on my face in the morning."

"No." *Hard no!*

Her face wrinkles in confusion. "No to what?"

"If you are going to hold anything while you sleep, that thing is me."

She laughs as if I'm joking. "I have never held or been held by someone while sleeping."

"I can't imagine that to be true."

"It is, but let me finish my list of sleep needs."

I gesture my hand for her to continue.

"I'm a very light sleeper, so I won't really sleep this first night. I need to know the sounds of a house before I'm comfortable enough to actually sleep."

"So, you just lay in a cold, dark room, listening for noises."

"No, I rest, fading in and out, but not really sleeping. Oh! I sleep best when it's raining outside, so I use a rain app. Will that bother you?"

"I..." My mouth stops mid-sentence, maybe because, at this point, I'm not sure she is kidding me or not. "I have never used an app while sleeping before, but I'm willing to try."

"I moisturize before bed, but I keep lip balm and hand cream on the nightstand. I can't sleep with dry skin. That might be a California thing because of the drier climate; I don't find myself using either at night when I'm in Buffalo, except when I visit in winter because the air does get dry and heating systems don't help."

"Do you need a glass of water on the nightstand too?"

"No, I hydrate really well during the day right up until bedtime, which is probably why I usually have to get up in the middle of the night to go pee."

I shake my head.

"I'm sorry. Is that too much information?"

"No, no. This is all good information. Nothing wrong with knowing what to expect." My head is swimming, but she doesn't need to know that, especially seeing her wringing her hands together.

"Trust me. I hear myself, and myself sounds high maintenance."

I wrap an arm around her shoulders, kiss the top of her head, then steer us around to the bathroom to figure out our nightly routine before bed.

"Ember, neither of us have ever lived with a significant other. We have many things to understand about each other, but I am so grateful to be given the time to know you."

"Does that mean you wouldn't mind if I slept naked? I really hate sleeping in clothes. I do when I'm a guest in other people's homes, but never in my own home."

"You think I will mind you sleeping naked?"

"Some people might feel uncomfortable."

"Ember, I am a man who is completely obsessed with your body. No, I would not mind you sleeping naked next to me. Just don't be surprised if, things happen."

"I don't mind things happening." She winks before stepping into the bathroom before me.

This is going to be so much more difficult to keep myself from touching her how I want tonight.

The first thing that nudges me is the feeling of something missing. What wakes me up is the absence of November wrapped in my arms and legs. I reach for her, but she is no longer in bed. When I reach in the other direction for my cell phone to check the time, its blue light burns my retinas, but I register two-something in the morning before my eyelids squeeze shut in resistance.

"November?" I speak into the dark room.

When she doesn't respond, I sit up and listen. I switch my phone on again, but this time don't look at it. I use the glow to see where I am going as I shuffle to exit the bedroom. I open the door just as November exits the bathroom at the far end of the hallway.

I rub the sleep from my eye with the heel of my hand. "You could have used the bathroom in here."

Softly illuminated by the recessed lighting near the baseboard, she walks toward me. Her hair is tousled, eyes partially hooded from sleep, and she's wearing the short pink robe she placed on the chair by the bed before going to sleep.

"I didn't want to wake you."

"You weren't in my arms; that's enough to wake me."

She wraps her arms around my waist, rests her head against my chest, and breathes me in. "Sorry."

"Don't be." I fold her into my arms, then whisper against her temple, "You are a very interesting sleeper."

"I know," she murmurs. "I told you."

"No, no. It's so much more than side sleeping naked in the cold with bathroom breaks."

She pulls away to look up at my face, not detaching from me fully, waiting for me to continue.

"Your limbs have a mind of their own. They go everywhere. I finally figured out, to avoid possible injury, I had to lock you down with my arms and legs. So, I apologize if it wasn't easy for you to get out of bed."

She giggles quietly. "I had no idea I flail around like that."

I lead her back into the bedroom. "You're also an escape artist."

"What?"

"You were sleeping on your back when I first tried to contain you, but your limbs were not having it."

"Oh no!" She cringes. "If I was on my back, you heard me snore."

"You don't snore, but you do whimper."

"I... What? Whimper?"

"Yeah, every now and then, these little, soft whimpers escape your mouth." Every time I heard these noises, I had to actively push thoughts of her whimpering in other ways out of my head. "I think it was in response to something you were dreaming about."

She walks around to her side of the bed, thoughtful. "Strange. I don't remember what I was dreaming."

As dim as the light from cellphone may be, I still have to avert my eyes as November slips out of her robe before crawling back into bed.

"Rhys, you don't have to look away."

I can hear her smile as I make myself comfortable on my side, facing her. "Yes, I do."

"Why?" Scooching in closer to me, her hand slips under the hem of my T-shirt to rest against the naked skin of my waist.

"Because looking at you naked gives me ideas I don't want to indulge in your first night here. Would it be okay if I hold you?"

She smiles her answer. "You mean lock me down."

I smile too. "No, I mean hold you."

Her fingers slowly trace the edge of the waistband of my boxer briefs.

She licks her lips. "I'd rather explore the ideas my nakedness gives you instead. It is morning now, so no promises to yourself will be broken."

The tips of her fingers barely slide under the waistband of my boxer briefs, her smooth leg moves enticingly up and down my own, and my cock pulses awake, ready for anything November has on offer.

I palm the curve of her waist and move a thigh between hers; my cock is half hard now. "You are absolutely right."

Her warm hand slips fully inside my briefs, cupping my

ass cheek and giving it a squeeze. My dick is wide awake now, hard and ready for the tight, wet pussy rubbing gently against my thigh.

There will be no going to sleep now.

I claim her lips with my own, a kiss immediately hot and wet and needy. She clamps her thighs around mine, and her throaty moan vibrates along my tongue, through my body, down to my dick. I am excruciatingly hard for her.

"I want you on top." I'm already rolling her on me as she yanks down my briefs. "I want to watch you ride my dick."

She attacks my T-shirt next, as if she's offended it dares come between my skin and hers. I grip my throbbing shaft at the base and hold it straight up as invitation.

"Ride me good, Ember."

Her eyes flash as she comes up on her knees, positioning her slick entrance against the head. I begin to salivate thinking about her sweet taste, and I almost want to flip her to her back to suck between her legs. Almost. Because when that wet pussy begins the slow, tight slide down my length, the cast of the blue light against her skin, against that pretty pussy swallowing my length – I am exactly where I need to be.

"Fuck, Rhys!" Her voice quivers, just like her thighs. "I don't think... I don't think I can go all the way down."

I grip her hip with one hand to steady her. The other moves down to where we are joined together; she is so close to taking me all the way. My thumb reaches upward, finding her swollen clit, and I rub narrow circles.

So wet for me!

She clenches around my cock.

"You can take it, Angel," I grit out, holding myself back from bucking up into her for the friction I need.

Her hips sway forward and back, getting lost in the feel

of my thumb massaging her. She slides the remaining distance down, and groans.

"That's it." It's my turn to groan. "Fuck! I need you to move now."

She raises her hips and comes back down, just like the good girl I know she is, and I don't hold back anymore, my hips coming up to meet her as she slides down to me, gripping her ass, finding our rhythm.

"Damn! You look good on my dick like this!"

"You feel better," she pants out.

I push myself up in a seated position, needing to put my mouth on her, anywhere they can. Her bouncing tits catch my attention first, and I suck a peaked nipple between my lips. She gasps, but that's not enough for me. I take a little bite, wanting to fucking eat her up, and she gives me the response I am craving – she squeals!

She rides me harder as I lick over the sting, my hands a vise on her hips to help her fuck my dick how she needs. I take a nip of her collarbone, and receive another squeal.

"You taste so fucking good." I lick against her skin.

I glide a hand up her spine, curling my fingers around her shoulder as I bring her down on my cock again and again.

"Oh!" November rakes her fingers through my hair. "Take me how you want."

That does something to the wiring of my brain, something that makes my cock impossibly harder for this woman. Without one thought of what I want, I flip her onto her back, still inside her. I give each of her tits a good suck, hoping to see marks there in the light of day.

"I'm going to fuck you hard, right now," I rasp.

And she doesn't hesitate: "Give it to me."

That husky voice vibrates through my tense body, breaching every bit of control I was clinging to. I slide my hands underneath her arms and grip her shoulders, so she can't slide away from me. My mouth crashes into hers, a messy kiss she moans into, and I start fucking her – HARD.

She raises a bent knee as far as she can towards her chest to take me deeper; her cries and pants urge me on. She feels so fucking good; her walls tightening around me, the wet sounds bringing me to the edge.

I recognize the change in November's breathing; she's on the brink. I break a kiss to watch her, eyes flaring in antic-ipation of the moment she falls over that cliff. Desperate for that moment, I reach my hand down between us and firmly stroke my thumb over her tiny knob of nerves. Her hips jerk at the intense sensation of thumb and cock. I know I'm going to come any second, but she must go first.

"My pretty girl is taking my dick so perfect." My voice sounds like I swallowed fire. "So damn good fucking you."

She's a reader. She gets off on the words. And mine were the lit match she needed to set her off like fireworks, her mouth opening in a soundless scream, eyes shut tight. I hold my own orgasm back long enough to watch her, feel her wet warmth begin to coat me. Now, I can let go.

I go deep, slipping through her tightness as my cock has had all the friction it can take, and explodes over and over with a few last jagged thrusts. My face burrows into her hair, her neck, breathing in her spicy vanilla scent mixed with the heat of sex. My arms band underneath her body to hold her flush against me, not wanting to ever let her go.

And November is holding onto me just as tight.

CHAPTER 19

November

My eyes flutter open for the second time this morning. The first thing I'm aware of is, holding a pillow instead of Rhys. I listen to the quiet of the house. When I pick up my cell phone off the nightstand, it is just past eight o'clock – I rarely sleep in this late - and I realize Rhys has already left for work.

Then I see his text waiting for me.

Good morning, Idiosyncratic Sleep Angel!

If you need anything, text or call anytime.
I'll be home by 6 pm. Have a great day!

Good morning, Handsome Limb
Wrangler!

Thank you for letting me sleep in, but I
missed out on good morning and
goodbye kisses.

He is quick to respond.

> You looked too peaceful to wake up, but I did kiss you on the cheek. Going forward, I'll make sure to give you a proper kiss goodbye.

Butterflies take flight in my stomach, make a soaring circle, then settle again.

> Always kiss me good morning, good night, hello, and goodbye.

> I have no problems with your kiss requirements, but thinking about kissing you is overly distracting in a meeting.

That's right, work. I pull the covers back and get out of bed.

> Sorry. I'll let you get to it.

> Please, don't be sorry. I always have time for you.

> I love knowing that, but you have stuff to do and I have stuff to do.

> Have a great day!

> You too!

I text a kiss emoji and sigh, then make the bed, take a quick shower, and dress in leggings and a sweater. A little hungry, I go downstairs to the kitchen, but when I investigate the refrigerator, well, Rhys did say he doesn't really cook and has a meal delivery service. Several black containers with clear lids are stacked neatly on one shelf. There are some condiment jars in the door and a few apples in the crisper, but nothing else.

When I open the freezer door, I laugh because there are more pints of ice cream than there are refrigerator items. The pantry isn't any better. A few boxes of protein bars, which I grab one for my breakfast, a couple flavors of protein powders, and a few other items that don't register to me as anything I can make a meal from.

There is a fancy espresso machine on one counter, but no sense putting it to use when I really want a latte and there is no milk in the house. To be completely sure, I open every cabinet in the kitchen only to realize that quite a few of them are empty and cookware is sparse.

I sigh. And sigh again.

No need to make a grocery list, because he needs everything. *We* need everything.

I grab my handbag and head toward the garage.

My first stop is a cute coffee shop about a mile outside of Rhys' neighborhood. I decide to have a seat and scratch off work emails from today's to-do list, while sipping a latte to wash down this chocolate peanut butter protein bar atrocity. I couldn't eat it all. It didn't taste like chocolate and it didn't taste like peanut butter.

Next, I stop at a couple shops to buy a few kitchen necessities, then drive to Trader Joe's where I overstuff the red shopping cart with everything I need to make meals for the week, plus all my favorite snacks to introduce Rhys to. When I return home, I make several trips between the garage and the kitchen to unload, then set to task organizing the kitchen. I have decided to claim this space as my own. King of the Mountain.

After camping out in the front sitting room for the last several hours, working on research for clients and writing my findings, the alarm I set to start preparing dinner chimes on my cell phone. I save the documents, close my laptop, and sit for a moment. Other than the kitchen, I think this may be my favorite room in the house. It is sparsely furnished with only a couple upholstered armchairs, each with their own ottoman, set in front of a large, white fireplace carved with roses and vines in relief. With only one picture window facing the front yard, what this room needs are bookshelves. It would be the perfect little library. Dare I dream!

My phone chimes again when I am pouring out a pot of steaming hot water with perfectly boiled potato chunks into a colander. I carefully place the empty pot in the other half of the sink, before looking to see who is calling. Seeing Rhys' name across the screen lights me up inside like a sparkler and I can hear it in my voice when I answer.

"Hello there!"

"Hello, Angel. How was your day?" I can hear his smile, he's happy to be talking with me, and I love that I can do that for him.

"Good. I got a lot of work done. And you?"

"Good. I am closing up now and will be leaving in a few minutes. What would you like me to pick up for dinner? Or we could go out. Whichever you choose is fine with me."

Is it strange this normal conversation feels important to me?

"Neither. I am making dinner as we speak."

There is a long pause at his end, but I know he's still there.

"November, you didn't have to do that." His voice is not chiding, but it is a tone I have not heard him use before. I can't put my finger on it.

"No, I didn't. I wanted to. As beautiful as you have maintained this kitchen, I sense its sadness from neglect."

"You got me there." He chuckles. "Still, you don't have to cook for me."

"Then let's say I am cooking for myself, but made enough for you to have some. Besides, I prefer making my own meals. I enjoy going out to eat, but I don't make it a regular thing."

He seems to mull that information over for a few seconds before responding.

"What did you make?" I know he's grinning.

"You'll see when you get home." I grin back.

"I'm on my way. See you in twenty minutes or less."

"See you soon."

The moment I hear the door to the garage open, an automatic giddiness radiates through my entire body. In a few seconds, I will be near Rhys. I realize, as busy as I was today, I missed him.

"It smells incredible in here!" he exclaims, stalking around the counter to get to where I am slicing meatloaf, to get to me.

"Is that a first for this kitchen?" I set the knife on the cutting board.

"Nothing before has come remotely close."

He wastes no time pulling me into his arms, and I sink into the feel of him. I breathe in the familiar hint of the vetiver and sandalwood cologne he wears. When I look up, his entire face is happy, content to hold me, to come home to me – my heart is sailing!

"Hi," I whisper.

"Hi." He leans in. "I recall talking about a hello kiss rule this morning."

He brushes his lips against mine in the lightest of kisses, and I bloom under his attention.

He's home!

I eagerly accept his hello kiss, and his desire for me is palpable as his tongue explores my own.

His stomach growls.

I laugh against his mouth before breaking the kiss. "I think your stomach wants dinner more than any other part of your body wants other things."

He groans his disappointment.

"You open the wine, and I'll finish plating dinner."

Rhys steals one more kiss, a second, before doing as instructed.

"Would you like red or white?" he asks, moving away from me.

"As much as I like red, it doesn't make me feel great most of the time, so white, but no chardonnay, please."

Rhys studies his wine storage. "Does Sauvignon Blanc sound good?"

"Perfect."

He fishes a corkscrew out of a nearby drawer and makes quick work of opening the wine bottle. He's quiet, glancing around the kitchen, maybe looking for something, no, noticing something.

"I know you went grocery shopping." He opens the refrigerator, peeks inside, then closes it. "You did a lot of shopping."

He joins me at the dining table, and pours wine into my glass as I take my seat.

"Thank you," I begin. "Yes, I bought ingredients for dinners and some other things. By the way, after dinner, will you show me how to use your espresso machine? I have one in LA, but it's not nearly as fancy as yours and I don't want to do anything that might break it."

After pouring his glass, he takes the seat in front of the plate I set out for him.

"Sure." He smiles wide. "Is this meatloaf?"

"I was slicing it when you walked in."

"My eyes were only on you."

I place a napkin in my lap to give me something to focus instead of getting up and hopping into his lap.

"Turkey meatloaf. My own recipe. I always try to fit in veggies where I can. This has spinach, carrot, red bell pepper, garlic, and onion."

Rhys places his napkin over his lap. "And homemade mashed potatoes."

"Nothing goes better with meatloaf."

He picks up his wine glass to toast. "My compliments to the chef."

"You haven't even tasted anything yet." Regardless, I pick up my glass and clink his. "I know dinner will be delicious. Thank you."

"You're welcome."

We sip our wine, place our glasses on the table, and pick up our forks. I can't help notice we each have a piece of meatloaf with a bit of mashed potatoes as our first bites.

He closes his eyes as he chews, humming his approval.

After he swallows, he looks to me. "Ember, this is fantastic."

"Thank you. It's one of those comfort meals I love to make from time to time."

While chewing another bite, Rhys seems lost in thought. "I can't tell you the last time I ate meatloaf. Probably when I was home from college. My mom would make it as one of her staple meals."

"Oh, the memories woven into food," I speak wistfully. Hearing him mention his mother makes me think of my own. "I am grateful every time I step in front of the stove that my mom taught me how to cook when I was very young. I've come a long way since then."

He extends his hand to cover my own, giving me a

commiserating smile. "You've had a busy day with work and shopping and cooking. I'll clean up after dinner."

"Deal."

"Also, let me know how much I owe you for everything."

That stops me mid-bite. I chew. He chews. We look at each other.

It never occurred to me Rhys would want to pay me for something I normally do. It feels peculiar. I've never depended on anyone for money since I turned eighteen.

I swallow. "You don't owe me anything."

Rhys forks another piece of meatloaf, then swipes it through the mashed potatoes.

"Yes, I do. Let me know if you want cash or the money sent electronically," he states before his laden fork slides into his mouth.

I set my fork at the edge of my plate. "If that's the case, how much should I pay you to stay here?"

He looks so confused. "Nothing."

"So, monetarily, how does this work?" I sound more agitated than I know I should be, but money talk hasn't always led to the best place with men in my past.

"November, I don't want you paying for anything while you're here. You're already paying for your household back in Los Angeles."

"True. And that makes complete sense to me. Although, I'm working from your home, spending a lot of time here during the day, which means higher utility bills. I'll be eating up the gas in your car when I run errands and such." I take a breath. "I just want to know how I'm expected to contribute."

He frowns, rests his fork against his plate, then reaches for my hand, holding it tenderly.

"I was hoping, while you're here, that you would look at this house as... home."

My voice softens, "I have never had anyone pay my way before. I don't want our relationship to become transactional. I've been there before. If I do this for you, what will you do for me? I don't want that for us."

"I would never do that, but I do want to take care of you. I've never had a woman in my life that brings this desire to take care before. You have awakened something so instinctual, primal, in me, it feels like a privilege to care for you. I want more of that."

Rhys' eyes are the clearest blue I have seen them yet, so sincere. I believe him. I'm not sure how to navigate this situation, how to lean into someone, to allow them to take care of me. It's new, and scary, and I don't know how to let go.

Yet, my head is bobbing in the slightest of moves.

"I can't have you reimburse me for what I bought today. It's too weird. But perhaps I wait to do the next shopping trip with you and you can pay for that. It's the best I can do right now." I wave my hand around in a gesture to everything around me. "All of this. Being here with you. I have these moments when I feel like I belong here, then I doubt that feeling because... How can I when everything is still so new between us?"

"You are not alone in that. I was thinking the same thing at work today. But when I thought about you being here, about me coming home to you, it feels right. Regardless of the short time we have known each other, I have to do what feels right. It's how I have always lived my life and it hasn't failed me yet."

I study his face. Instead of thinking, I feel. The way he makes me smile. The way he makes me feels safe. The way my heart warms when he's near.

"Then we follow what feels right."

We finish our dinner while discussing lighter topics. Our plans for the remainder of the week. Rhys becoming an uncle for the first time. Inviting Plum over for a sleepover to give Alex and Mark a night to themselves, while giving Rhys a trial at being a good uncle.

Rhys clears the table and loads the dishwasher while I place the leftovers in the refrigerator.

"Oh! How could I forget dessert? I bought Snapdragon and Cortland apples and made a skillet crisp. It's just hanging out in the oven. And I saw you have vanilla bean ice cream in the freezer."

I move to the oven, but Rhys catches my hand and leads me back to the dining table. He returns to his chair and pulls me between his legs, pushing my ass against the table's edge. His eyes are hungry, but I don't think it's for the dessert I intended.

"I'm sure it's as delicious as dinner was," he rasps out, reaching for the hem of my sweater and slowly pulling it upwards. "But my dessert is spreading you wide on this table, licking you like the tasty treat you are until you are raw and pink and begging me to stop."

And just like that, my panties are wet. In a flash, they're chucked to the wayside as Rhys proves, as I'm beginning to understand, he is a man of his word.

CHAPTER 20

Rhys

The smile on my face, however subtle or wide, is now a permanent fixture, utilizing certain facial muscles more often that it feels like the burn of a hard workout at times. It's a good burn.

My first week of November living with me couldn't have gone smoother or made me happier. Have we had some growing pains? Of course. We are still figuring each other out, but I don't regret one thing. The more time we spend together, the more I know her, the more I am becoming attached. I can't even think about her returning to Los Angeles, because it makes no sense to my heart. Yes, my heart.

Before Plum's soccer game on Saturday, we invited her to spend next Saturday with us for a sleepover. November cleared it with Alex the day before to make sure they didn't have any plans written in stone. Plum was so excited; I think it boosted her adrenaline during the game. Maybe it was my imagination, but I thought she ran faster, and she scored three goals, something she has never done before, I was told.

On Sunday, both our families met for brunch again.

This time we went where I took November for our first dinner date. We were both in the feel of that memory together; we sat closer, we constantly touched. If my arm was around her, she leaned into me. If my hand was on her thigh, hers was covering mine. There came a point where all I wanted was brunch to be over so I could take November to bed and have my way with her the rest of the day.

Gareth was able to join us for brunch this time. He remained quiet, only speaking when spoken to, not unfriendly, but definitely not himself. I originally chalked it up to him being new to the blended family dynamic. It may have only been a week, but so much has transpired. In addition, Plum was there, and it's possible Gareth doesn't know how to act around kids. Maybe it's sinking in that Carys will be a mom soon and there will be a whole new member of our expanding family. I can presume anything I want, but I did make a mental note to spend some time with Gareth and figure out where his head is besides what is going on at work.

That brings me to problems that have occurred with the deal we made with Fourthwrite. Contracts were signed. Work has begun. Asher has been putting in many hours to create new software. We are holding up our end of the bargain, but I believe the other company is having second thoughts and attempting to pull back in a shady way. My fear is that they will badmouth my company. In today's technology age, with social media and the internet, when something gets out, it's very difficult to make it go away. Morgan Security isn't just my livelihood, it's the livelihood of all my employees. If Jon and Don think for one second they can bring my company down, they will never know what hit them.

That said, I have had a few erratic work days, and November has remained so understanding. Something else I have learned about her: she doesn't need constant attention. She doesn't need me to entertain her. She has her own work and spends time with family. She's been exploring Buffalo on her own, making a list of where she wants to revisit with me

November is an emotional book reader. She cries during sad parts, which I cannot tolerate to watch. I have to hold her and attempt to heal her heart in some way. When something she reads hits her as funny, she laughs out loud, making me laugh because it is so damn infectious. And when she reads a spicy scene...

During a rainy evening this past week, I joined November in the sitting room she loves so much. She was reading in one of the armchairs facing the crackling fireplace and I sat in the other, working on my laptop. In my peripheral, her nearly bare legs stretched before her and crossed at the ankles on the ottoman, flexed. It was only a slight movement, but I realized she was pressing her thighs together. When I glanced at her face, she was wearing that same smirk when she was reading that sex scene the day we met. To be sure, I watched her read a couple more pages, watched her body go through a series of responses; more thigh squeezing, lip chewing, the small shifts she made by clenching her ass. The glow on her skin wasn't just from the light of the fire.

Watching her become so aroused was mesmerizing, until my own arousal became painfully relevant in my pants. I couldn't stand watching her, knowing that if my fingers traveled underneath the hem of her oversized sweatshirt, I would discover her need. After all, one thing I have made clear is, I want to take care of her; every single one of her needs.

"Do you need help with something?" I ask, my voice pure gravel.

"What?" I obviously surprised her by the way her eyes went wide, as if caught.

I close my laptop and set it on my ottoman before moving to the rug on my knees. As I raise her legs with one hand, I push her ottoman out of my way with the other.

"What's the scene about, Ember?"

She swallows, her eyes reflecting the fire, turning her irises molten. "You obviously know it's a sex scene. What gave it away?"

I unclasp her ankles and rest both her feet on the floor. My hands move up the petal pink fuzzy fabric of her over-the-knee socks until my fingers reach the top, tempting myself by playing with the edge.

"You have a tell. If you hadn't given me your book to read on the plane, I would never be the wiser."

"Which means, you were watching me for a while as I read."

She is about to set the book aside, but I stop her by gently clasping her wrist, directing her book back in front of her.

"I won't deny that you captivated me on day one and you still captivate me." I will never hold back the truth from her. "Tell me what you're reading."

"Rhys, you know it's a sex scene."

"There are many, many ways sex can be had. Tell me specifically what's happening in this scene."

Finally, I allow my fingers to traverse the soft skin of her thighs up to the hem of her sweatshirt. She sucks in a long, low breath and my dick jumps.

"He... He just finished going down on her."

I rest a hand atop each her knees, spreading her thighs apart while my hands glide upward along her heated skin; this time under that fuchsia sweatshirt I want to strip off her.

"That's a good man. Did she get off?"

Whether she is aware of it or not, she parts her thighs a little wider for me.

"Yes," she hisses, just as my fingertips swipe over the damp fabric of her cotton panties.

I slide her gusset to the side and test her wetness with my thumb, moving through her slick. My mouth waters.

"Is there anything in particular he did to her that you're curious about?" I lean forward and press my lips against the skin of her inner thigh, my tongue taking a little taste.

"Nothing you can't do better," she sighs out, her breathing labored.

"Good answer." I grin against her skin. "Do you need me to take care of you?"

She eagerly nods. "Please."

I take hold of one knee, raising it until it rests atop the armrest, spreading her wide for me. No easing into it. My tongue takes a deep dive into her glistening pussy and I groan at the flavor of her. Luscious cream sweetened with honey and a dash of cinnamon. And I hungrily lap up every drop, the addictive flavor coating my tongue and throat.

She squirms, hands gripping the book tight. "Oh my God! That feels intense!"

I don't stop my ferocious eating, even as her hips buck. No, instead, I brace an arm across her pelvis to hold her down as I finish my meal.

She tosses her closed book aside. Her hands move to the back of my head and pulls me closer, sparking a mental image of getting her upstairs so she could ride my face while holding onto the headboard. My dick goes steel hard. I need her to come hard and fast; need to own her when I know, in reality, she can slip away from me in a moment.

Without words, she pulls and shoves and tugs me upward until I am standing before her. She looks up at me with lust-filled eyes, pupils blown wide. Her skin flush from her fast orgasm.

"You want to play like that?" she fires at me as she wrenches the fly of my pants open.

No tempting. No teasing. Her hot, wet mouth sucks in the whole length of my hard cock to the back of her throat. She hollows out her cheeks, sucking me tight on the slide back.

"Fuck!" I force out between my clenched teeth.

I fist a handful of her hair at the back of her head.

She rolls my balls in her warm hand as she grips my ass with her other hand.

My toes curl. My thighs shake. Instead of me fucking her mouth, she fucks my dick with her mouth.

And when I come, hard and fast down her throat, just the way she needs me to, I know November needs to own me when she knows, in reality, I can slip away from her in a moment.

But I won't.

CHAPTER 21

November

Other than a few errands here and there, I haven't really been out of Rhys' house. I love his home. There's a home gym I've been using almost daily, a great kitchen, fireplaces, comfortable outdoor furniture for nice days – why would I leave? Yet, I elected to take a Pilates class at A New Day before meeting with Alex, just to pry myself out of becoming a hermit.

"I think we have three solid options for Morgan Security." I scan my laptop screen one more time. "And you're one hundred percent comfortable with offering these packages?"

"I created plans for absorbing the fifty new customers via Morgan, plus room for growth in the new year." Alex sighs. "Actually, this was the push I needed to implement expansion plans. I've been putting it off for no good reason other than what if it doesn't work. Now, it has to work."

"As long as you feel good about it."

"I do. Nervous, but excited too."

I save the documents and close my laptop.

"Alex, I'm really proud of you and what you have done with this studio."

"Thank you. It was always our..." She doesn't finish, doesn't need to. I know she's thinking about Roman and how this studio was their dream. "Anyway, thank you."

I stand to pack up my tote bag to be on my way, and to do something so I don't shed tears. My brother would have loved how the studio turned out. He would have loved to know his wife built it up on the foundation they created together. He would have loved to know his wife never gave the dream up.

"How is the great experiment going?" she asks.

"Great experiment?"

She comes around her desk and walks with me out of the small office.

"That's what I'm calling you shacking up with that sickeningly handsome man of yours."

I snort. "The great experiment is going well. I have no complaints."

We pass the weight room and the locker rooms, before entering the front of the studio.

"What are you doing for Thanksgiving?"

That's right. It is November, after all. I usually spend the holiday with Genevieve, but this year, I will be spending it with Rhys in one way or another.

That's weird. And not.

"I'm sure it would have come to me at some point, but I'll ask Rhys what he usually does."

"I can ask Mark's parents if you two can come with us to their cabin. They have plenty of room and they have always liked you."

"Thank you, but I kind of want to stick around Buffalo."

"I understand that."

We stop near the exit.

"Make sure Plum has everything with her at soccer for our sleepover."

"Are you sure Rhys is okay with this?"

"Honestly, I wasn't sure myself, but when he mentioned doing s'mores in the backyard fireplace and maybe buying a projector to watch movies outside, I knew he's on board."

"He's a keeper. S'mores and outdoor movies? Now, I want to sleep over."

I hug her. "Sorry, Alex, Plum loves you, but I don't think she would appreciate you tagging along this time."

She squeezes me. "Yeah, this sleepover is all she's been talking about since you invited her."

We let go of each other and I open the door to leave the studio.

"I'm glad she's excited. I'll see you Saturday. Love you."

"Love you."

When I turn into Rhys' driveway, my gaze snags on what looks like two large boxes on the front porch. I proceed to the garage to park since I won't be going out for the remainder of the day. Once the garage is locked, I walk through the house to the front door.

As I open the door, I see I was correct. Both boxes are addressed to me in familiar handwriting, and when I look at the sender's name, yes, they're from Genevieve. I pull my cell phone from the thigh pocket of my leggings and open up a text.

> What in the world did you send me?

I return my phone to its pocket before testing the weight

of the box closest to the door. It's heavy, but not prohibitive of me picking it up and tossing it inside the house. When I reach for the second box, my phone vibrates, and I pull it out again.

> YAY!!!

> Did both boxes arrive? I haven't had time today to track them.

> I received both. What's inside?

> Some things I thought you might need.

> Some?

> These boxes are huge. The end of the month is not that far away.

> I have a feeling you might be there longer.

> I have a meeting to get to now.

> Talk soon. Thank you! Love you!

> Love you!

Before organizing my side of the closet, I took a shower, changed into cozy loungewear, and had a solo dinner of peanut butter chocolate ice cream. Rhys had called to let me know he was going to miss dinner. Work has not been kind to him this week.

When I hear a stirring downstairs, it's after nine o'clock; Rhys worked a sixteen-hour day. He has to be completely wiped out.

"Ember?" he calls from the hallway.

"In the closet!"

Within seconds, Rhys appears in the doorway, looking

even more tired than I imagined. He looks at me with soft, weary eyes, then looks at the various articles of clothing surrounding me where I sit on the floor.

"Did you go shopping?" he asks as he enters the closet, careful not to step on anything, then joins me on the floor, legs stretched out in front of him, back against the drawers on his side of the closet.

I finish folding a charcoal gray sweater, place it into the open drawer beside me, then climb into his lap. His arms are instantly holding me tight.

"Genevieve sent me part of my closet... from Los Angeles."

It feels odd to call LA home right now, so I don't. And I don't mention how she thinks I will be here longer.

"That was nice of her."

"It was."

I give Rhys a lingering hello kiss, not sexual; I just want him to know I am here for him. When I break the kiss, I hug him and he buries his face in my hair.

"Hi," I whisper.

"Hi," he whispers into my neck.

"Did you have dinner?"

"We had Chinese delivered to the office for everyone."

"Did you actually eat?"

He chuckles. "I did. Did you?"

"I did." He doesn't need to know I ate ice cream.

"I'm sorry I'm so late."

I know Rhys feels bad for spending time at work when he feels he should be spending time with me. To get through to him, I pull back, forcing him to look at me.

He looks so tired.

"Rhys, this is real life, and work emergencies happen in real life. Wasn't the point of me staying with you is to see if we work in a relationship?"

"Yes, but –"

"No. I need you to understand, I don't feel neglected. I'm glad you're home now, and I hope your problems come to a conclusion soon. Not so I can monopolize your time, but so you won't feel so stressed."

He answers by giving me a chaste kiss on the lips and holding me close again.

"Thank you for understanding," he says, and I can feel his body begin to relax.

"Why don't you take a shower and get ready for bed? I'm going to finish up in here. Then we can both turn in early."

"Can I just hold you a little while longer?"

"I will never refuse you that."

"Then I will hold you while you talk."

He missed me.

"Okay," I smile warmly. "Alex asked what my Thanksgiving plans are and I have no idea. My family will be away the week of Thanksgiving."

Rhys pulls his face out of my hair to look at me again. "Usually, Carys hosts dinner, but she and Gregory are taking a road trip to Savannah and Hilton Head while Carys can still somewhat comfortably travel. Since they will be away for the holiday, they're hosting a Friendsgiving the Saturday before. I've been so busy; I forget to tell you about it."

"That sounds like fun. What about Gareth?"

"He will be in Manhattan for the long weekend with Asher. I can make a dinner reservation for us somewhere."

"I'd rather stay home with you on Thanksgiving."

"I like the sound of that." He gives me another kiss, then rests his head back against the drawers behind him.

"Are we expected to bring anything to Friendsgiving?"

"I usually order the wine, champagne, and desserts for

Thanksgiving, so I imagine those duties will stand for this. But I'll verify with Carys."

"I'll handle the desserts. You handle the booze."

"Sounds like a plan."

I kiss him one more time before crawling off him, so he can take his shower. Rhys still looks exhausted, but his mood has shifted to something lighter. I will take credit for that. It makes me feel warm inside that a little time with me can make a shitty day less shitty for Rhys.

CHAPTER 22

Rhys

Gareth paces the space behind the couch in my office, waving a pair of chopsticks in his right hand, and holding a takeout box of beef and broccoli in his left. With all the ranting he's been doing, I don't think he's taken one bite yet.

"We have done enough, Rhys. You have exhausted all your tactics to resolve this issue with Fourthwrite. Beyond reasonable."

I haven't touched my food yet either. It's sitting on the coffee table getting cold as I lean back in my armchair and close my eyes.

My head is killing me.

"I know," I murmur.

"And might I add the play on words with their company name when, in fact, Jon and Don have not been forthright at all. Assholes."

"I know."

There's a knock on the open office door before Asher walks in. He closes the door behind him before taking a seat in the chair opposite me. The lack of expression on his face gives away nothing, but that's typical Asher. He looks to me, then Gareth before speaking.

"I have some information you are not going to like."

I blow out a breath, then gesture with my hand for him to continue.

"I did some digging."

My body goes still, because the type of digging he would be doing might not be information we should have in our possession.

I look to Gareth. He looks at me. Our non-verbal conversation lasts several seconds before we agree to continue.

We both turn back to Asher.

"Go ahead," Gareth states, giving Asher explicit permission.

"I found a press release that's scheduled to post on Monday morning. Fourthwrite will announce their partnership with your competitor, Vault Systems."

So, that's who was in that meeting. I know what the CEO of Vault looks like; he wouldn't be able to show his face, but he had his cronies attend in his stead.

Gareth cuts in, "Vault is no competitor; they cut corners with their garbage products to offer cheaper cost. The lawsuits against Vault alone..."

Asher shrugs. "Regardless, Fourthwrite signed a contract with Vault. Furthermore, there are email correspondence between the heads of Vault and Fourthwrite discussing how to get out of the contract Fourthwrite signed with Morgan. Basically, Vault states Morgan will play nice and by the time the press release is out, Morgan won't chance bad publicity and bow out."

My blood is boiling.

"Where did you find this information?" Gareth is

seething. I can tell by his calm, monotone voice. He is not playing around.

"Technically, I didn't do anything wrong. The contract between Fourthwrite and Morgan Security allows me access into their servers for just about anything I want. If they actually read the procedures, and I don't think they did, my job requires me to hack into their systems in order to rebuild them stronger. It's up to Gareth to find the loophole that will allow us to use the information I found in a legal way."

For every night their deceit has kept me away from November...

"Gareth, do what you must."

It is after eleven o'clock when I arrive home after a complete shit of a day. We made some headway toward a plan, but decided to start again with fresh eyes in the morning. I know Gareth and Asher will continue to work through the night, even though I told them to go home. Then I remembered Gareth is only thirty-two, Asher thirty; the hours I put in when I was their age felt like nothing. I know I'm not old, but it's times like this when I feel my forty-two years.

I park my SUV in the garage and sit a minute. I do the box breathing technique November taught during the meditation class I attended. Every time I need to calm down, to focus, I have used this method; numerous times this week. But it's not enough when all I want is to not have to call November another night to tell her I won't be home until late. To explain to her this isn't the norm and hope she believes me.

Hope she doesn't decide a life with me is not worth it.

Finally, I enter the house, kick off my shoes and don't

bother putting them in a cubby when I am just going to put them back on at dawn. I left my coat at work. By the time I realized I left it behind, I was already down in the parking garage, walking to my car. I wasn't about to waste one more minute separated from November tonight. Even if she is asleep, just to hold her one more minute.

The kitchen light is on, which was considerate of November to leave for me. When I pass through, I turn off the lights, then head down the hallway toward the staircase. But the closer I get to the front of the house; I notice a dim light radiating from the living room.

Is the fireplace on?

The moment I step foot in the large living room, I halt. Standing there is November, leaning against the sofa, backlit by the red-orange glow of the fireplace.

She is dressed for, dare I think, dark deeds.

I soak the view in. Thick hair pulled up in a high, sleek braid. Black bra, if you can even call it that; two scraps of fabric, each with red ribbon tied in a bow right over each nipple. Barely a triangle of black satin covering her cunt with three thin straps over each hip. And her feet? The highest fucking heels I have ever seen. Shiny black, thin ankle straps, platformed. The stiletto heel is so high, when I take the few steps to her, she is only a few inches shorter than I am.

She says nothing. Does nothing but stand there. Yet her eyes tell me everything I need to know about what this night could be.

What my pulsing cock wants, is to fuck her over this sofa.

As if she can read my thoughts, the temptress says in that dreamy voice of hers, "Sex is many things. Fucking, and I mean the most carnal fucking, can be the ultimate stress reliever."

I have heard November say 'fuck' many times. Usually during sex, the word comes tumbling out of her mouth, but to hear her use it now, in her most sultry tone – it's maddening, the need to bury my cock inside her. Maddening.

"If you're too tired, we can revisit this another time."

Her little smile taunts me as she gives me a flirty shoulder shrug, and as she is about to step around me, two of my fingers curl into one of the thin straps on her hip, preventing her from stealing away.

My hand cups her cheek. My thumb swipes across her cherry-stained lower lip. Every time I look at this woman, so many emotions swirl inside me. The dominant one in this moment – pure unadulterated lust.

She flicks her tongue against my thumb, a quick taste. In response, my thumb presses into her talented mouth. Her lips wrap around and she sucks, her teeth biting down to almost pain. My other hand grips her hip tight. She releases my thumb and grins, wickedly.

If I was tired before, it has been forgotten.

She steps in close. The bows on her nipples brush close to my own through the fabric of my midnight blue dress shirt. The warmth of her breath, her whispered words, makes my skin buzz.

"Use me."

When she pulls back, in the span of a few heartbeats my blue eyes read the permission in her brown ones, because, maybe, I am dreaming. If I am, please, please, never wake me up.

My mouth slams into hers for the most ferocious kiss we have had to date. We are heavy breaths and fucking tongues. No, this is not a delicate kiss. This is pent up lust unbound. This is my need to be with November at the very base level of human instinct.

Her fingers fight with the buttons on my shirt, and I

wouldn't be surprised to be missing some. I don't care; my fingers may have broken the zipper of my pants when I freed my hot, hard dick.

I spin November around and bend her over the back of the sofa so fast, she shrieks in surprise. Those tiny straps on her hips end in a red satin bow as if her beautiful round ass is a present. For me.

At her current height, when I lean forward, my chest to her back, the length of my cock presses in between the globes of her ass. I press further, enjoying the hardness of me against the soft of her.

"You are so fucking pretty bent over like this."

My fingers reach underneath her, past the patch of satin to what should be the gusset, but it's basically a string and that string is drenched. I rest my forehead against her shoulder. All the filthy ways I can fuck her flash through my mind.

"Do your worst." It's said as a command. Encouragement.

I grip the base of my cock and it jerks, like it knows it's two seconds from slamming into tight, wet splendor. And, fuck, it does.

November cries out.

I stand tall, my cock inside her to the hilt. I grab her hips hard, pull all the way out and fill her full again. Her words 'use me' wrap around my brain, and the unspeakable things I want to do to this body.

The braid.

My hand wraps once, twice around her thick braid, and the hold I have on her, the image of her back bowing when I pull, makes my cock swell and I can't hold back anymore. My hips piston into the dripping mess of her. She cries and moans and pants in response, angling her ass to take more of me.

"Rhys! Fuck me just like that!"

"My pretty girl likes it hard from behind," I grit out.

"Yes!"

The friction is intense and I don't know how long I will last inside her tight cunt. I underestimate how far gone she is, because before I can reach around to rub her clit, she's already falling apart. My surprise halts my thrusts.

"No! No! Don't stop!"

I let go of her braid, take hold of her ass with a slap, and ride her hard again.

When she comes a second time, I come with her, releasing as deep inside as I am able, and echoing her moans.

Completely spent, my hands smooth along the curve of her waist, her ribcage, holding there to gently guide her upright. As I pull out, we both wince, my raw dick and her abused pussy enduring the unwelcome drag. The mix of our cum trickles down the inside of her legs. I take off my dress shirt and bend over to clean November's skin the best I can, then pull up my pants as I stand again.

She turns to face me, kisses me lightly on the lips; the opposite of how this fuck session began.

"That was amazing."

I pick her up, bridal-style, and head to the stairs.

"I need to clean you up properly and take you to bed."

She wraps her arms around my neck as I climb the stairs, loving every second of her in my arms this way.

"Take me to bed? I don't think my pussy can take you again tonight after that."

"To sleep, November. Do you really think my fucked raw dick could handle more?"

"Maybe."

I have to laugh. "Definitely not tonight. I am officially wiped."

At the top of the stairs, I turn left to our bedroom.

Our bedroom.

"Tell me, is this one of the things Genevieve sent to you?" I ask, glancing at her supposed bra thing.

She giggles. "She sent the whole ensemble wrapped as a housewarming gift."

A housewarming gift. Not a gift just because. It sounds like Genevieve is in support of my relationship with her best friend even though we are on the other side of the country. I will take every bit of support I can hold on to.

"She's a very good friend."

"The best."

I am going to do my damnedest to hold on to November Day.

CHAPTER 23
November

What a difference a day makes!

Each day this week, Rhys gave me the highlights of what was going on at work, but never too deep into the weeds, which I understand for his line of work. He was as open with me as he could in order for me to understand why his time at work took away time from me. I told him he didn't have to explain because he has never given me a reason not to trust him, then I realized it's because of his transparency that I trust him.

All I know for sure, whatever plan he, Gareth, and Asher executed yesterday, worked. And, with a little more sleep than usual this morning, Rhys is relaxed and in a much better mood. What Rhys could say is, because Fourthwrite signed with two companies and was in breach of contract, Morgan Security will receive a lot of money for what he considers very little work. The contract is terminated, and Fourthwrite is free to stick with the other company. He might think it's a lot of money for very little, but I saw what he went through last week; he deserves every penny for

Fourthwrite's dishonesty and the aggravation Rhys' staff endured.

With Rhys more rested than he has been, we spent a few hours before Plum's soccer game to prepare for the sleepover.

I bought, no, I conceded and allowed Rhys to pay for a few items to transform one of guest bedrooms into something more to Plum's taste, currently, light pink and blue. New bedding, drapes, a fluffy area rug, and I created a small reading corner near one window, with a beanbag chair and throw blanket. On top of the bed, I placed a welcome basket filled with her favorite candy for movie night, a few sheet masks and eye gels she loves, a pair of autumn fuzzy socks, and a new book I thought she might like. I paid for the basket items.

When I'm done, it occurs to me that, however easy it is to change this room back to how it looked before, I created something for my niece in Rhys' house. And he was more than happy to contribute.

After Plum's bedroom is done, I join Rhys in the backyard to see if he needs any help with his tasks. If I had any doubt he wasn't completely okay with my young niece spending twenty-four hours with us, those thoughts have vanished.

The patio furniture is rearranged so the largest outdoor sofa with three matching ottomans faces an exterior house wall to be used to project the movies on. That's far from being all he did. There are throw pillows and blankets he brought out from the living room, fairy lights hung from the ceiling, a new badminton net spiked into the grass, wood in the fireplace ready to go, and a new pizza oven set on the outdoor kitchen counter. I planned for us to make home-made pizzas, but I was going to use the kitchen oven inside.

"I read the instructions for the pizza oven, so I think I

know how it works. And I found these cool LED lit birdies for a nighttime badminton game if Plum feels like it. It might be fun to play in the winter too. Maybe."

There are no words. I simply grab Rhys by the hand and lead him back inside, to the living room, where I show him how much I appreciate his attention to the details, and have my way with him.

~

Sex only made us a few minutes late to Plum's first soccer game, but I texted Alex to give her a heads up. When we arrive, Alex takes one look at me and laughs.

"Good you got it out of your system, because knowing you, you will never have sex with Plum in the house, and Rhys will have to wait."

After the games (one won, one lost), Plum barely manages to switch out her soccer bag for her overnight bag and hug her parents goodbye, before pulling me and Rhys to the SUV.

Excited much?

I feel a little bad, but when I look over my shoulder at Alex and Mark, they are walking to their car, holding hands, and laughing.

Plum insists Rhys give her the tour of his home, but we both show her to her bedroom.

"This is mine?" she squeals, tossing herself onto the bed to tear open the gift basket.

I take a quick video with my cell phone to send to Alex and Mark.

"We want you to feel comfortable here," Rhys answers.

She jumps off the bed, and runs to give us a joint hug. "Thank you, thank you, thank you!

Thank you so much Auntie Novie and Uncle Rhys!"

He heard it, and the resulting expression on his face is a funny mix of uncertainty and happiness. He looks to me as if seeking my approval to which I give him a nod over Plum's head, and he hugs her back.

"You're welcome." He swallows.

We eat an early dinner of individual pizzas and a garden salad. As soon as the sun begins to set, Rhys and Plum play badminton until dark. They watch the birdies glow and change colors, more trying to keep the birdie in the air than a competitive game. I chose to sit by the fire, binge on s'mores, and watch Rhys build a memory and a relationship with my treasure of a niece. If I think about it too long, I might burst into tears over how sweet they are together.

I don't know. Maybe I thought Rhys might grow tired, so I watch and wait for any sign he might need an out. But he continues to be so patient with Plum, listening to her and being thoughtful about his answers to any questions she might have. Never once does he pick up his cell phone – I don't think he has his phone on him.

After we change into warm pajamas, hoodies, and socks, we make popcorn and hot cocoa, and assemble our junk food trays. Give me all the fruity, sour gummy candies. Rhys is all about the dark chocolate peanut butter cups, a rather large bowl full. Plum ran upstairs to gather her Hello Panda, Hi Chews, and mochi candy. We let Plum choose the movies. Since she wanted to 'prolong the Halloween vibe,' we watch the first *Halloweentown* movie, then she was willing to watch *The Nightmare Before Christmas* again this season because she told Rhys it was a 'must see' which I have to agree.

Plum doesn't quite make it to midnight, which I am not surprised with back-to-back soccer games, badminton, and a whole lot of junk food. I cut off the snacks before ten o'clock, and made Plum go brush her teeth before starting our last movie, so I don't have to wake her up now. Rhys carries her upstairs with ease as I lock doors and turn off lights along the way.

After tucking Plum into bed, Rhys and I head toward ours.

Halfway down the hall, Rhys stops and leans his back against the wall. I stand against the opposite wall and wait for him to organize his thoughts to speak them.

"Ember, I am eight years older than you are."

"Eight years is not a big difference when I'm in my thirties and you aren't that far past forty."

"Still, I think this is an important conversation we haven't touched on yet, and we should. Especially if either of us, or both of us want to have children."

I nod, understanding why he has been so quiet since the last movie we watched, when Plum fell asleep in between us. I know he kept glancing at her, and me.

"I agree, but that topic has nothing to do with our ages."

"Have you ever thought about being a mom?"

"Yes. In the context of my mother raising me and my brother all on her own. My dad left when I was a toddler, never to be seen or heard from again. She was a great mom, but the older I became, I realized how hard on her single parenting was with no support system. I made up my mind, if I ever were to have a kid, I wouldn't want to do it alone. I understand there are no guarantees, but I wouldn't want to do it alone if I had the choice."

Rhys looks to the floor. He doesn't comment, perhaps allowing my words to find their spot in his brain, so I ask, "Do you want children?"

He blows out a breath. "I don't know. Even though I don't have kids, I feel like I was a parent already."

"You absolutely were."

"Yet, so much time has passed since Carys and Gareth went to college, and I am still unsure if I want children of my own."

"Well, that makes two of us. Maybe it isn't a pressing issue now. All I know is, I'm thirty-four-years-old. Up until this point, I haven't had the overwhelming desire to raise children. Will that change in the future? Your guess is as good as mine. Do we need to work this out now? No. Let's just see where the end of this month takes us first."

He pushes his back off the wall, takes my hand in his, then brings it to his lips to place a kiss on my palm. "Thank you for always being honest with me."

I wrap one arm around his waist and his arm goes around my shoulder as we turn back to our bedroom. Rhys' thoughts are still swirling. I can tell by the furrow between his brows and I don't want him to go to sleep with heavy issues on his mind.

"You know, it was cold outside, but I was completely comfortable with all the blankets. I bet I could sleep out there through the night and it would be the best sleep ever."

"No," he states firmly.

"No?"

"If you discover you sleep better out there, you will never sleep in our bed again and that is unacceptable."

I stifle my laugh as Rhys closes our bedroom door.

CHAPTER 24
Rhys

The chime of my morning alarm is fucking annoying. It's Thursday and the alarm is only a reminder of how fast time is speeding along when I need it to slow down. My eyes still shut, I reach behind me, my hand feeling around for my cell phone to turn off the noise. Then I become hyperaware of the 6:00 a.m. morning wood in my briefs. How can that even be possible? I took November three delicious times last night.

November.

I reach for the warm, sexy body next to me only to discover cold, empty sheets. I finally open my eyes and blink a few times before my vision is able to make out the general features of the dark bedroom. No sign of her.

One foot on the floor after another, I sit on the edge of the bed, feel around for the T-shirt I tossed on the comforter last night, and slip it over my head as I rise from the bed. The search begins for my missing female I need to be close to right now.

Female?

I have been reading those Romantasy novels of November's too much.

When I shuffle down the hall, I hear movement coming from somewhere downstairs, and descend the steps. On the main floor, it becomes clear to me, November is doing something in the kitchen. The noise; the sweet, slightly spicy smell of something my brain can't quite identify while still waking up is getting stronger the closer I get.

My eyes squint as I step into the brightness of the kitchen lighting, then lean against the wall to watch my beautiful November at work: messy bun, flour marked apron, cupcake printed pajama pants, tank top, and all. By the production she is orchestrating, she's been awake for a while. The sweet little smile on her lips indicates she knows I'm here without having to look up. I step up behind her, widen my stance to completely wrap my arms around her waist and place a kiss against her soft cheek.

She reaches across the counter to press the screen of her cell phone; it's then I realize she has an AirPod in her ear, listening to what I think is an audiobook.

"Good morning." She turns her face to gently brush her lips against mine, lingering a beat, but I want to go so much deeper, but I also don't want to disturb her work. I break the kiss and tighten my arms around her; feeling the curves of her is going to have to be enough for now.

"Good morning to you too. What are you listening to?"

"A romance novel I love so much by Tarah DeWitt. The MMC is a chef and I thought the story would pair well with my Friendsgiving preparations. Since the book is a reread for me, I can stop it anytime I need to, like when a disheveled, handsome man strolls into my kitchen."

Main Male Character. The bookish lingo November has taught me over the past month is starting to sink in.

"Your kitchen?" I tease her, kissing her again through my smile.

I love she's staking claim.

"My kitchen." She smiles against my lips.

November continues pinching dough into pretty curves around a pie plate. There are five identical ones lined up in front of her, plus six of another type of pie crust that I assume are already baked, on wire racks further away.

"How long have you been awake?" I rest my chin on her shoulder as she works.

"A few hours. It's two days before Friendsgiving. If you're looking for me over the next two days, this is where you'll find me."

"This looks like a lot of work."

"It is, but it's fun work. At least, fun for me."

Fully awake now, I scan the counters, the stand mixer, food processor... I know I don't own pie plates and wire racks.

"Ember?"

"Yes?"

"I barely cook, and I certainly don't bake. Where did all this equipment come from?" "Yeah, you didn't have much to work with in this gorgeous, wasted kitchen." She finishes crimping the crust, and sets it in row with the others.

"Yes, I know how bare my kitchen is, was, so I'll ask again. Where did all this come from?" "Some of it locally, some from online."

After wiggling out of my hold, she walks around the counter to open one oven door, and proceeds to place the first crust inside.

I follow her, then pick up two crusts, handing them to her one by one.

"Why did you spend all this money? You could have picked a bakery and ordered the pies."

When all the pie crusts are tucked inside, she closes the oven door, then sets the timer on her phone.

"I wanted to make everything homemade. I enjoy baking and needed the equipment."

My hand catches her by the hip before she can go skittering off again. As she turns to me, I place my other hand on her other hip. I get momentarily distracted by her big, brown eyes.

I will never get over such lovely eyes.

"Angel, why didn't you tell me you needed all this? I would have given you my credit card."

She huffs, folds her arms across her chest. "I know we had this conversation about you wanting to take care of me, but this was far too expensive to ask of you. It is way too much."

"Nothing you could ask of me is too much."

"A puppy?"

She's playing, so I will play. "We could go adopt one after work today."

"A pony?"

"I don't know where we would keep that, but I'll figure it out."

"How about a yacht?"

"We could dock it in the marina. No sweat."

She snorts, but she unfolds her arms and allows them to relax at her sides. I realize, when it comes to money in the future, I need to be gentler with her. The situation with her mom and past men have really done a number on her. I will give her all the patience, if she will one day be more open to allowing me to take some of the financial burden from her. All of the burden is just my wishful thinking.

I place my hands on the sides of her neck, my thumbs swiping the softness of the pink skin of her cheeks, and I'm wondering how I can get through to her that I want to be able to do things for her, make her life easier in any way possible.

"I appreciate all the work you're doing for Friendsgiving. Please understand, I am here for anything you need. And one of the best things I can do is help with costs."

She doesn't say anything at first, her eyes searching mine, then widening when she feels I mean what I said.

"Okay." She exhales, her voice soft. It's almost reluctant, but it's approval. "But I need you to know that I don't want you for your money."

"Ember, if there is one thing I know without a hint of doubt, is that. And it's because of that, I want to take care of you."

Relief is what I feel as I lean in to kiss her lips tenderly, but I remember my early morning conference call, and pull my lips away reluctantly. "I have to get ready for work, but would you like me to make you a latte before I head upstairs?"

The alarm on November's cell phone pings, announcing the pie crusts are ready.

She rises on her toes to give me a quick kiss before turning away from me to open the oven door.

"I would appreciate it, thank you."

As she makes another batch of dough, I make us both lattes, finishing them with several shakes of cinnamon. After I set the latte in front of her, I fold her into my arms and breathe her in for one more moment before I really do need to leave.

"You smell like the best thing in the world. At first, I thought it was a perfume you wore. Now, I think it's all the baking you do, all that vanilla and cinnamon you use and eat permeating your skin."

"Aren't you glad it's not onions and cilantro?"

My laugh bounces off the kitchen walls.

∾

During my years in business, I have learned, everyone has a distinctive door knock. That's why I don't look up right away when I hear Carys' and finish typing the last few words of an email before giving her my attention.

"I wanted to see if you need me for anything important today, and to remind you I will be out of the office starting tomorrow." She eases herself into the chair on the other side of my desk. "Gregory and I are both taking off to prep for the party and get trip packing done."

My sister looks great, healthy, in good spirits, but it doesn't prevent me from worrying about her taking this trip.

I still can't believe my baby sister is having a baby.

"What's your staffing like for next week?" I ask.

"Meg is in charge while I'm on vacation. Most of my employees are taking time off; it will be skeleton crew, but I expect it to be a quiet few days before the holiday. Everyone knows they can reach me by phone, if necessary. I'll send out a company-wide email so everyone knows."

"Thanks. Now that the Fourthwrite fiasco is behind us, I expect next week to be quiet too, but I'll be around; November and I aren't going anywhere, and Gareth doesn't leave for Manhattan until late Wednesday morning."

"I think I forgot to text you, we received the wine and champagne delivery yesterday, thank you. Are you all set with the dessert order?"

I want to brag, but decide to keep November's baking as a surprise.

"November is handling it."

"You gave her the headcount, right?"

"I think she said she was planning on ordering for more people, in case the guests want to take more dessert home."

"Smart lady you have there."

"Don't I know it."

Carys assesses me, the corners of her mouth inching upward into something truly happy. "You're obsessed!"

"I am."

Her eyes look like they may fall out of her head. "Wow! I can't believe you just owned that."

"Why bother denying it?"

"Does that mean November is staying? I would love that for you, and me too. But I'm also truly loving her family. Alex has put my mind at ease so many times over pregnancy issues. She has really helped with what's necessary to have and what's kind of a waste as I'm finishing the nursery."

"I'm glad to know you have support like that."

"So, is November going to stay?"

My deep sigh is earnest. "I'd keep her forever if she will let me. If I'm being this honest, I think I have known since I met her.

"Have you had a discussion about her staying permanently?"

"When she moved in, we agreed to wait until the end of the month to have that conversation."

She opens her mouth as if trying to decide whether or not to speak further, then does. "Do you think she feels the same about you?"

"I think so. I hope so."

"Have you told her you love her? Because it's written all over your face every time you talk about her."

My eyes turn their focus to the rich wood of the desk; I drum my fingers.

"No. I have wanted to tell her a hundred times in the last week alone. But I don't want my words to interfere with her choices."

"I can respect that. I just hope your actions are proving your love."

"I can only hope."

Carys eases out of her chair to stand. "Well, big brother, I have been waiting a long time for true love to come your way, and I really do feel this is it for you. And when you tell me November is staying permanently, we'll celebrate."

I stand and walk around my desk to give my big-hearted sister a squeeze, being very careful of my future niece or nephew, which she nor Gregory has informed us yet.

"Thank you. I love you, kid."

"Love you too."

"Rhys!"

Startled for a heartbeat by the unexpected screech of my name, I stop mid-chew, pause to gauge how mad November might be before I swallow.

"This is the best pumpkin pie I have ever tasted. You are a pie making queen." I take another forkful into my mouth and let the perfectly smooth custard texture roll over my tongue.

She pads over to where I'm seated on a stool at the kitchen counter, plants her hands on her waist, and juts out one hip. Long hair tousled. Sleepy eyes. Short magenta robe. Bare feet.

Fucking adorable!

"Is that supposed to make me forgive you for ruining a pie?"

"This pie is so delicious I really don't care if you forgive me." I ready another bite on my fork. "Totally worth your wrath."

"I can't believe you said that." Her giggle turns into a yawn that she covers with her hand.

"I will never lie to you. And on that note, I'm keeping another pie; you'll be short two."

"That's not happening. It's bad enough you demolished one."

"You have twenty thousand pies and desserts for less than forty guests."

"Stop exaggerating!" she chides. "I like guests to have options, and be able to take some dessert home."

"Then I will keep an extra pie back and that will be my take-home dessert."

That bright laugh of hers is addicting; it seeps into my bones, and I want to play with her some more like this to feed my addiction. "You think I'm being cute, but I am dead serious."

I pull out the stool next to me for her, an invitation to stay with me.

Stay with me, Ember!

"There's no talking to you." She concedes, taking the seat, her robe riding up to display more of those luscious thighs I love to be between.

She doesn't confiscate my pie, so I lean in and plant a kiss through her hair, right behind the ear. She smells like the lavender body wash she bathes with at night, the vanilla scent that is just her, and the warmth of sleep. The sensation of missing her washes over me for some unknown reason, causing me to frown. Not wanting her to see, I turn back to my pie.

November grazes her fingers through my hair, the soothing touch makes my eyes close; it feels so good. She does it because she senses I need it and it is one more thing for me to love about her.

Love.

Yes, I can say it to myself. I am in love with this woman. My whole heart belongs to her and I never want it back. I am at her complete mercy, and can only hope she chooses me, loves me. If she offers it, I will take even a fraction of what I feel from her. I don't want to imagine how I could let her go. A life without her. I won't.

"What's wrong?" she asks softly.

Nothing. Everything.

The last thing I want is talk about is the near future. Instead, I grab the seat of her stool and pull it as close to mine as possible, then gather her into my arms. Breathing her into memory. Feeling her arms around my shoulders, holding me tight, but I am holding tighter. My actions tell her exactly what's wrong, and she's answering me back. We are that good together.

"Are you going to at least share some of that stolen pie with me?" she whispers.

I take one hand away from her body, and blindly find the pie plate to push it out of her reach. "No. But you could take a walk on the wild side and get your own."

She bites my shoulder through the cotton of my T-shirt, and laughs.

All is right in the world.

CHAPTER 25

November

The weather could not be more perfect for today. It's chilly enough to wear my red wool coat Genevieve shipped to me, but the sky is a brilliant shade of blue with those white puffy clouds I love so much, hovering like in a boldly colored landscape painting. Makes me wish we were driving out to the country, somewhere isolated, for a picnic with all the desserts securely packed in the trunk. Instead, we're driving to Carys' house for Friendsgiving, and I know it's wrong to feel like it's a consolation prize, but what I want more than anything is to be alone with Rhys.

"I can't believe you counted the boxes." Rhys taunts me as he slows toward a stop sign. His thumb smooths over my skin while holding my hand. "I can't believe you don't trust me."

"I counted them first thing this morning just in case you got any ideas of holding back another pie, or two, or three."

I wish the beautiful sky and Rhys' playful words were enough to distract me, but the truth is, I'm nervous. Friendsgiving sounded like a lovely idea, and all the baking was so much fun, something I haven't done on this scale in a long time. Until I realized ALL the baking I was doing.

Put me in front of an audience of one hundred strangers and I am perfectly fine to work the room. Running a team building exercise or leading a retreat is a performance for me. What I'm about to face is close to forty guests, the vast majority unknown to me and I of them, but not to Rhys. In some capacity or other, they know Rhys, and will judge whether or not I'm a good fit for him; I can almost feel my bones shake. Try as I might to be inconspicuous about my nerves, I think he senses it, and it's why he's trying to bait me into joking with him.

"I'm glad I didn't hide one in the garage. Believe me, the thought crossed my mind."

That actually makes me smile. "See, you've just proven you cannot be trusted with desserts."

Rhys brings my hand to his lips and softly presses them against my knuckles, letting them linger as he speaks. "Only desserts you make, and one other."

"Other?" I'm very confused.

He gives me a pointed look; the simmering lust in his eyes tells me exactly what that dessert is, and I feel warmth creeping up my neck. As he makes a left turn, I shift in my seat, crossing my legs right over left. I feel his grin against the back of my hand, sending a shiver down my spine.

I know what he's doing, and I appreciate him so much right now.

He wasn't kidding when he said Carys lives close by. We were barely in the car ten minutes before we are parked in the driveway, grabbing a few bags from the back of the SUV to carry into a house about the size of Rhys'. And as we approach the stairs to the porch, I remember this is the home he grew up in and, now, I'm seeing it through a whole other lens than just a house.

"Did Carys and Gregory change the exterior of the house during the remodel?"

"No. They painted and made some changes to the landscape, but it looks pretty much the same. The interior is another story. They went deep in the renovation."

"Where was your bedroom located?"

He gestures upward with a hand, careful not to jostle the bag he's carrying. "This one in the front. They kept it as a bedroom, but it doesn't look anything like it did when I slept there."

Rhys doesn't bother ringing the doorbell, just opens the door and holds it for me to enter. Oh, this place smells delicious! Melted butter, roasting turkey, baked sweet potatoes, a medley of vegetables cooking, and an array of spices.

Thanksgiving yumminess!

"Hello!" he calls into the house.

Carys is the first to pop her head out from down the wide hallway, where I presume the kitchen is located. "Gregory and I are back here."

We walk side by side toward Carys.

If I thought Rhys has the ideal kitchen, Carys' is that by double. And there are several people bustling about. By the uniforms of black polo shirts and black pants, definitely hired staff for the dinner party.

"Hi!" I exclaim. "I love your home."

Carys gives me a warm hug. "Thank you. I am so happy you are here with Rhys, and that your family will be here too."

"Thank you so much for extending the invite to them."

Carys hugs her brother. "I love Alex. And her family is fabulous. Of course, I had to have them here. It's a party for friends."

She peeks at the craft brown bakery boxes in the two bags hanging from my hands, her brows scrunched in question. "Where did you order the desserts from? I don't recognize the packaging."

"My girlfriend knows how to bake." Rhys beams.

My girlfriend! My heart is melting like the butter I smell.

Carys eyes the four bags amongst Rhys and me. "November! You baked all this?" She waves us over to a side counter to unload.

"That's not all. There's a few more bags in the car," he adds in a boasting tone, proud to show off my skills.

Gregory immediately spots his guests as he enters the house through a sliding glass door, the bright sunlight turning his hair a lighter blond from his usual golden.

"Hey! Welcome! Happy Friendsgiving!"

He side-hugs me, as I smile. "Happy Friendsgiving to you too."

This is the easy part. I'm so glad we arrived way before the other guests will. I can set up, get the lay of the land, maybe have a drink. Hopefully, Alex, Mark and Plum will be some of the first to arrive. They'll be three more anchors to ground me.

After Gregory and Rhys clap each other on the back, Rhys asks, "Will you help me get the rest of the bags from the car?"

Gregory already starts down the hallway towards the front door. "Let's do it."

Rhys takes my coat, plants a quick kiss to my cheek, then follows after his brother-in-law.

Carys is already unpacking the boxes of desserts. "I can't believe you did all this."

"It's no big deal." I'm feeling that spotlight on me again and need to deflect.

"Yes, November, it is a big deal. No one coming to this party knows how to bake, that I know of. This is a huge deal and I appreciate you so much." She hugs me again. "And I can see plainly that Rhys appreciates you too. I am so happy he found you."

I break the hug, so I can get a good look at Carys, and what I see is nothing but the truth. I didn't know how much I needed to hear that. Acceptance is powerful medicine when you are feeling the outsider.

"Thank you. I'm happy he and I found each other." My voice is a little tight as I speak, and I clear my throat before I continue. "Anyway, I made pumpkin pie with a graham cracker crust, and individual gluten free, pumpkin pies. There are old-fashioned apple pies, and apple salted caramel pies. The chocolate cream pies need to be refrigerated or just placed outside since it's so cold. Pear cranberry tart, and a couple trays of blueberry crisp."

The men return with the remaining bags, and set them where there is space on the counter.

"Since not everyone is a pie lover like Rhys, the pie thief." I elbow him, and Carys raises an eyebrow.

"Can't believe you just ratted me out." He shakes his head.

I talk over him. "I made lemon bars, German Chocolate squares and a few Bundt cakes. Oh! I also brought caramel sauce in a small crockpot to serve hot, and whipped cream."

The jaws of Carys and Gregory drop, both sets of eyes look to Rhys, and he just shrugs in their non-verbal conversation.

"Is there a place for me to set up the desserts? A table somewhere?" I ask, looking about the kitchen.

"Yes, let me show you." Carys starts crossing the kitchen, careful not to get in any of the staff's way.

I follow her but say over my shoulder to Rhys, "Remember, I know exactly how many boxes there are."

He just grins at me, but I'm just playing with him. I

know I went way overboard with the desserts, and if he did hide one, no matter.

Once in the dining room, Carys steps aside for me to take in the preparations. "Since we're doing dinner on the patio, I thought having dessert inside would be nice and give the staff peace to clean up and get out of here at a decent time."

The long dining table is already staged with tablecloths, tiers, plates, utensils, and fall foliage accents.

"This is really beautiful, Carys."

"I hire good people. Is there anything that you see missing? Knives maybe?"

"All the desserts are precut, but I brought extra servers that are sharp just in case."

"Of course, you did." Carys chuffs. "Rhys found the perfect woman for himself. Smart, sweet, capable, and insanely beautiful."

Rhys comes up behind me and wraps his arms around my waist. "Beautiful? You must be talking about November." He doesn't wait for an answer. "What can I do to help?"

This!

All I need is Rhys nearby and all feels right in the world.

The people Carys and Gregory hired did an outstanding job of transforming the backyard patio into an autumnal wonderland. Clusters of tall, faux fall trees strung with fairy lights in the corners, lit chandeliers overhead made of branches and colorful leaves and flowers, more leaves and flowers connecting the long line of glass and brass hurricane lanterns along the middle of the table. I took as many pictures with my cell phone as I could, including a few selfies alone, of Rhys, and of me with Rhys.

I have to thank Carys for seating me between Rhys and Asher.

"Of all the other guests, Asher has to be seated on your other side." Rhys is only joking when he whispers in my ear. I think he's joking.

Plum is seated on Rhys' other side, then Mark, then Alex. Carys heads this side of the table with a college friend of hers, Lily, who is in town for a short while, and Gareth to Lily's right and across from me. I am eternally grateful to be seated far away from Gregory's three beautiful, similar looking cousins, Ashleigh, Kayla, and Anabelle, who are whispering amongst each other, and throwing interesting looks my way. If Rhys notices, he doesn't let on, just continues his conversation about favorite Thanksgiving things with my niece, which is completely adorable.

"November?" Asher's voice is low, but instantly gains my attention to turn to him. "Don't give them another second of your attention."

"Am I missing something?"

He casts an almost undetectable glance their way before focusing only on me. "Rhys chose you."

"I don't understand."

"Each one of them and a slew of other women around town have been in competition to land him."

"Competition?"

Oh!

Rhys' words from a few conversations come to mind, especially when he told me he doesn't date. I don't date either, but our reasons are very different. I lost interest in having no luck in searching for 'the one' and only ending up with the wrong ones. For Rhys, he is 'the one' for many, but only for his money.

Asher must read the understanding on my face, because he doesn't reply.

"What about Gareth?" I ask.

He winces. "Gareth has made it painfully clear to them, he is not interested, and never will be. Still, I think they'll hold some hope there until he's married."

"Rhys isn't married."

"I believe it is obvious to everyone here, Rhys has found his one, married or not. Also, they know you're living together. And I wouldn't put it past Carys to have informed them that Rhys is off the market in order to lower their expectations."

My knee-jerk reaction here would be to deny what Asher has said, but how can I when I feel in my heart what he said is true? I can't. I won't.

"What about you?" I ask.

There's a shadow of a grimace on his lips, a sadness that makes me wish I could take back my question.

"I am insignificant to them, but it doesn't matter."

He makes that statement as if it's all he knows. All he has ever known in his life. Heartbreaking to hear. Horrifying.

Asher barely spoke during dinner, but I could tell he was listening to everything going on around him up to our talk. I respected his privacy and introverted personality, but he set that aside to put me at ease and that speaks volumes to the person he is.

"Are you done eating?"

Rhys' voice snaps me out of my reflection. When I turn to face him, he must read my expression, because he frowns, wraps an arm around me, and leans in.

"What's wrong?"

I pull my lips into a smile. "Nothing I want to say here."

Guests are getting up from the table, mingling, and

slowly making their way inside the house. Asher was one of the first to leave the table. I wouldn't be surprised if he went home.

"Did I do something wrong?" Rhys looks devastated that he may have hurt me in some way.

"Not at all." I place a hand on each side of his face and kiss him fully on the mouth.

He doesn't care who's around or watching, he pulls me in as close as he can, and kisses me like we have been apart for weeks instead of sitting side by side for most of the evening.

Isn't that the epiphany of the day.

Why waste time wondering who is watching?

CHAPTER 26

Rhys

As soon as November's family left the party, we made the rounds to say our goodbyes as well. We decide not to take leftovers; we'll have our own Thanksgiving dinner on Thursday. Although, I was going to take a hunk of the pumpkin pie I have clearly become addicted to, but my considerate girl told me she has a whole pie waiting for me at home.

My girl.

Mine.

The ultimate thought. I want this woman to be mine more than anything I have wanted in a long, long time. November feels so right for me. Made for me. And all these feelings I have, complex and true, is nothing I have ever felt before. My head and heart are overwhelmed by her.

I introduced her as my girlfriend to everyone at the party; the term doesn't feel like enough, but it will have to do for now. If I am given an inch of a chance, I will make her mine forever, and never take that chance for granted.

When we reach my SUV, I unlock the doors, but November hesitates to get inside. She stands there looking up at the night sky. The half moon is bright, backlighting the few clouds lingering from the day, but not bright enough to wash out the blinking stars.

"The sky is so beautiful here. In Los Angeles, with all the city lights, I don't see as many stars as I do here. One time, Genevieve and I drove out on a byway to the desert at night. In the middle of nowhere, no other cars to be seen in either direction, we turned off the headlights, and just laid on the car hood watching the stars in the pitch-black silence. Something so simple was one of the most moving experiences of my life."

God, she's beautiful!

The stars above hold no candle, and I cannot look away from her.

It's no wonder Gregory's cousins were seething down the dinner table. If they gave her a chance, they would experience her kindness, her open heart, and truly know a good soul. But they won't. I hate to judge, but from my past observations, they are more comfortable tearing other people down to make themselves feel better. To prove my point, when they found out November made the desserts, they put down their plates and walked out of the dining room. Petty. If November saw their reaction, she never let on, and I hope she didn't.

When I don't say a word in response, she looks to me, a smile on her lips that implies I have been caught. That's fine. I want to be caught by her, especially when she smiles like that at me, only for me. I want to collect every single one of her smiles, overstuff my heart with them. Hoard them.

"How much have you been drinking, Mr. Morgan? Will I be driving us home?"

"The one whiskey earlier and I nursed that glass of wine at dinner. That's all. I would never put such precious cargo in jeopardy."

She steps in close to me, threading her arms into my open coat and clasping her hands at my back. I allow her to take my body heat as I hold her against my chest; she can take anything she wants from me. Leave me with nothing, I couldn't care less.

"There was a moment at dinner when you looked sad." I have to know if there is something I can fix. "Why?"

"It was something that Asher said." Her smile turns to a pout, and I instantly hate myself for asking.

My brain can't compute that Asher would ever say anything to intentionally hurt someone.

November looks up at my face. "I can feel the tension in your body. Calm down. What Asher said was about himself, but he did give me the head's up about the triplets."

My brain is really confused, then it clicks, and I chuckle. "Gregory's cousins."

"They are something else."

"I'm sorry if they made you feel bad."

"Oh, they didn't. Honestly, I actually feel kind of sorry for them. To go through life that angry with the world, yourself, your life, is not a good headspace to be in."

She is far more empathetic than I am. "Then what made you feel bad?"

Absentmindedly, her hands toy with the buttons on my burgundy dress shirt. "Asher said he was insignificant. It was in context of the triplets not interested in him, not that he's interested, but when he said it, it felt like... more. Something else. Darkness."

To see November frown, and to know Asher feels like that about himself, kills me. Gareth knows more about Asher than I do, but I know enough that his life has never been easy, especially growing up.

"Do you know what Asher is doing for Thanksgiving?" she asks.

"Yes, he will be with Gareth in Manhattan."

"Good. I'm going to bake banana bread tomorrow. Will you take a loaf to Asher on Monday?"

"Of course."

My sweet lady.

She smiles, but it's not as bright as it was when she was talking about the stars. "The cold air feels good, but I'm ready to go home. My energy is about wiped out. Too many strangers today."

Home.

I like hearing November call my house, home, and I have one more week to help her make the decision to stay in *our* home permanently. It's a walk on a tightrope, allowing her to come to the decision on her own, and trying not to beg her to stay. All I can do is live with her, love her, each day and hope it's enough to show that we belong together. Because we do belong together; I feel it in every cell in my body. There is no way she doesn't feel it too. I can't be imagining what she feels for me. This can't be wishful thinking.

I place a kiss on her forehead near the hairline, and hope she can't sense I'm spiraling.

"Let's go home, Angel."

CHAPTER 27

November

Sunday brunch felt bittersweet.

It felt final.

I'm glad Rhys and I had one last get together with our families before everyone jets off for their holidays. At the same time, it was Sunday; an alarm bell announcing this is the day that begins the last week of November. It was an imaginary bell, but I bet Rhys heard it too.

It was not lost on me how clingy he was during the day, and making love to me at night like he was trying to press every emotion he feels into me. With his lips. With his body. His words of adoration murmured against my skin.

I have been just as clingy too.

Rhys worked yesterday, will work today, then off beginning tomorrow. He will be solely mine for the remainder of the week and I plan to enjoy every moment, regardless of the end looming near.

And every moment means waking up with him to have lattes together and talk about meaningful things. And the normal things like what to prepare for Thanksgiving dinner as I make a grocery list.

"You're going to be so sick of pumpkin pie when the week is over," I say as I write the ingredients I need to make yet another one for him. I love pumpkin pie too, but I'll make a mixed berry one for me.

"Blasphemy!" He fakes a scowl, then raises his mug to his lips all the while glaring at me comedically over the rim.

Ignoring him, I continue, "It's just the two of us, so what are your absolute need to have items for dinner?"

"Turkey and your mashed potatoes." He winks at me.

I wink back. "Do you want stuffing?"

"I can take it or leave it."

"Me too. We'll leave it." I hum my indecision over other items. "I have to have cranberry sauce, sautéed mushrooms and onions, and corn. And my mom's cucumber salad. I know that may sound odd, but it's a holiday meal tradition in my family."

"I look forward to trying it."

"I love the taste, but I'm only allowed a tiny bit because I have a mild allergy to cucumbers."

Rhys nearly spits his coffee out when he laughs. "You eat food you're allergic to? What else are you allergic to?"

"Strawberries." I smile at how entertained he sounds at my misfortune. "There's this brand of strawberry ice cream I absolutely love, but when I buy it, I eat too much of it, and I'll start to break out in streaks of red on my skin."

"Does that happen when you eat too much cucumber salad?"

"No, I just throw up the salad. That's why I will only have a taste."

"Oh, Ember!" Rhys lets his head drop chin to chest, then raises it again to look at me. "I don't know if you're fooling me or not. Seriously, I know it's late in the game, but I really should know if you have any severe allergies."

"Rosemary makes my tongue feel funny, like it's

swelling, but I don't think it does. Nothing serious I'm aware of and I have eaten all kinds of different foods. And you?"

"None."

"Lucky."

I assess the ingredient list I created and add sweet potatoes. I may not add them to the Thanksgiving menu, but I want them at some point this week.

Rhys takes his mug to rinse in the sink, then places it in the dishwasher. I appreciate that he doesn't expect me to clean up his messes and vice versa. He has a cleaning service come in every Monday, but doesn't leave everything to them. He pitches in wherever he can.

"I think I'll add a couple vegetable dishes to the menu. Anything else you can think of?"

"I am completely happy with mashed potatoes, so anything else you make is a plus."

"Anything particular you want for dinner tonight?"

"I can pick something up if you want."

"I'd rather cook my own food after eating out yesterday and Friendsgiving."

He walks back around the counter to where I am seated in my usual stool.

"You and I are on the exact same page."

"I like soup on a rainy day; I'll make soup."

Rhys gives me a succession of three quick kisses on my lips. "I'm not kidding when I say everything you cook is outstanding. Whatever you decide, I'm a lucky man for it."

One more kiss and he's out the kitchen, probably taking the stairs two at a time, to get ready for work.

I have another hour before the grocery stores open. I wish I could call Genevieve right now. Actually, if I did call, she would answer, but I know she's sound asleep. That's one bad thing about living in Buffalo when my best friend is in another time zone, three hours behind me.

At the same time, I should be able to figure out what I want on my own. This is my life. Yet...

One moment I'm one hundred percent positive I will stay in Buffalo. The next, I think it is madness that I'm living with a man I have known barely a month. Is that enough time to love someone? Love a man so much, you will pick up your life and move across the country to be with him? What if we fail? What if the relationship ends? Where will I go from there? Then, I ask myself, am I really considering giving up my life in Los Angeles for a man? That thought leads to: you have had more of a life here in Buffalo this last month, than you have in Los Angeles for the past year. But I read a lot of great books!

I quiet my brain, and allow myself to feel...

I am in love with Rhys Morgan.

Love is never wrong, regardless of the hows, whats, whys, wheres, and whos.

I love Rhys Morgan.

CHAPTER 28

Rhys

The company I created when I was basically a kid, and developed over the past two decades, is something that gives me great pride. The people I hire not only possess the best skills to benefit my company, but they are good people who have created a family environment. In return, I pay them well, offer a benefit plan that they can choose what's best for them, and, when I'm able, I talk with them, listen to them.

That's why I like days like yesterday and today; the only two days of work during Thanksgiving week. The building is quiet, each department lightly staffed. I only handle what work is urgent and the rest can wait until next week. I have breakfast and lunch catered for the employees these two days, allow them to leave two hours early, and I spend time roaming the other two floor in the building instead of staying in my office. I know every single employee by name and enough information about each of them to engage in a genuine conversation. It's fun for me, reminds me why I do what I do, and I hope they appreciate what I do for them as much as I appreciate what they do to make Morgan Security the best in its industry.

My last stop of the day is Gareth's office on the third floor. I was surprised when he chose that floor for his office and his team instead of the fourth floor, but there is a staircase door a few steps from his office that leads right to the door that spits out into my guest 'living room' near Sophie's desk. Gareth wanted to be able to 'bother me at will' and this staircase is closest to the most direct route to me.

But Gareth hasn't bothered me in a while. Yes, I saw him at Sunday brunch, but our party was too large to have a one-on-one conversation, and anything we discussed last week was purely Fourthwrite problem solving.

His office door is wide open, so I let myself in.

"Hey, I didn't see you at breakfast this morning." I begin as I walk over to his desk and take a seat in one of the guest chairs. "What can you possibly be doing to keep you away from a goof off day?"

"I went to workout at A New Day to see what the fuss is all about. You were right to partner with them. It's a great facility." He sighs as if in recall. "Great staff."

"I hope our employees feel the same. Carys had Accounting pay for the company membership on Friday. We'll include all the information with the bonuses right before Christmas break."

"Good. Are you going out with November for Thanksgiving dinner?"

"I asked her, but she wants to cook dinner herself."

"Her pumpkin pie is amazing! I would take her cooking over dining out too."

I smile. "She wanted to invite you and Asher to dinner, but you already had plans."

"Maybe the two of you should host Thanksgiving next year."

I can picture that so clearly. My head and my heart are clearly in sync in wanting that scene to come to fruition.

"If November decides to stay, I know she will want us to host."

"The way the two of you look at each other, she will stay or you will go, but you two will be together."

My thoughts and emotions are an overwhelming swirl of complexity over Gareth's statement. I decide to change the subject.

"Do you and Asher have plans in Manhattan?"

"Other than a Thanksgiving dinner reservation, we have very different ideas of what constitutes fun. He wants to see an opera, visit a couple museums, and walk around the city. Surprisingly, he's only been to New York a couple times for work, but never saw anything. I want to do nightclubs and sleep in, so we may not see each other much." He pauses, watching his index finger make invisible shapes on the smooth desk top, before continuing. "Maybe Asher has a point."

Work aside, I can't recall the last time Gareth has been in such a serious mood.

"And that point is?"

"I don't know. That there's something beyond making money and partying?" He doesn't look at me when he attempts to joke, but it falls flatter than a pancake.

Here it is. The thing that I could see in my brother that seems off.

Because of our age difference, I had the privilege of more time with our parents. More time to learn how to be soft and tough from our mother. More time to learn how to be a man from the great example of our father. To glean the best advice from both.

I did the best I could with the tools I had to finish raising my brother and sister, and when I look at who they have become today, I like to think my parents would be proud I didn't allow all their work to go to hell. I'm definitely not going to allow my brother to erase all of it by thinking less of himself.

"Gareth, I hope you don't think those two things make up the entirety of who you are. Making money because you love what you do and are good at it, is not wrong. Going out and having fun is your way of blowing off steam. You are not hurting anyone by doing either. But I think you forget that because of the money you earn, you are able to do all the pro bono work you do. When it counts, you have always stepped up to do the right thing. And, personally, I couldn't ask for a better brother."

"I hate to admit this... Shit. This is going to make me sound like a real asshole instead of the one I pretend to be." He shuts his laptop and stands up, then begins to pace his office. "When Carys married Gregory, I was happy for her. When they announced they were having a baby, I was happy for them both. The idea of being an uncle was intangible to me, but I thought I would get there. You and I would have a laugh over being single uncles, figuring it all out in how to support our sister."

He stops and leans his back against one window, folding his arms across his chest, and focuses on a spot on the wood floor.

"Then you met November. Don't get me wrong, I really like her for you, but I saw a very different dynamic. She has been an aunt for years now, and she will show you how to be an uncle. You sort of already are doing that with her niece. I'm okay with all of it. I want you to be happy. You deserve all the happiness for what you have had to sacrifice. But I look at it from that perspective, and I feel everyone is moving forward except me. And my life doesn't feel as good anymore."

I stand and walk over to my brother. Small raindrops skim the window behind him, and when I place my hand on his shoulder, my knuckles graze the cold glass.

"Just because other lives are changing, doesn't mean there is something wrong with yours. If you change your perspective, you might see that you are beginning to identify other things you want for yourself. You are not an asshole for wanting to change what a good life means to you. If I know you at all, once you figure out what you want, I know you will do what you can to get it."

Gareth nods his head, but I know what I have said is only scratching the surface. I will make it a point to spend some time with him after this holiday is over.

I pull my brother into a hug, something we haven't done in a very long time.

"Go home, Gareth, and get ready for your trip. And when you're in New York, maybe go with Asher to one or two sights."

He pulls away. "Definitely not the opera."

"Then get Asher to go to one club."

"I already tried, and I remember his answer being, 'over my cold, dead body.'"

I can't imagine Asher saying those words, but it would be funny to hear them come out of his mouth.

"Whatever you end up doing, have a great trip." I start for the door.

"Tell November happy Thanksgiving for me and to save me some pie."

Over my shoulder, I tell him, "Yes, I will tell her, but I will be eating all the pie myself."

I take the stairs down to my floor. When I exit the stairwell, I see Sophie cleaning and organizing her desk drawers. Yes, that is how slow today has been.

"Sophie, it's so quiet, you don't need to be here, go home," I say as I approach my office door.

Rarely does she hesitate an invitation to leave early, but she continues to replenish a stack of neon colored Post-Its in her top right drawer before looking up in my direction.

"You look like you've been through it," she comments.

"I'm fine, just looking forward to going home."

"Home to Lady Love. I find it interesting, and heart-warming, to have experienced the pre-November, worka-holic, lonely Rhys and the post-November, lovesick Rhys. I may not have known post-November Rhys long, but I like him better."

"I like post-November Rhys better too. Let's hope he's here to stay."

"There's no hoping. What does my son say? It's facts? I don't know about the lingo of kids anymore."

I give Sophie a hug. "Happy Thanksgiving, Sophie. Tell your family the same from me."

"Happy Thanksgiving. Give your girl a hug from me."

That's a request I have no problem seeing through and in four hours, I can do just that.

"It's a no-brainer that you would be down here eating pie. I just didn't expect you to be eating *my* pie."

Part of our bedroom is over the kitchen, so when I heard light footsteps and running water above, I knew November would be downstairs soon. There is a steaming hot latte, a napkin and a fork waiting for her on the counter in front of the stool beside me. Her stool. The one she has been sitting in since the first time she came to my house.

"For me, pumpkin pie is more a nighttime thing. Your

berry pie? Breakfast of champions," I joke, but I hear the words and I know my heart isn't in it.

She steps between my stool and hers to give me my good morning kiss before sitting. It is my first real look at her, and she is already dressed in black leggings and that violet hoodie she wore the morning I brought her a latte before flying to Manhattan.

"You're lucky that's a decoy pie. I had a feeling you might want an advance tasting. The other one is in the pantry." Her heart doesn't sound in it either.

I slide the pie plate between us as she picks up her fork. We eat pie and drink coffee in silence. Bite after bite, sip after sip, I just don't want to be silent anymore.

"It's the end of the month."

"Technically, we have a few more days," she replies.

"Is three days going to make that much of a difference?"

"Unless I find dead bodies in the basement, no."

"If there are dead bodies, it's not by my hand." I allow our banter to fizzle out before speaking again. "What are we going to do?"

She takes a long sip from her mug, faint steam tendrils reaching upward. After she sets her mug down, she lays out her plan.

"We go out today to buy a Christmas tree or two or three, and decorate them with all the strings of lights I bought. I like buying my trees before Thanksgiving to avoid the day after crowds."

My heart beats a steady drum in my chest.

"And tomorrow?" I want to push my luck as far as it will go.

She turns her body to face me. At first I see no tell on her beautiful face of what she will say, but her eyes sparkle when she looks into mine.

"In one of my favorite romances, Macy and Elliot spend

Thanksgiving in their underwear, eating turkey on the living room floor. We can have an indoor picnic under the living room Christmas tree."

"And take turns reading from that book to each other."

"Or listen to the audiobook."

"I haven't had a Christmas tree in this house in years."

"Looks like you will break your streak this Christmas, because I must have a tree. And I want one in the bedroom too. And maybe my kitchen."

November can have a forest in this house for all I care, as long as she will stay with me.

"I know you fly to Florida next week, but does this mean you will come home to Buffalo?"

"The short answer, yes. The long answer..." She takes a deep breath. "When I think about going back to my apartment, in my heart, it doesn't feel like home. I know it's because you aren't there. I won't be coming home to Buffalo; I'm coming home to you."

My fork clatters on the floor; I hadn't realized I was holding it. I do know I'm standing, my palms on each side of her neck, her pulse jumping when I capture her mouth with mine. I kiss her hard, thoroughly, until I need to catch my breath. My forehead rests on hers, my body not wanting to be disconnected from her ever again.

"I love you, Ember," I pant out. "I. Love. You."

Words are not nearly enough when I feel like I have waited lifetimes for November Day. I met her five weeks ago, but there is no way my heart would let go of her for something as insignificant as time.

Love has its own timeline.

"And I love you," she whispers, yet her words are clear and true.

I am thankful!

Epilogue

FEBRUARY 14 OF THE FOLLOWING YEAR

November

On the day of Christmas Eve, as big, fat snowflakes fell from the sky, blanketing Buffalo in two feet of snow, Rhys and I discussed a future together. The conclusion was for me to move in permanently, and for the remainder of the day, we made detailed plans. The lease on my LA apartment was up at the end of February anyway, and I typed a letter to my landlord to start the ball rolling that same day. Rhys was so excited, he made love to me under the living room Christmas tree.

On Christmas morning, after I made a breakfast of eggnog pancakes with cranberry compote, and crispy turkey bacon on the side, Rhys presented me with three gifts: the pink slip to his sedan; gift cards to my favorite all-romance bookstores across the nation; and the business card to the best carpenter in all of Western New York. The pink slip made me laugh, because we had discussed the day before what I was going to do with my car in LA. I told him I had become attached to his sedan and perhaps I would donate my car to charity. He asked if he could buy me a new car, but the Mercedes is practically new in my opinion.

The gift cards made me swoon - all the pre-order incentives and special editions I will have! But the carpenter business card was a question mark for me, until Rhys explained he wanted me to pick one of the bedrooms and work with the carpenter to turn it into the wardrobe closet of my dreams. And, MY sitting room into a home library.

I was so excited, we made love under the living room Christmas tree. Again.

In January, I flew back to Los Angeles to sort through my stuff and pack. Of course, all my kitchen items and books were moving with me, but I donated so much other stuff, and most of my furniture with the exception of my sofa, which I will never part with, that I plan to reupholster and place in the library after it is complete.

Rhys wanted to fly to Los Angeles with me to help, but Genevieve took a week off from work to spend time with me, so Rhys joined me during my final week. I introduced him to what I love most about Los Angeles, but more important, I was able to introduce the two loves of my life in person instead of through a video chat.

When Rhys and I flew back home to Buffalo, I wept inconsolable tears as he held me against his chest for the entire flight from Los Angeles to Chicago. By the time we boarded our flight from Chicago to Buffalo, I was all cried out. That is, until I realized Rhys had booked us the exact same seats in row seven: me by the window, him on the aisle, no one in between.

This man!

Today is Valentine's Day. A Saturday. Before I left for LA, the carpenter had asked which room I would prefer he start work; I chose the home library. The work was completed yesterday and, with Rhys, I'm taking a few hours to free my books from the moving boxes, and set them on the beautiful built-in shelves the carpenter created, including replicas of the roses and vines of the fireplace.

Rhys left the library under the guise of making us another round of lattes, but really to give me privacy to video chat with Genevieve when she called sounding blue. We always wish each other a happy Valentine's Day, sending each other an arrangement of hot pink roses, and her call was just for us to thank each other, but I detected her despondence even though she tried to hide it. Sometimes, Genevieve can be a tough nut to crack.

We talked.

I gave her an option, but I could tell she wanted to be alone with her thoughts. She will resurface when she's ready.

"Really think about it, Gen, don't brush it aside. You know I will support you in any way I can. Okay?"

"Okay." She sounds noncommittal, but maybe I planted a seed.

"I love you." I feel my eyes begin to sting. Living here with Rhys is everything good and loving; not being able to see or talk to Genevieve whenever I want has been the only difficult adjustment.

"I love you too. Talk soon."

Less than a minute after I disconnect the call, Rhys appears with two lattes that might not be as steamy hot as they were when he made them. I could hear his footsteps several times outside the library to check whether or not he could come back into the room.

"How is Genevieve?" he asks with true concern as he hands me my coffee.

I wrap my hands around the oversized mug with black and gold tile accents, and it registers how odd it is for something I used every day in Los Angeles to be here in Buffalo. Sometimes, I catch a glance of something of my former life chapter in a room here and it takes me off guard for a moment, yet it makes me smile.

I blow out a breath. "My best friend is in the middle of a life crisis and has decisions to make."

Rhys takes a seat on the floor with me, leaning his back against the sofa that traveled nearly three thousand miles to be here.

"Anything you can share?"

"Gen has wanted to open her own bookstore for years, but in Los Angeles, like most big cities, retail space is expensive. She has savings and could apply for a loan, but it's high risk. I suggested she move here, open her bookstore here. Like me, Los Angeles is all she's ever known and she has a great paying job that offers security, but the work has never been something she loves."

"Sounds like Gen has some serious thinking to do." Rhys takes a sip from his mug. "You would have your best friend in the same city again."

"I know it sounds biased, even to me, but I really do think her bookstore concept is brilliant. I've seen her business plan and her little nest egg could get her through her first year while getting the store up and running. I just feel so bad that she feels stuck and doesn't know what to do. Genevieve is one of the best people I know."

He sets his mug on the floor beside him, then gently wraps his arms around me, careful not to jostle my latte.

"Is there anything I can do to tip the scales in your favor of getting her here?"

"Probably not. If you thought I was stubborn in allowing you to care for me, Genevieve is on a whole other level."

"She sounds like the type of person who would not take a personal loan."

"Definitely not."

"There are many ways we can sweeten the deal, though. I have contacts that can be utilized to help pull everything into place."

"Like?"

"A commercial realtor to help find reasonably priced retail space, for one. If she's looking for a business loan or investors that support small businesses, I can point her in the right direction." He glances around the library. "I even have a carpenter that does excellent work, and she will need that recommendation."

I must have the most doubtful expression on my face, because Rhys laughs, warm and hearty.

"I am not talking about pulling strings, just cutting down her research time, lessening her struggle. The sooner she is able to open for business, the better."

Rhys reaches for my mug, removes it carefully from my hands, then sets it aside before tugging me into his lap.

"I do have an ulterior motive." He grins. "I will do anything to see you happy. If tipping the scales in Gen's favor to get her to Buffalo will make you happy, then that's what I will do."

"Tomorrow. I will give her the day to stew, then text tomorrow."

He brushes a loose lock of hair spilled from my messy bun over my ear. His palm rests against my neck.

"Are you okay with not going out to a fancy dinner or something else?"

Rhys wants to do right by me in every way; he has proven it over and again. I think he's having a difficult time understanding, *this* is special to me. His time, his attention, his mind, his heart is everything to me. He will understand as I prove it to him over and again.

"More than okay. I am exactly where I always want to

be. With you. In your arms." I press a light kiss onto his lips. "I love you so very much."

The light in his eyes is breathtaking, bright with a happiness that didn't exist the day we met on an airplane, the beginning of falling.

"I love you more than you will ever know, Ember."

By the content smile on Rhys' lips, I am certain he sees the same sparkly bliss reflected back to him.

Acknowledgments

Writing the Falling manuscript was like hiking Runyon Canyon before dawn when you haven't hiked in a long time. During the ascent in the dark, your heart, lungs and leg muscles work so hard that your contemplate giving up and turning back several times, but watching the sunrise when you reach the top and the city become brighter during the descent is completely worth the agony. If writing Falling is hiking Runyon Canyon, I will liken navigating self-publishing and marketing to what I believe climbing Mount Everest must be: every aspect is something to learn, a decision to make, and a problem to solve. Demanding of you.

Along my debut author journey, I had good people to support me, places to inspire me, and tools to get me through. Without these, I know I would have had several more days of tears and self-sabotage than I did.

My mom taught me to figure things out for myself, going so far as to hide instructions for anything I needed to assemble or learn to operate. Those lessons prepared me for the ultimate puzzle of self-publishing. As frustrating as the learning was as a kid, I now love jigsaw puzzles and use them to think. Thank you, Mom! You will always be a huge part of my heart.

Like November and Rhys, my close family unit is small. I love my family, but love them even more for encouraging my writing, being a sounding board, and having faith I would make it to the end of the Falling publishing process.

There are two areas in self-publishing I didn't mind

spending money on: editing services and book cover design. I laughed when I ended up contracting two Sams. Thank you to Sam Stringert for making the editing process as painless as possible for a debut author. And thank you to Sam Palencia for creating the stunning art for Falling, and bringing Rhys and November to full color life.

Thank you, Azeret Moreno, for your support and your fabulous social media graphics! You're an angel for helping my lost self through the scary marketing game.

I had no idea where the backdrop of Falling would be until I spent half of 2024 in Buffalo, New York. Nearly six months of morning walks with my dog pal, Coco, meeting friendly people, and exploring the city. Frankly, it was all the water in and surrounding Buffalo that sold me on using the city as the location of the entire Love's Own Timeline Series. The inspiration for the cover of Falling was Hoyt Lake in Delaware Park – beautiful during every season, but autumn will always be special to me.

Grateful for the plethora of snacks in the world to get an author, who emotionally eats and had little time to cook, through the learning process of self-publishing. Not grateful for the weight I gained from the plethora of snacks I ate and now have to drop said weight. Hopefully, book two will balance better with a healthy lifestyle.

November's Vanilla Caramel Candy Recipe

Makes approximately 240 pieces.

Ingredients:
- 4 cups heavy cream
- 1 cup sweetened condensed milk
- 4 cups light corn syrup
- 1 cup room temperature water
- 4 cups sugar
- 1 teaspoon salt
- 2 sticks unsalted butter, cut into 16 pieces
- 2 tablespoons pure vanilla extract
- Vegetable oil cooking spray
- Wax paper or food grade cellophane, 4-inch squares

Spray a 12 ½- by 17 ½-inch baking pan with vegetable oil spray. Set aside on cooling rack in a spot where it will not be moved. In a 2-quart saucepan, combine cream and sweetened condensed milk; set aside.

In a heavy 8-quart stockpot, combine corn syrup, water, sugar, and salt. Clip on candy thermometer. Over high heat, cook until sugar is dissolved, stirring with a wooden spoon, 8 to 12 minutes. Brush down sides of pot with a pastry brush dipped in water to remove any sugar crystals.

Stop stirring, reduce heat to medium, and bring to a boil. Cook, without stirring, until temperature reaches 250° (hard-ball stage), 45 to 60 minutes. Meanwhile, heat cream mixture over low heat until it is just warm – do not boil. When sugar reaches 250°, slowly stir in butter and warmed cream mixture, keeping mixture boiling at all times. Stirring constantly, cook over medium heat until thermometer reaches 244° (firm-ball stage), 55 to 75 minutes. Stir in vanilla. Immediately pour into prepared pan without scraping pot. Let stand uncovered at room temperature for 24 hours without moving.

To cut, spray a large cutting board generously with vegetable oil spray. Unmold caramel from pan onto sprayed surface. With a long chef's knife, cut a 1 ¼-inch strip of caramel, then cut strip into 1 ¼-inch pieces. Wrap each piece in cellophane or wax paper.

November's Banana Oat Bread Recipe

Ingredients:

 2 1/2 cups oat flour
 2 teaspoons ground cinnamon
 2 teaspoons baking powder
 1 teaspoon baking soda
 1/2 teaspoon salt
 4 very ripe bananas, mashed
 1 teaspoon vanilla extract
 1/2 cup whole milk Greek yogurt
 2 large eggs
 1/4 cup coconut sugar

Preheat oven to 325°F. Grease a 9"x5" loaf pan; set aside. In a medium mixing bowl, mix together the flour, cinnamon, baking powder, baking soda, and salt. (I use a dinner fork for this step, but a whisk works well too.)

In a large mixing bowl, thoroughly stir together the bananas, vanilla, yogurt, and eggs. Mix in sugar thoroughly. Add the flour mixture to the bowl and stir until just combined.

Pour the batter into the prepared pan to about 3/4 full. Bake until the loaf is golden brown and a toothpick inserted into the center of the loaf comes out clean, about 45-60 minutes. Transfer pan to a wire rack and let cool for about 10 minutes, then unmold the loaf onto the rack and let cool completely before slicing.

November's Turkey Meatloaf Recipe

This is a large, family-size loaf. If you are single or have a small family, I suggest creating two or more loaves (remember to reduce oven time). This meatloaf freezes well in airtight container.

Ingredients:
- 1/3 cup quinoa
- 2/3 cup chicken broth or water
- 1 large onion, finely chopped
- 1 large carrot, large hole grated
- 1 1/2 large red bell peppers, finely chopped
- 1 cup overly packed fresh spinach, finely chopped
- 4 cloves garlic, minced
- 2 lbs ground turkey, 99% lean
- 2 tablespoons tomato paste
- 1 teaspoon garlic powder
- 1 teaspoon onion powder
- 2 tablespoons Worcestershire sauce
- 2 large eggs
- 1 1/2 teaspoons sea salt
- 1 1/2 teaspoons ground black pepper
- 1/2 cup ketchup
- 2 tablespoons coconut sugar
- 2 teaspoons Worcestershire sauce

Bring the quinoa and broth or water to a boil in a saucepan over high heat. Reduce heat to medium-low, cover and simmer until the quinoa is tender and the liquid has been absorbed, about 10 to 15 minutes. Set aside to cool.

Heat olive oil in a skillet over medium heat. Stir in the

onion, carrot, bell pepper, and garlic. Sauté until the onion has softened and turned translucent, about 5 minutes. Turn off heat, then stir in spinach. Let veggie mixture cool.

Heat oven to 350º F. Line a rimmed baking sheet with foil or parchment.

In a large mixing bowl, add the turkey, cooked quinoa, cooked veggies, tomato paste, onion powder, garlic powder, 2 tablespoons Worcestershire sauce, eggs, salt, and pepper. Using your clean hands, mix thoroughly to evenly distribute ingredients in the turkey. Shape mixture into a loaf (or two) on the lined baking sheet.

In a small mixing bowl, combine the brown sugar, ketchup, and 2 teaspoons Worcestershire sauce. Rub mixture over the top and sides of meatloaf.

Bake in the preheated oven until no pink in the center, about 50 minutes. An instant read thermometer inserted in the center should read at least 160º F. Let the meatloaf cool for about 10 minutes before slicing and serving.

"Mine"
Book two of the
Love's Own Timeline Series
coming early 2026!